T0011739

Benita Renee Jenkins 2:

Boxing Rings and Cages

Benita Renee Jenkins 2:

Boxing Rings and Cages

Lorisa Bates

www.urbanbooks.net

Urban Books, LLC
300 Farmingdale Road, NY-Route 109
Farmingdale, NY 11735

Benita Renee Jenkins 2: Boxing Rings and Cages

Copyright © 2021 Lorisa Bates

All rights reserved. No part of this book may be reproduced in any form or by any means without prior consent of the Publisher, except brief quotes used in reviews.

ISBN 13: 978-1-64556-326-6
ISBN 10: 1-64556-326-X

First Mass Market Printing December 2022
First Trade Paperback Printing November 2021
Printed in the United States of America

10 9 8 7 6 5 4 3 2 1

This is a work of fiction. Any references or similarities to actual events, real people, living or dead, or to real locales are intended to give the novel a sense of reality. Any similarity in other names, characters, places, and incidents is entirely coincidental.

Distributed by Kensington Publishing Corp.
Submit Orders to:
Customer Service
400 Hahn Road
Westminster, MD 21157-4627
Phone: 1-800-733-3000
Fax: 1-800-659-2436

Prologue

Doug Gibson was walking out of the gym when his brother, Sean, stopped him. "Hey, little brother, lookin' good in the ring."

Doug was none too pleased to see his absentee sibling and knew he only came around when he needed something. He frowned and kept walking past Sean without speaking to him.

Sean blocked his path. "Doug, what up?"

"Man, what the hell do you want?"

Sean was about to say something that he knew he would regret and instead retained his composure. "Bro, how you gonna talk to me like that? We fam, and fam stick together."

Doug broke out into laughter. "Fam? What do you know about fam? The last time I saw you, you stole from the fam. Almost got your fam kicked out of their apartment. Remember that?"

"Listen, I am gonna pay y'all back. How's Nana?"

Doug fought back the urge to punch Sean dead in the face. He had heard his brother's promises a million times before, and tonight was no different.

Instead, he used his shoulder to push his deadbeat brother out of his way. "I gotta get to work."

Sean was not letting Doug go without making him listen to what he had to say. "Doug, come on, man. You know that shit just went a little crazy last time. I'm sorry. I'll make it right. I promise."

"You act like this is the first time you did some crazy shit like this. It's not. And now, Nana and me have to pick up extra shifts to cover your debts."

"What do you want from me?"

Doug looked his no-good brother up and down before answering. "You can't do anything ever to make this right. Not with me anyway." Before Sean could respond, Doug walked away, leaving his brother contemplating what he would do next.

"Oh, it's like that? Oh, okay. Well, I gotta be somewhere too. Keep walking then." Doug didn't look back, and this only made Sean more anxious. "Doug, come on, man. Don't be like that. Why can't you just accept my apology? I said I was sorry. A'ight? I'll get up witcha later."

As he watched his brother walk farther away from him, Sean put his hands into his pockets and crossed the street, jumping into the passenger side of a black Escalade.

Reggie looked directly at Sean. "Well? What did he say? Is he down or what?"

"Didn't have a chance to ask him," Sean replied.

"What? Man, what were you two talking about all this time? You got me straight trippin' right now. I know I just didn't hear you say that you didn't ask your brother to help you out of this jam we're in. You have *got* to me kidding me. Here you got me driving to this two-bit gym, and all you can say is that you didn't have a chance to ask? Shiiiitttt."

"Reggie, chill out, man. I'm gonna holla at him lata tonight after he gets off work."

"For the love of God, Sean, if you don't handle this shit soon . . ."

"I know. I know. You ain't got to remind me. Damn," Sean whined.

Sean had been friends with Reggie since middle school, and he had always been a loose cannon. They were road dogs, but at any given time, Reggie would blow a gasket if he didn't get what he wanted. And tonight was no exception. Sean also knew that Reggie would always go to bat for him, no matter how mad he got. But his tattooed friend was beyond pissed, and he was scared that he would indeed take matters into his own hands. He took a deep breath and started biting his nails.

"Sean, I am not playing around with your non-confrontational ass. You should have let me handle this shit."

"Reggie, you need to chill out. I got this covered," Sean answered.

"Right. Sure you got it covered. That's why we're sitting here in this damn car trying to figure out how to stay alive. All because your dumb-ass bet on a loser."

Sean knew Reggie was right and that he had been reckless with his bets. But he just knew that Joaquin Buckley was going to win his latest match against Kevin Holland. When he ended up losing the match, Sean realized that he was in serious hot water. The local bookie wanted his money, and he didn't have it to give. Reggie had warned him not to bet a large amount of money, but he didn't listen. He had borrowed $5,000 for a five-to-one bet, but then Buckley lost in the last round. It was lights out, and now Sean needed to convince his brother to fight on his behalf.

As he looked out the window, he could only hear a high-pitched voice from Reggie, but he didn't understand what was coming out of his mouth.

"Sean! Sean! Do you hear what I'm saying right now?"

Sean remained silent as Reggie continued to scold him. "I'm telling you right now, if you don't handle this shit, then I swear to God, I will rip your throat out. I'm not going down for this. You hear me?"

Sean closed his eyes and worked on tuning out Reggie's voice. He needed some time to think about what he planned on doing next. It was coming down to the wire for the deadline to repay A-Roc. "Can we just drive?" Sean asked his hotheaded friend.

"Can we just drive? Can *we* drive? Sure, Sean. Whatever the fuck you wanna do. We can just drive." Reggie pounded on the steering wheel. "Fuck. Why did you put us in this predicament, huh? Why?"

"I got this handled."

"Hell no. You ain't got shit handled. Well, you better figure out how to get shit handled because if you don't, it will be all of our asses on the line."

Reggie cranked up the ignition, put the car in drive, and pulled off. Neither one had anything else to say to the other.

As Sean rubbed his hand over his bald head to calm himself, he needed to figure out how to get his little brother's help, but he knew he needed a miracle to make that happen. Maybe it was time for him to reach out to his grandmother so that she could talk to Doug. All he knew right now was how much his younger brother hated him. He saw it in his eyes. How could things get so bad between them? They used to be so close, but that was a lifetime ago.

Sean knew he had made mistakes, but he had promised himself to do better by his family. Even when he pleaded for forgiveness, Doug had made it clear that he was done with Sean after he had stolen money from their grandmother. They had almost gotten kicked out of the apartment when she couldn't come up with the money to pay for rent. If it weren't for a family friend, they would have been on the streets. Doug was so angry that he clocked Sean in the chin, leaving him with a broken jaw.

After that, Sean stayed clear of the firecracker and promised his grandmother that he would never do anything again to put the family in any kind of compromising situation. However, in true Sean style, he didn't keep his word. Now, he needed his little brother to fight in an illegal boxing match. He would figure out a way to convince him, even if he had to stoop to the lowest levels to make it happen.

"Reggie, I'll convince my brother to get on board for all our sakes."

Reggie didn't even look over at Sean as he kept his eyes on the road. He knew that if Sean didn't come through, then it would be all of their asses that had to pay.

Chapter 1

Benita was covered in sweat after an intense workout with her father, Leroy Jones. They ran ten miles and arrived at Grady's Boxing Gym, where they sparred for another half hour. She slowly climbed out of the ring and plopped down on an empty chair.

"Damn, if I didn't know better, I would think that you were trying to kill me, Sensei Leroy."

Showing a huge, toothy grin, he smiled at his daughter, who was stretching out her sore limbs. "It' s been a long time since we trained together, and I wanted to make sure that you were still in tip-top condition."

"It hasn't been that long. You keep forgetting that they whipped me into shape—correction—kicked my ass when I first joined the DTCU. You know, the same organization that you worked for?"

"Oh yeah. How could I forget?"

"Yeah, how could you forget?" Benita and Leroy chuckled at her question.

Leroy wrapped a white towel around his neck and wiped the sweat off his face. He had recently discovered that Benita was his daughter. When he found out that she had been recruited into the Domestic Terrorism Crime Unit, better known as DTCU, he went ballistic on Director Jeremiah Bolden.

"Jeremiah, I should kick your ass for bringing my daughter into the fold."

"First of all, I didn't know she was your daughter, and second, I don't owe you anything."

"Well, I'm going to tell you right now, if anything happens to my daughter, then I'm coming after you."

"Leroy, you need to calm the fuck down before you get yourself hurt."

If it weren't for Samantha DeVreau, the two men would have been fighting in Jeremiah's office.

"What's going on with you, Leroy? Calm down."

"You knew about this?" Leroy turned to Samantha with anger in his eyes.

"I had no idea that she was your daughter. And if I do remember, one of our agents asked you about Benita before we recruited her."

"Well, now that we all know that Benita is my daughter, make no mistake, I will do everything in my power to protect her. And if that means I will

*have to go over your head to do it, I will," Leroy
screamed before storming out of Jeremiah's office.*

Leroy thought about that last encounter with
Jeremiah and Samantha while watching his daughter stretch. He and Jeremiah had always had their
differences, but there would be a major fight on
Jeremiah's hands if he interfered with Leroy teach-
ing his daughter the lay of the land. He knew first-
hand how tough working for this organization
could be, especially when agents had to go undercover for long bouts of time. Sometimes, they
would get so deep undercover that they would lose
their way. He was not going to let that happen to
Benita. No matter what, Benita was now his priority, and he was going to protect her, no matter the
cost.

Even with the years of training that prepared
Benita to become a jujitsu champion, it was not
necessarily enough to protect her from the unknown. She would be assigned some of the toughest cases, and that scared him. No matter how
strong Benita may come across, she was still naïve
to the streets and not fully prepared to navigate
through bureaucratic bullshit.

He had always had a bond with this young lady
from their very first meeting. He had grown to
love her as his student, but now, he loved her even

more as his daughter. Not a single moment would be wasted as he continued to build a relationship with her. He remembered the confusion that came with him telling Benita the truth the day that she visited him in the hospital.

"Sensei Leroy, why would you put your life in danger for me?" Benita had pushed.

"Because you're my daughter," he remembered answering.

"Wait, daughter? What are you talking about? How can this be?"

"I know, it sounds crazy, but it's true. Benita, I just don't know where to begin," he commented.

Benita had pulled up the chair next to his bedside and took hold of his hand. "Why don't you start at the beginning?"

"When I first started working at the DTCU, I met your mother while I was undercover."

Benita was utterly shocked when she heard her sensei tell his story, but she remained quiet.

"If it weren't for your grandmother, I would have never known that you were my daughter. How surprised was I when she came to my studio to tell me the truth."

"Grams told you?" Benita asked.

"Yeah, she must have really been desperate to keep that secret from me all of these years." Leroy *chuckled and then winced at the pain from his injuries.*

"I can't believe it. You're my father?"

"I think I always knew the truth. Even the first time you came into my studio. There was always a connection between us. I know it's a lot to take in, but I hope that one day you will see me as more than just your sensei."

Benita stood up, took a deep breath, and walked to the window.

"Benita, you okay?"

"I don't know. I'm shocked. Really shocked." Benita had turned toward Leroy with her arms folded. "Tell me about you and my mom. I wanna know everything. I wanna know what happened and why you left us."

Leroy pulled himself away from that memory and walked over to the water dispenser. Taking a breath, he poured two cups of cold water and handed one to Benita. "Here you go. Drink up."

"Thanks." She took a big gulp and threw the empty cup in the nearby trash. "This felt good. You and me. Back at it again. I miss training at your school."

"I miss having you there. You were one of my best students."

Benita placed her hands on Leroy's shoulders. "I was always your *best* student. Who would have thought that same man who trained me would turn out to be my father?"

Leroy gave a hearty laugh. "Right. But you know what? I couldn't ask for a better daughter. I trained you well, Grasshoppa. And we owe it all to your grandmother."

Benita walked over to the dispenser and got herself another cup of water. "Yup. Grams went straight gangsta on you, didn't she?"

"You can say that again. She's a tough old bird. Scary, actually."

"I cannot believe she never told me the truth about you and Mom," Benita said.

"It wasn't her story to tell."

"Hope you're checking in on her."

"I'm keeping my promise, although it's one of the hardest promises I've ever had to keep. She really doesn't like me much," admitted Leroy.

"Not even a little." Benita laughed as she finished drinking her water. She remembered the first time Grace took her to visit Leroy's school, and she was surprised by how rude her grandmother was to Leroy. Grace instructed Benita to join the other students interested in signing up for the next round of classes while she talked to the instructor. As soon as she walked away, Benita noticed that her grandmother was extremely aggressive toward him, but he remained quiet. She later discovered that Grace told Leroy that she knew he was the man who had broken her daughter's heart, and she would never forgive him. However, she also knew how much Benita wanted to learn jujitsu and that Leroy had gained an excellent reputation for having the best school in the city. No matter how much she disliked him, she wanted Benita to learn from the best.

Tossing his cup in the trash, he changed the subject. "So, when do you start your new assignment?"

"I have no idea. I mean, it's been a few months since Carl's arrest, but all I've been doing is sitting on my ass waiting for that call. You know, it's hard. I did all of this training. Got thrown into my first case that I really wasn't ready for, and now? Nothing. I feel antsy. Like, you can't get me revved up, but then pull back when I'm ready to go."

"I know. But, Benita, this is a part of the process. The right project will come along at the right time. Remember when I told you that patience is key for success?"

Leroy placed his large hands on top of Benita's shoulders. "Sit on the floor so I can stretch you out."

Benita plopped down and spread-eagle while Leroy stood behind her and firmly pushed her forward until her chest touched the mat.

"Yowza. I didn't realize how tight I was," she whined.

"Breathe through the pain," Leroy suggested.

"Of course, you can say that, Sensei. You're not the one being stretched out like a rubber band."

Leroy eventually released her, patting her on the back. "Good girl. Now, let's get out of here. I'm starving."

He pulled Benita up from the mat. She gave herself one last stretch before heading toward the ladies' locker room. As they walked past the ring, she noticed two thugs watching the young fighters who were currently boxing. She tapped Leroy on the arm, stopping him before he passed the ropes.

"Wait. Let's watch these two guys for a minute," she suggested as Leroy sighed.

"Benita, it's time to eat, my dear."

"Just a few minutes. Please?"

Leroy stood next to his daughter, watching the two boxers.

"Check out that brutha's technique. He's weak on the left," Benita commented.

Just then, the tall, dark, chocolate man lost his footing, and all of a sudden, the smaller Hispanic guy took control and started using body blows to the left side of the body.

"Doug, you're weak on the left. Block yourself. Keep your hands up. *Hands up.*"

Benita turned to see a slender, middle-aged white man yelling at the young Black boxer. She whispered in her father's ear, "I guess I'm not the only one who's been pushed to the limit, huh?"

Leroy placed his arm around his sweaty daughter. "What are coaches for? Can we go now? I have a class to teach tonight."

Benita looked around the gym, watching different athletes working out.

"How did you find this place?" she asked her father.

"Grady's Boxing Gym has been around longer than you've been born. I used to come here when I was a kid."

"Dang. What was that like, 100 years ago?"

"Ah, you got jokes. Well, Ms. Comedienne, can you please go get dressed so we can leave?"

"All right, already. So bossy."

Leroy laughed at his kid and shook his head. "I'll see you in a few minutes."

As he headed toward the men's locker room, Benita continued to be distracted by the guys transfixed on the young men in the ring. She glanced at them one final time before walking into the ladies' room. Something felt off about these guys, and what she knew about herself was that her gut was screaming that they were bad news. Making a mental note, she would talk to her father about her concerns once they got to the restaurant.

Chapter 2

Benita stepped out of her shiny black Mustang GT and headed toward the elevator. Although she heard footsteps behind her, she never changed her stride. She repositioned her gym bag in case she had to drop it. Ever since she joined DTCU, she had developed a certain paranoia and was always prepared for an attack. Everyone had to be watched. There were only a few people she trusted.

Pulling out a small three-pound weight, she turned around, ready to whack the person who was walking too close behind her. Just as she was about to go into full swing, an arm blocked her aim. Her intense demeanor changed when she realized that it was her lover staring back at her.

"Miguel, what the hell, man? I was about to clock your ass."

He pulled her close and gave her a passionate kiss. "I've been waiting for hours for you to get home."

"You couldn't have called? Texted? You know, like *normal* people?"

"We're not normal people, Benita. We're trained operatives."

"Whatever. Well, your trained operative ass almost got a knot upside your head. When did you get back in town? I thought you were recruiting the next crop of androids."

"Androids? Ha. You got serious jokes. Just got back. Came straight here."

"Yeah, I know, hiding in the damn shadows. At least, you didn't break into my apartment like the last time."

"You're never gonna let me live that down, are you?"

"Nope. Never." Benita turned around and headed toward the elevator. She wasn't interested in talking to him.

"Hey, you just gonna walk away? Did you miss me?"

Miguel tugged on Benita's arm and turned her around. As he pulled her closer, she struggled to break free. "What's going on with you?" Miguel asked.

Benita stopped moving, but she remained stone-faced. When he tried kissing her again, she turned her head. "Will you let me go, please?"

Miguel released his beautiful lover but pleaded for her to stop being so mean to him. "Why don't we go upstairs and talk about what's got you all pissed off at me?"

Benita rolled her eyes and pressed the up button. Although she was happy to see him, she continued to have an attitude.

The elevator door opened, but Benita blocked Miguel's entry.

"Oh no, my Dominican prince, no can do tonight."

"What are you talking about?"

"It's time you do *your* job and find *my* next case. I'm getting tired of hanging around with too much time on my hands. And you know what? I just may get myself in trouble, and we know how much you hate me getting in trouble."

"Benita, why does everything have to be a thing with you?"

Benita placed her hands on her hips and gave him a smirk. "Find me an assignment, Agent Perkins. Because if you don't, you won't be stepping into my crib anytime soon. You feel me?"

Before Miguel could reply, the elevator door closed. He wasn't too shocked by Benita's behavior. He knew she was angry at him, but he had explained that there was a protocol that she had to follow. Every agent had to go through a three-month hiatus to deprogram from the previous case. All agents had to do this before jumping into a new assignment. Benita's first case had put her in a dangerous situation when she took down Carl "Holiday" Johnson, a big-time music mogul who had his hands in different illegal enterprises.

Miguel was not only responsible for her well-being, but he also forced her to give up contacting her family. The guilt sometimes overpowered him, but he knew he'd made the right decision to have Benita work for him. What he didn't plan on was falling in love with the feisty beauty.

The agent slowly walked down the long and lonely parking garage toward his car. He thought about turning around and heading back to her apartment but knew that Benita was not in the mood to hear him out. It was time for her to get back out in the field . . . for both of their sakes.

Taking out his phone, he sent a text to Benita's phone. I promise to find you a new assignment. Love, M. He placed his phone back into this jacket and jumped in his Dodge Durango. He was too tired to deal with Benita's antics tonight and would tackle the task tomorrow. Cranking up his vehicle, the disappointed agent headed to his place for a long, hot shower and a good night's sleep.

Just as Benita's phone buzzed, she walked out on the tenth floor toward her apartment. She knew that her attitude was overkill, but she didn't care. She wanted Miguel to know just how pissed off she was at him. When she got to her apartment, she punched in a five-digit code and unlocked her door. First, flipping on the light, she looked around to make sure that everything was in place before closing the door behind her.

Then she pulled out her phone and quickly read the message from Miguel. Her annoyance faded away as she thought about her Dominican lover. She remembered the first time she met him at the club in Brooklyn, and she was instantly attracted. That smile. Those perfect teeth. He was tall, handsome, and straight-up sexy. Pure perfection. But little did she know that he had set his sights on her long before they met. In fact, he wasn't thinking of her as a love interest but as a recruit for the Domestic Terrorism Crime Unit. She was pissed off at him for the longest time, but eventually, she let her guard down and gave in to her feelings. Miguel became her protector. Her lover. Her everything.

It still felt like a dream when she thought about how she ended up at the DTCU. Most people wouldn't understand how she could forgive the man who set her up for a crime she didn't commit. However, when she thought about how she was living a life she had never dreamed of, the resentment turned to gratitude, and she owed it all to Miguel.

Benita replied, Thank you, M. I'm sorry that I'm such a bitch. Let's connect tomorrow after I get a good night's rest. Leroy kicked my ass today at the gym. Love, B.

Walking down the hallway toward her bedroom, she flicked on the light switch and dropped her gym bag onto the floor. Then she slowly peeled off her clothes, feeling every part of her aching body. "Sensei Leroy, you seriously tried to kill me today." She grinned when she thought about her instructor. "I mean, Dad." Chuckling to herself, she walked to the bathroom and took a long, hot shower.

Twenty minutes later, Benita put on her favorite white fluffy robe and strolled into the kitchen, where she poured herself a hot cup of herbal green tea. She often thought about all the times when she came home from work, karate class, or school and sat down with her grandmother Grace to catch up on the day's events.

She could almost hear her saying, *"Benita Renee Jenkins, come on in here and join your gramma. You hungry? I got a plate for you."*

To which she would reply, "Thank you, Grams. but I'm not really hungry."

"You always say that you ain't hungry. But I'm here to tell you that you need to eat. I don't want to see my grandbaby waste away. Not only do you need to feed your stomach, but you also need to feed your soul. It takes a lot of energy to accomplish all of the things you're doing with your life."

"You're right, Grams."

**

Benita sat at her kitchen table thinking about how she missed her grandmother's sweet face and the way her nose would wrinkle when she was passionate about a topic. She wiped away the tears that ran down her face. She laughed when she thought about how her grandmother would spew her conspiracy theories. And come to find out, many of those theories turned out to be true. Grace had a sixth sense like none other, and Benita knew she'd inherited her grandmother's discernment.

As Benita sipped on her tea, she heard the buzz from another phone where she kept it hidden in a cutout book strategically placed on a shelf. It was a text from her brother, Wes.

Hey, B. Just checking in on you. Saw Sensei Leroy tonight. Good looking out for me to join his class.

Benita typed her reply. Glad to hear that news. It's about time you're doing something with your life. How's Grams?

Grams still crazy. But you gotta love her. Well, I gotta bounce. Hope to see you soon.

Love, Wes.

All she could think about was dropping by her family's home. Her father told her to be careful not to get caught because the last thing she needed was for anyone to find out that she wasn't following orders. Miguel had made it clear to her that she was forbidden to reach out to her family.

"So, are you telling me that if I choose to work for the DTCU, I have to cut off all contact with my family?" Benita asked.

"Benita, if you want to stay out of prison and keep your family safe, then, yes, that is what I'm telling you. No ifs or buts about it," Miguel warned.

Benita begrudgingly accepted Miguel's offer to come work for him. However, that wouldn't stop her from keeping in touch with Wes, who had almost gotten killed while in the crossfire of her last case. She put her life on the line to save his. Nothing was going to stop her from saving her little brother. Once Carl was captured, Benita had worked it out with Miguel to allow Wes to live a normal life if he promised to keep her secret to himself. Because if he didn't, there would be some serious repercussions for the entire family. Little did Miguel know, Benita had bought Wes a burner phone to use when he needed to contact her. Benita had made Wes promise always to keep their secret.

She hated keeping secrets from Miguel about her communicating with Wes, but she knew that he would shut it down had he known. Not only would he blow a gasket, but he would also make sure that she would never see her family again. She wasn't willing to take that chance. He was always telling her she needed to follow the rules, but this was one rule she wasn't going to.

Although she knew Miguel was right because she *was* putting her family in danger, she just couldn't listen to him. *No way am I going to cut off my family—no matter what*. Her brother was the only lifeline she had to her grandmother and cousin Deon, and she refused to give them up.

Benita sent one last text. Love you, little bro. Stay safe. She placed the burner phone back in the cutout book and returned it to the shelf. Plopping down on her white leather couch, she grabbed the remote and switched on her flat-screen television to watch her favorite movie, *La Femme Nikita*. She covered herself with her blanket and got cozy, thinking about her sexy lover. Soon, she picked up the phone and called Miguel, who was driving back to his apartment.

"Hello?" Miguel answered.

"Hi. Sorry about earlier. You know I can be extra sometimes."

Miguel chuckled because he knew that his beautiful lover was still a fiery one. "I promise you that

I'll do what I have to do to get back into your good graces. I want it to be the perfect case for you."

"Understood. Now, tell me about your trip and how much you missed me."

They spent the next hour talking about the last three weeks since Miguel had been gone on his assignment in Africa. Before they finally got off the phone, Benita commented, "Sweet dreams, my love. Sweet dreams."

Chapter 3

Miguel woke up super early to go for his morning run. He was happy to have been able to talk to Benita before finally heading to bed. He hated seeing her mad, and more importantly, he didn't want to disappoint her. He checked his phone and saw that she had left him a cute message. Good morning, handsome. Can't wait to see you tonight.

He smiled when he thought about how much he cared for her. He had promised her before they got off the phone that he would work on finding her a case today. Hopefully, it would happen before he saw her later on that evening. He thought about how much he missed his firecracker girlfriend while he was in Johannesburg. It had been a long time since he felt so strongly for a woman. The entire time he was away from her, he kept thinking about making love to her and seeing her beautiful face.

But last night threw him for a loop when she gave him a frosty reception. It didn't matter that he had been gone for the past month. She was being typical Benita when she didn't get her way. He knew that she was mad at him, but he never thought she would reject him the way she did. Even after telling her that she had to be patient, she still punished him. However, he felt better after she called him back, asking about his trip.

He looked over at the empty side of his bed and took a deep breath. As much as he wanted his woman next to him, he couldn't make it happen this morning. It had been a long time since they had snuggled up to each other and had made love all night. He loved how she would purr like a kitten when she fell asleep. He smiled when he thought about seeing her tonight.

The first time he saw this beautiful woman was before he recruited her into the organization. She was standing at the Brooklyn bus stop when two neighborhood thugs accosted her. Along with two of his fellow agents, Alex Stratsburg and Carlos Santos, he was sitting in an unmarked van located across the street. He was shocked at how well this woman handled herself in a situation that could have ended up badly. All he could think about at the time was to find out just who this badass lady was. *Never in a million years would I have thought I would have fallen in love with you, but I did.*

Finally, sitting on the edge of the bed, he thought about his friend, Agent Willard Cole. *Maybe Willard can help me out.* After a few more minutes of contemplating his next move, Miguel called his buddy.

Willard was at the gun range and saw Miguel's number pop up on his phone. "Perkins, what's happening, my friend? You back from Africa already?" Willard asked.

"Yup. I'm back. Never a dull day at the DTCU," Miguel replied.

"You got that right. So, what's up?"

"I was hoping you could help me with one of my agents. You know, hook me up with one of your cases."

Willard's rumbling laughter filled the phone. "You must really need my help if you're calling me this early. What's the little bastard's name?"

Miguel held the phone against his forehead, wondering if he should tell him or not.

"Hello, you still there?"

"Ah, yeah. Her name is Benita Renee Jenkins."

"Crap," Cole said. "What the fuck, Miguel? You know I don't generally take women on my cases. Shit, she must be a handful if you're trying to land her an assignment. Wait . . . Something you want to tell me?"

"No. Of course not. She's anxious to get on another assignment. And since I just got back into town, I don't have any active cases," Miguel muttered. "Plus, I immediately thought of you.

You have a special way of handling new agents. You know what I'm saying?"

"Whatever you need, my man. How soon do you need an assignment?" Willard asked.

"Like yesterday," he replied.

"Like yesterday, huh? Well, that's a big order. I got a pile of special assignments that I can go through. You coming in later today? We can go through them together, and you can see what jumps out at you."

"Yeah, that sounds like a plan."

"Great. I'm finishing up at the gun range, and then I'm off to the track. See ya later."

"Thanks, man," Miguel replied.

"No problem. Anything for you, my friend."

Willard hung up the phone and smiled when he thought about Miguel's request. He knew that either Miguel owed a major favor or had a hidden agenda if he was reaching out to him. Most people didn't like working with him, but Miguel was one of the good ones who appreciated his set of skills that only he could bring to a case. Willard had an uncanny ability to use his quick wit and judgment to handle any situation. He could spot a criminal a mile away and assess if he were going to be trouble. He was praised for thinking quickly on his feet and making sound judgments when closing a case.

Willard studied his training manual daily to stay prepared for all of his cases, working hard to maintain perfect mental and physical fitness. He was a master in self-defense, firearms, operational training, and the written manuals used at the academy to prepare new agents for the field. Unfortunately, Willard lacked strong interpersonal skills, which made him unpopular among the new agents and his colleagues. He never allowed anyone to get over on him for any reason. He knew the importance of each case, and he would push his agents to the brink to make sure that they did everything by the book. He reminded the agents that they needed to take their cases seriously in their pursuit of justice. Willard had a strong, creative mind and high intelligence with exceptional problem-solving abilities. He loved his job and demonstrated great patriotism. Although the top agents respected him, he was less popular among his colleagues due to his lack of social skills.

Standing only five feet tall, he overcompensated for his lack of height by using all his other skills to command respect. Most of the time, he would bark orders to get what he needed to be done. He would stop at nothing to close a case, and if that meant he worked his agents to the bone, then so be it.

For the past fifteen years, he had trained over 400 agents and closed more than 100 gang-related cases, surpassing all other agents working at the DTCU. What he loved most about his job was people's willingness to look beyond a tough exterior and allow him to excel in his career.

Although Agent Cole was generally not well-liked, Miguel interacted with him differently. He had always treated Willard with respect. They had become friends over their tenure at DTCU, and after working on a few assignments together, Miguel saw through Willard's façade. He wasn't fazed by Willard's violent outbursts and accepted him for who he was: a hardworking overachiever who always wanted to win.

Willard remembered when he and Miguel were having drinks after a long day at the office, and a guy began harassing Willard's friend, Geraldine, who was walking back from the bathroom. As she passed by the disorderly guy, he became a little too friendly toward her. That's when Willard lost it and started yelling at the man to leave his friend alone.

"Hey, let her pass," Willard barked.

"Fuck you, man. Why you even taking up for this ho?"

"Whatchu say, asshole?" Willard shouted back.

"Keep a-stepping, little man."

Willard balled up his fists as he moved one step closer to the drunken guy sitting on a high stool. The guy turned his back on Willard and shooed him away.

"Bartender, pour me another drink, please."

"Hey, you don't talk to a lady like that," Willard shouted again.

"What? Listen, I talk to all the hoes that way. I guess that makes you a ho lover, huh?"

As the drunk laughed, Willard pushed him in the shoulder.

"Willard, it's okay. Let's go." Geraldine, who tried to defuse the situation, pleaded with him to leave with her, but it was too late for this spitfire.

"Geraldine, it's okay. I'll handle this," Willard responded.

Taking a swig of his rum and Coke, the drunk slurred his words. "Yeah, Willard, why don't you go away? I'm trying to mind my own business, and you should do the same thing, little man."

"Did you just call me . . . little man?"

The stranger pushed his stool back and stood up, facing Willard.

"Yeah. And whatchu gonna do now?"

"This." Willard kicked the man in the balls and punched him in the face, causing him to grab his crotch before falling to his knees in agony.

Willard was about to kick him again, but Miguel pulled him away.

"Hey, now, Willard. Stop, man."

"Let go of me, Perkins. Let go."

"Calm the hell down, would ya? It's time to go. Like now," Miguel responded.

Then the guy stood up and charged at Willard. However, Miguel spotted him out of the corner of his eye and punched him in the stomach. This time, the drunk doubled over. Then he charged at Miguel, who swiftly moved out of the way and pushed the man in the back, causing him to fall into a few neighboring stools, where he hit the floor with a thud.

"Damn, Perkins. I didn't know you had it in ya."

Miguel looked at Willard and shook his head. "You ready to go?"

Willard looked down at the unconscious man and took his girlfriend's hand as they walked out of the bar.

Willard smiled when he thought about how Miguel had always had his back ever since that night at the bar. He had never had someone to take up for him as Miguel did, and from that point on, whatever Miguel needed, he was there to give it to him. Because in the end, loyalty was the name of the game.

"Can't wait to find out what's going on with you, Miguel." He reloaded his gun and continued working on his aim. Bull's-eye every time.

Chapter 4

Benita and her sparring partner, Evan Green, had been in the ring at Grady's for about forty-five minutes. Since Leroy introduced her to this little, wonderful hole-in-the-wall, she came in several times a week with her father or Evan. She thought about asking Miguel, but he had spent the last few months out of the country. Plus, she was still salty that she hadn't been assigned a new case. Neither she nor Evan had been assigned to a new case, and both were anxious to get things moving.

"Come on, Evan, you hit like a girl." Benita gave him a quick uppercut and a body blow, causing him to wince.

"Ow, Benita. What happened to a 'friendly' round of sparring?"

Benita flashed him a devious smile and gave him one of her famous swivel kicks. Evan lost his balance and landed on his backside.

"Okay, okay. I'm done," he snapped.

"Oops. I'm sorry. I don't know what came over me. I guess I just have a little bit too much energy to work off." As she stretched out her hand to help her friend to his feet, he pulled her down to the floor.

"Dammit. That was a low blow," Benita complained.

He burst into laughter. "And now you know how *I* feel. My ribs are gonna be sore for at least a week."

Benita remembered the first time that she had met Evan. She had walked into the exercise room at the DTCU building with Miguel and had noticed a tall, chocolate recruit drinking a cup of water. Their eyes immediately locked, and a warm feeling came over her. He had flashed his pearly white smile. However, when Miguel took notice, Evan's entire demeanor changed. He stood straight and serious. Benita has spent the morning sparring with her new boss, and when Samantha DeVreau entered the room, the beautiful agent asked Evan to show Benita around the facility while she spoke to Miguel.

"So, how does it feel becoming a new agent?" Benita asked as Evan gave her the tour.

"You know, this is a dream come true for me. Would you believe I started in the mail room? And thanks to Director Bolden, I have a chance to do something great with my life."

"Director Bolden?"

"Yeah, he believed in me, and I will be forever grateful to him for getting me into this training program."

After they graduated from the program and became full-fledged agents, they were assigned to the same case. They quickly learned how to work together and, importantly, became friends.

"Remember the first time we sparred?" Evan asked as he stood up.

"Oh, how could I forget?" Benita laughed. "You said you didn't want to hurt me because I was a girl."

Evan laughed as he stretched out his back. "Clearly, I didn't know what I was saying. I mean, you kicked my ass. I'm just happy you didn't put a hurting on me like you did our friend Carl."

Benita nodded in agreement when she thought about the fight she had with Carl. When she recalled how he had almost killed her brother, Wes, the anger began to seep through. She shook off the bad feelings and bent over to stretch out her arms and shoulder blades. Noticing a young man shadow boxing by himself, Benita tapped Evan on the arm.

"Hey, check that guy out. I saw him the other night. He's got great form, but something feels off."

"Really? Maybe you should give him some point-ers."

Benita playfully punched Evan in the side. "Maybe I will, smarty-pants."

"Smarty-pants? What are we, like five?"

Benita climbed out of the ring and walked up to the young man, who was focused on perfecting his punch combinations.

"Hey, love your form. Somebody's training you, right?"

Without stopping his routine, he replied, "Thanks. My coach is always riding me, telling me I need to practice."

"Don't they all? Listen, if you ever want a spar-ring partner, I'm here a lot. I can help you out."

"Thanks, but I don't spar with girls."

"Really? Is that right? Why's that?" Benita ques-tioned the intense athlete.

"Because girls can't pack a punch."

Benita turned to face Evan, who shrugged his shoulders. Evan tapped Benita on the arm, but she was ignoring him. "B, let's leave this guy to his practice, okay?"

"What's your name?" Benita asked.

"Doug."

"Well, Doug, I see you have a distorted opinion of women, but sometimes you should be open to opportunities that come your way. You just might be surprised what girls can do."

"I'll keep that in mind. Can I get back to my training?"

Benita threw her arms in the air, signaling that she was giving up. She turned toward Evan, and they headed to the locker room.

"Benita, is it that hard to believe that he doesn't *need* your help?"

"I was only trying to be friendly. I don't get men."

Evan laughed at her comment. "Just like men don't get women."

Benita cocked her head to the side with a curious look on her face. "Really? Men don't get women?"

"No, we don't. You say that you want one thing, but you actually want something else. Very complicated."

"Oh, puh-leeze. Men claim that they are so simple, but how many times have you guys changed your mind about things? Never satisfied . . . Always wanting something more. Never clear about your intentions."

"Hey, I beg to differ. We know *exactly* what we want, when we want it. In fact, we are very intentional in our approach. I don't know who you've dealt with in the past, but clearly, you haven't had a man who has both good intentions and integrity. When you have those two things, everything else falls into place. But enough talking about men and women. I think Doug over there has made it clear that he doesn't want to be bothered by you."

"You know what, Evan?"

"What, Benita?" he laughed.

"Whatever, man."

"Yeah, that's right. I said what I said."

Benita smirked at him, relented, and nodded in agreement.

"Wow. Benita finally stands down. I better move out of the way because lightning may strike right here and now. Okay, can we go now?" Evan smiled as he headed to the shower. "See you in ten."

Benita yelled at her friend as he walked away. "Well, don't get used to that. You know I always speak my mind. Plus, I'm always right."

Although Benita was annoyed by Evan's comments, she agreed that the young boxer wasn't interested in sparring with her. Disappointed, she shrugged her shoulders and finally walked into the women's locker room to shower. Ten minutes later, she exited, half-expecting to see Evan waiting for her. Peeking around the corner, she saw that he had not come out of the locker room yet. *Why am I not surprised?* Her prima donna friend was notorious for being late. He spent more time grooming than she ever did. *How many more "ten minutes" do you need, Evan?*

Leaning against the wall, Benita noticed a petite, older lady carrying a large shopping bag walking toward Doug. Expecting him to be rude, she waited for him to mouth something nasty. However, she was pleasantly surprised when he hugged and kissed her on the cheek. Benita soon realized that Doug was interacting with his grandmother. She instantly became sad when she thought about her own grandmother. *I miss Grams. I wonder what she's doing right now.*

"Nana, what are you doing here?" Doug asked.

"Well, how else am I going to see my grandbaby? You work all night and then come to this gym and spend half the day here. I know you're not eating like you should. So, I thought I'd come here on my day off." She handed him his lunch. "Now, I didn't bring enough for all your friends here at the gym—"

"They're not my friends, Nana." He guided the elderly woman to a small table and chairs by the window and said, "Why don't we sit here?" and he pulled out the chair for her to sit.

"Doug, now, don't be rude."

"Sorry, Nana. I know how you love taking care of people, but you don't need to do that here. These people . . ."

Nana patted her grandson on his hand. "The good Lord put us on this earth to help one another. As long as I have strength in these bones, I'll always help. Now, eat your food, will ya?"

Doug nodded at his grandmother and opened the bag of food. His eyes lit up when he pulled out a container of fried macaroni and cheese balls and a jerk chicken sub sandwich.

"Nana, you do know that I'm in training, right?"

"Of course, my dear grandson. And I know you'll burn those calories off in no time," she replied. "Now, eat up."

The young boxer took a bite out of the sub and closed his eyes, savoring every morsel.

Nana looked around the gym and noticed a young beauty leaning against the wall. The young lady was glancing over at her and Doug. She smiled. "Doug, do you know that gorgeous young lady?"

"Who?" Turning around, he saw Benita. "Oh, her. No, not really. I mean, I met her earlier."

Nana raised her eyebrow and cocked her head to the side. "Okay, Doug. What happened?"

"Nothing. I mean, she wanted to work out with me, but I told her that I don't spar with girls."

"Well, she looks like she can handle herself just fine."

Doug bit into the sub and tried to ignore his grandmother's comments. He knew what she was trying to insinuate, but he refused to give her any energy when it came to her pestering about finding a girlfriend. He needed to remain focused on his training since his next fight was coming up in a few weeks.

"She's pretty too."

"All right, Nana. So, what else do you have planned for the day since you have the day off?"

Elsie chuckled at her grandson because she knew how much he hated her trying to play matchmaker. He was all business with no intentions of dating. She wanted him to have some kind of balance in his life and not just focus on boxing. But she didn't want to push him. "Well, I got some errands to run before heading home." She couldn't help but glance over at the young woman standing by the bathroom. Maybe Doug would change his mind and work out with her. At one point, Elsie gave her a casual wave while Doug wasn't looking. This caused Benita to wave back.

Benita kept glancing over at Doug and his grandmother as they enjoyed a meal together. Her heart filled with sorrow when she thought about her own grandmother. It had been a long time since she had laid eyes on Grace, and at that moment, the pain was too much for her. She blinked to hold back the tears. Evan finally came out of the locker room and noticed Benita's distraction.

"Hey, my friend. You ready to go?" he asked.

Without looking in Evan's direction, Benita picked up her bag and started walking toward the exit. "Yup. Let's get that drink. I definitely need one," she muttered to him.

Chapter 5

By the time Miguel had arrived at the agency, he found Willard sitting in the conference room separating a stack of folders into piles for Miguel to review. He was writing on multicolored notes and sticking them on different folders to prioritize the cases from the most recent to the oldest.

"Hey, Perkins, I see you finally made it to the office," he commented without looking up. "I thought you had forgotten about me."

"Well, after running five miles, taking a shower, and checking in with my boss, I needed a beat to prepare mentally for your shenanigans," Miguel replied.

"Shenanigans, indeed," he laughed.

Miguel walked over to the coffee machine and poured himself a cup. He looked back over his shoulder and watched as Willard meticulously positioned the folders in perfect stacks. "Wow. Look at all of those files. I didn't realize you had that many open cases, Willard."

"That's what happens when there are so many criminal activities happening at the same time. Shit builds up. And with the limited number of agents that I trust to close a case, I'm stuck with these. And they just keep coming. I think I got at least another ten this morning to review."

Miguel sat down across from Willard and sipped his coffee. "Well, I'm sure you're gearing up for the next batch of agents you can boss around and work to death," he chuckled.

"Hey, somebody's got to whip these fuckers into shape. And if the organization trusts me to do it, then who am I to say no? Plus, I'm damn great at it. Love training those little bastards. You know I can't stand lazy asses."

Miguel continued sipping on his coffee. "Yup, I know you do. So, whatchu got for me?"

"It all depends on what kind of case you're looking for. Let's talk about your agent. What's her name again?" Willard asked.

Miguel rubbed his chin and went into deep thought.

"Earth to Perkins. Hello?" Willard sat back in his chair and removed the glasses he was wearing.

"What?" Miguel asked. "Oh, her name is Benita."

"Care to explain what's going on here?"

Miguel looked at his friend with a straight face because he didn't want him to read his true reaction.

"Yeah, her. And I need to lock her in fast or—"

"Or what? Miguel, are you involved with this agent? Is she trying to blackmail you?"

Miguel smiled. "Blackmail? What are you talking about, blackmail? No. Of course not. Blackmail. What kind of guy do you think I am?"

"Miguel, you and I go way back. You and I know this isn't the first time a woman has caused some drama in your life, and I'm sure it won't be the last. And now, with this damn 'Me Too' movement, I don't want you to get caught out there and risk your career. You feel me?"

"Yeah, I feel ya. Look, I brought her in on a case last year, and I just want to make sure that she's taken care of. That's all. Now, can we get back to your cases? Which ones should I look through first?" Miguel reached for the group of folders currently in front of him.

"Did you reach out to any of the other agents and check on which cases they had?" Willard asked.

"No. Why would I do that when I knew you had openings?"

Willard nodded at his friend and continued writing on his notepad. "Okay, then. Tell me about this agent. What's she like? What are her skills? Why is she so important to you?"

Miguel continued to keep his same composure. He was not going to allow Willard to see him crack. "Well, she's extremely intelligent. Very street savvy.

Quick thinking . . . like yourself. And very head-strong. She's the kind of agent who will find her own case if she has too much time on her hands. Like now."

"Oh, she's a wild card. And I bet you she loves pursuing cases simply because her gut tells her to."

"Yeah, and if I don't rein her in soon, then—"

"Let me guess. Director Jeremiah Bolden will have your ass."

"Bingo. And we know you don't want the direc-tor to get involved. Not if I can help it. I don't even wanna think about how bad it could go. That's what I'm trying to avoid at all costs." Miguel tried not to look his friend in the eye because he knew he would see right through his façade. No way was he going to tell him the truth about his re-lationship with Benita, no matter how much he wanted to share.

"Look, she's still green but is an excellent agent. I loved how she worked hard to bring down a major thug in Brooklyn, and it was her first case. I just want to keep her engaged so as not to go rogue on me," Miguel said.

"Well, Daddy Bird, all you can do is hope that when they jump out of the nest, they learn how to fly," Willard chuckled.

"Yeah yeah yeah. I hear ya. That's why I know you're going to find the perfect case for me."

"Okay, I'll keep looking, but you owe me, Perkins."

Miguel smiled and nodded in agreement. "You know I gotchu."

Willard smirked as he stood up to leave the conference room. "Well, one day, I'm taking you up on that promise. But for now, I'll settle for you taking these folders to my office after you finish looking through them. I got a briefing in ten minutes. Enjoy, my friend."

"Thanks, Willard."

Miguel muttered to himself that it would be a long day and sighed as he began to comb through the many piles of folders currently stacked on the table. No matter the time, he was committed to finding Benita the next case in order for her to remain happy.

Chapter 6

Benita and Evan drank their bottles of Dos Equis while munching on nachos and guacamole. They watched mixed martial arts on several flat-screen televisions located behind the bar at Los Mintos. "Do you wish you could still compete?" Evan stared at Benita as she gulped down the last of her beer.

"Yeah. It was definitely one of the things on my bucket list, but between work and school, I barely had enough time to keep up with my jujitsu classes." She quickly changed the subject. "Hey, any word on your new assignment?"

"Nope, not yet. You?" he asked.

"Not a word. Here, I thought we would be swimming in new cases. But, noooo, we got to wait and keep a low profile. I'm seriously not the patient kind."

Evan popped a peanut in his mouth and nodded in agreement. "It's all good, B. I'm not mad about the time off. I mean, the last case was pretty intense. You should just roll with it. Enjoy the downtime. Trust me, we'll be in deep cover very soon."

"Well, I'm ready to go now. I wanna go where the action is. This sitting around waiting is driving me crazy. I can only work out and eat Mexican food for so long."

"You mean your boy Perkins hasn't found you a case yet? I thought he would make sure his star pupil would be set by now."

"What is that supposed to mean? I'm not his star pupil," Benita protested.

"Oh, okay."

"No, seriously. You act like I get special treatment. Well, I don't. Agent Perkins is always preaching proper protocol and probation. So, no, he didn't hook me up with any new cases. I gotta wait like everybody else. But I tell you what, though. I didn't sign up to play wait-and-see. You know what I'm saying?"

Evan took a long swig of his beer and nodded. "Girl, you're preaching to the choir."

"You know what we should do? We should go by the office tomorrow morning and demand that we get assigned a new case. And if they don't, then we'll find one ourselves."

"Really? *That's* what you want to do? Well, I think I'd rather chill out for a minute. A new case will come. Trust and believe that."

She drank more of her beer. "So, what do you think of Doug?"

"Who?" Evan asked.

Benita looked strangely at Evan as if he had two heads. "Umm, the guy from the gym? Remember him? His name is Doug."

"Oh, *that* Doug. What about him? What's your deal with him anyway?"

Benita picked up her bottle but placed it back down when she realized it was empty. "Something don't feel right about him. He's working hard. Real hard . . ."

"Of course, he's working hard. Clearly, he's in training, B. You don't expect him to be smiling and throwing up pleasantries, do you? Come on. If anyone should understand what's going on with him, it's you. It takes a lot of discipline to become a boxer. Plus, dude is a Black man trying to do something good with his life, and I'm sure he's staying clear of the streets."

"Of course, I know that, Evan. But—"

"But what?" he asked.

"Listen, I feel in my gut something's going to happen to him."

"What are you, a psychic or something? 'Something's going to happen to him.'" Evan shook his head and finished his beer along with a handful of peanuts. Annoyed that he didn't have any more food to eat, he searched for a server to come to their table. "Where's our waitress? I need more food."

"Evan, are you listening to me?"

"Yes, Benita. I'm listening to you. But I'm not understanding what you're saying. You don't make any sense."

Benita responded, "Okay. Hear me out, will you?"

Evan raised his hand to get his waitress's attention. When she looked his way, he held up his empty beer bottle in one hand and put up two fingers, signaling her to bring over two more bottles of beer.

"Hey, Earth to Evan. Focus, please?"

"Okay, already. I'm focused. Now, explain to me how you came up with this conclusion after seeing this guy earlier today."

"I've seen him several times at the gym."

"And?"

Benita took a long breath to stop before going into her explanation. "Well, I was just about to tell you . . . Leroy and I were at the gym earlier this week, and that's when I first saw Doug sparring in the ring. What was interesting to me was when I noticed these two shady characters checking him out. They were whispering and shit. You know, making gestures as if they were plotting something."

"That's all you got?" Evan frowned.

"What do you mean, is that all I got? I'm telling you that those guys are bad news and are up to no good. They want something from that kid. I have a bad feeling those guys are hanging around the gym for the wrong reasons, and it ain't because they want to work out."

"Girl, you're too much. I mean, you just found out this guy's name like an hour ago? And now, you've created this whole scenario in your head that he's in trouble or something? Are you so desperate to be on a case that you're making things up?"

Benita placed her arms on the table and clasped her hands together. "When it comes to my sixth sense, I'm *never* wrong. I know what I saw, and I know what I feel. And I'm telling you that things are not right, and shit is going to hit the fan."

"Okay, let's just say that you're right. What then? What are you gonna do about it?"

Evan smiled as the cute chocolate waitress brought over two beers and more guacamole and chips, placing them on the table. "Thank youuuu soooo much." He winked, signaling to the server that he was checking her out.

"You're welcome." The waitress but an extra wiggle in her step as she walked away from the table.

"You mean, what are *we* gonna do?"

"No way, sis. This is all on you. I'm not gonna be part of your off-duty project."

"What else you got going on? Huh? How many days are you just going to sit around and wait for something to happen? While we got the time off, let's do a little investigative work. Come on, Evan, how are we gonna get better as agents and stay on the top of our game if we don't solve cases?"

Evan grabbed a few chips and dipped them in the guacamole. "All right. All right. What have you got in mind?"

"Well, I thought we would reach out to Huey—"

"Wait. Huey? Nope. Not gonna do it. Not Huey. He'll rat us out. Dude has no loyalty to people. Only the company."

"Noooo. That's not true. He likes us."

"No. He likes *you*. That guy caves faster than a house of cards. Plus, you know he's afraid of his own shadow. More trouble than he's worth."

Benita knew that Evan was right, but that wasn't going to deter her from getting the information she wanted. "Evan, it's going to be fine. I'll call Huey in the morning and ask him for this little favor. It will take him like two seconds to pull up information on Grady's Gym. I'm sure he can let us know if there have been any kind of issues or situations happening in or around the gym like gambling or money laundering or something like that."

When Evan heard Benita's comments, he quickly became skittish. "Gambling? Money laundering? Really, B?"

"Listen, we gotta cover all bases. We'll head back to the gym tomorrow, snap some of the locals, and do a little bit of digging. We'll just check on Doug E. Fresh, making sure he's okay. You feel me?"

Benita and Evan picked up the bottles and toasted to their new case.

"Here's to partnership," she said.

"Whatever you say, B. I just hope that your little project doesn't backfire on us. I'm seriously not trying to get in trouble when we're still in our probationary period."

Benita smiled. "Oh, Evan, you worry too much. Everything's going to be fine. Trust me."

"Where have I heard that before?"

They finished watching the fight, and Benita felt a burst of excitement when she thought of getting back into the investigative mode with her partner and friend. An hour later, they left Los Mintos and headed toward her car parked two blocks away. She loved the little neighborhood of Perth Amboy, New Jersey. Smith Street had a small shopping center catering to working-class customers. It was a blue-collar town, and for the most part, it was quiet and close to major transportation. Most shops closed on the early side, but Los Mintos and Grady's Gym served the insomniacs and the nocturnal workout enthusiasts.

"That last fight was a good one, Evan. I mean, I knew Benny was gonna knock Curtis out."

"Nah, that was a lucky punch. That's all it was. They were going toe-to-toe for at least six rounds."

"If that's what you wanna believe, fine. But you owe me twenty bucks."

Benita stuck out her hand, waiting for Evan to pony up. After a bit of resistance, he eventually reached into his front pocket, pulling out a crumpled bill.

"Next time, remind me not to bet you on some MMA fighters."

"Hey, you forget that I know every fighter's stats. Sorry, playa." She snatched the money from his hand, playfully examining it to see if it were counterfeit. "Let me find out you're walking around with fake dollars in your pocket . . ."

"Oh no, my sister. My dollars are the real deal."

They playfully bantered back and forth when they spotted Doug leaving the gym with two men trailing him. As soon as the young fighter turned left out of the building, the thugs accosted him. They began pushing him against the wall, but Doug shoved them off of him. Suddenly, a loud argument ensued.

Benita looked at Evan. "Damn, those are the same guys that I saw earlier this week."

"Are you sure?" he asked.

"Oh, I'm sure. Those are the same muthafuckers. See? I told you something wasn't right with those guys."

"Yup. It looks like your sixth sense has paid off," he commented.

"Hey, what's going on over there?" Benita yelled.

One of the guys wearing a red and blue shirt turned toward Benita and Evan.

"Bitch, you need to mind your own business," he shouted back at the agents as he pulled up his shirt, revealing a gun secured by his belt buckle.

Shocked by the gangster's action, Benita looked over at Evan and said, "Wait. Did that guy just flash his gun at us?"

Chapter 7

Clay Garner and his friend, Loco, walked out of Grady's Gym, annoyed as they jumped into the back of Reggie's car, where he and Ace were waiting. The four men parked up the street from the establishment, then waited patiently for Doug to leave the gym. Reggie looked at the clock on the dashboard and saw that it was nine o'clock. An hour had passed since they first got there, and now he was irritated that Sean's brother was still working out.

"Is the little fucker even in there?" Ace asked.

"Yeah, he's there. Ninja acts like he ain't got a care in the world. Damn, I ain't never seen someone so committed as that dude," Loco commented.

"I just don't get it. Dude don't got a life? I mean, why he just wanna work out all the time at the damn gym?" Clay started vaping.

"All I know is that it ain't gonna be so easy to grab him. Dude is ripped and strong. He got a punch that will go through the wall. Reggie, he like Iron Man and shit," Loco commented.

Reggie frowned back at Loco. "Well, we got a job to do. So, I need for you and Clay to grab that muthafucka and throw him in the trunk so we can take him to my boy J's warehouse. He needs to understand that he must fight to pay off his brother Sean's debt."

"Reggie, like I said, dude is Iron Man, and I'm not going to fuck with him. You need to handle this shit," Loco replied.

Reggie turned around and stared at Loco until he withered in his seat. "Well, I can't do it because the little fucker knows who I am. So, Ace'll go with Clay since you're a scared little bitch."

"Who you calling a scared little bitch?" Loco whined.

Reggie pulled out his electronic cigarette and smirked back at Loco. "Well, I'm not the one concerned about getting beat up. All I know is that he needs to bring his boxer ass out, so we can get out of here," Reggie barked.

"Your boy Sean is straight-up gangsta for setting up his brother like this. That's really fucked up, you know what I'm saying? He's a stone-cold gangsta. Shit, they must hate each other if he's got to go through all of this trouble to ask for help," Ace commented.

"Well, unfortunately, shit happens, you know. This ain't nuthin' new. We just got a real Cain and Abel on our hands, believe that." Reggie remembered the day when he suggested that he and his crew have a come-to-Jesus talk with Doug, and at first, Sean was not interested in having any of that, but eventually, he consented.

"Man, listen, you need to let me handle this shit because clearly, your brother ain't listening to you." Reggie stared at his friend, who was pacing back and forth.

"I don't know, Reggie. What if something goes wrong? I can't have you and your boys hurt my brother," Sean replied.

"We not going to hurt your brother, but I think it's time that you need to take this situation more seriously. All I'm saying is that we just scare him a bit and make him understand that our lives are on the line if he doesn't participate in these fights."

"I know . . . but I don't know."

"Listen, I've already spoken to Jermaine, who's going to give you one more chance to repay the money. I'd rather deal with him than A-Roc, who is ruthless and will stop at nothing to get his money back."

Sean thought long and hard about what his friend was saying to him and finally agreed to speak to his brother about the fight. "Listen, let me speak to my brother, and I'll see if he'll do it."

"Well, you better hurry up because if he doesn't fight, then you're screwed. Nope, we're both screwed since I brought you into these dudes' world. Believe that," Reggie said with feeling.

Reggie took another puff and inhaled. He thought about how desperate Sean was after his brother turned him down. He finally came to his senses and asked Reggie for help. And ever since Reggie introduced Sean to the gangster who ran the boxing ring, he was responsible for paying off any debts that Sean didn't. Now, he was focused on grabbing Doug when he left the gym. He perked up when the boxer exited the building and tapped Ace on the arm, pointing in the young man's direction. "Finally. You know what to do."

Ace and Clay got out of the car and followed Doug. As they approached the young boxer who was carrying his gym bag, he didn't flinch when they stepped in front of him.

"Hey, you. Ain't you Doug Gibson? You that fighter, right?" Clay glanced around.

"What do you want?" Doug tried to walk around them.

"Wait, can we holla atchu for a second?" Ace asked.

"Actually, I'm late for work. Can't really talk right now," Doug responded.

Clay tapped Ace on the arm. "Oh, he can't talk right now? Well, I think you could holla at us for a minute or two."

Confused by the exchange, Doug wasn't sure what these guys wanted, but he knew that the best thing he could do was to keep walking because he didn't want any drama. All he wanted to do was to mind his own business and get to work.

"Sorry, fellas, I really can't talk right now," Doug reiterated.

Suddenly, Ace pushed Doug against the wall. "I think you can make time. Like right now."

"What the fuck is you doing? Who the hell are you, and what do you want from me?" Doug hollered.

"We got some business to discuss. So, you are gonna relax and come with us."

Doug pushed Ace off of him, but Ace and Clay pushed him against the wall again. "Get the hell off of me, or you're the one who is going to get hurt. I sure as hell ain't going anywhere with you two assholes."

"You'll do what I tell you to do. Don't make this shit harder than it needs to be," Ace ordered. "Now, come on."

Out of nowhere, a young woman began yelling at them from across the street. "Hey, what's going on over there?" the woman yelled.

Ace pulled up his shirt, revealing his gun. "You need to mind your own damn business."

The young thug was shocked when the woman didn't flinch when she saw his gun. "Hey, Clay, is that chick for real?"

Meanwhile, Benita yelled back again from across the street. "Did you just flash your gun at us?"

Evan was about to make a call, but Benita motioned for him to put away his phone. "Nope, we need to handle this right now," she stated as she started walking toward the men.

"If you're about to do what I think you're about to do, then don't. We need to call the police before things get out of hand," Evan replied.

"Let's just go have a little chat with these fellas. Like right now. You coming?" Benita asked.

Evan shook his head and started jogging to catch up with Benita as she walked fast toward the three men. "You know that this is not a good idea, right? Somebody's gonna get hurt," he said.

"Oh, I know, but I promise not to hurt them too badly," she responded.

They finally crossed the street and headed straight toward the thugs who were still harassing Doug. Benita did not flinch as she stood eye-to-eye with the main guy with the gun. "Hi. How are you fellas doing tonight? Question: did you flash a gun at me?" Benita asked.

"This chick here is crazy. What the hell are you doing? Are you stupid or what? Or just can't mind your own business? You need to step away before you get hurt," Ace commanded.

"E, this guy here is so funny. Well, I'm not stupid. But it seems *you* are. I mean, who harasses someone in plain sight? I have one question for you. What do you want with my friend?"

"This doesn't concern you," Clay chimed in.

When Clay reached into this pocket, Evan quickly stepped in front of him, blocking his path to Benita. "Now, I hope you're not going to do anything stupid," Evan commented.

Clay thought twice before making another move. Instead of reaching into his coat pocket, he pleaded to Ace about leaving.

"Ace, man, let's get out of here. We can handle things another day."

"Yeah, Ace, you should probably listen to your friend," Evan responded.

Ace took two steps toward Benita, but she was not intimidated by him at all.

"Yo, Doug, I see you got some chick trying to save you." Ace then turned back to Benita. "Listen here, little girl. I'ma only tell you one more time. You need to keep steppin' and mind your own damn business before you and your little punk-ass boyfriend get hurt. Now, fall back because I would hate to see your sweet ass splattered all across the sidewalk."

Benita was now in one of her defensive stances. "Sure, I'll leave, but not without Doug. He's coming with us."

The gym owner, Alan Grady, came to the door to see where the commotion was coming from and noticed Doug standing outside. "Hey, what's going on here? Doug, you okay? Who are these people?"

Doug looked over at the owner. "It's fine, Mr. Grady. Nothing for you to worry about."

"Right, pops. Nothing for you to worry about," Ace said.

"Well, things don't look fine. I'm about to call the police if you don't leave right now," Mr. Grady threatened the thugs.

"Doug, why don't you come with us? We'll take you home," said Benita.

"The hell you will. We got business with Doug, and you are *not* a part of it," Ace screamed.

"I'm not going anywhere with any of you. I'm outta here." Doug looked around, and just as he was about to leave, Clay pushed him against the wall once more. However, this time, Doug performed several body blows, knocking him to the ground. Clay was trying to reach for his gun, but Evan placed his foot on Clay's arm.

"Nope, not tonight, my friend. Don't move, or I'll break your arm," Evan warned. Then turning around to Doug, he asked, "You good?"

"Yeah, I'm good," Doug responded. He was also confused about who these two people were helping him.

As Ace tried to leap toward Evan, Benita tripped him, causing him to land on the ground.

"What the fuck, man?" Ace screamed.

Benita bent down and took the gun hidden in Ace's jeans. "That was a punk-ass move. How rude."

"Fuck off, bitch," Ace yelled.

He tried to stand up, but Benita knocked him back down. "I seriously wouldn't do that if I were you. E, do you know how much I hate that damned word?"

Evan smirked. "Yup, I certainly do."

Benita turned toward the owner, who was shocked to see how quickly they de-escalated the situation. "Mr. Grady, please call the police now. It's time for them to pick up the trash before these two cause any more problems."

"My pleasure, young lady. Doug, are you okay?"

"Yes, Mr. Grady. I'm fine."

Mr. Grady went back inside, allowing the door to shut behind him.

Benita looked over at Doug. "Doug, what do these guys want with you?"

Doug watched both of them. "I have no idea. I don't know them."

Benita looked down at Ace, who was shaking his head in disgust. "I saw you earlier this week checking out Doug. What do you want with him?"

"Fuck off, bitch," Clay bellowed.

"Damn—the language," Benita responded.

Benita noticed a car speeding toward them. Suddenly, the passenger window came down, and an arm came out, holding a gun pointed directly at them.

"What tha . . . Evan, grab Doug! We need to take cover."

Benita, Evan, and Doug ran behind a green dumpster, dodging bullets coming from the car. Ace and Clay quickly jumped into the backseat. Benita and Evan pulled out their 9 mms and got off a few shots, but not before the car sped away.

Doug caught his breath before turning to Benita and Evan. "Who the hell are you two?"

Chapter 8

Miguel had spent hours looking through a stack of folders that Willard left for him. None of the cases were appealing. *Damn*. It had been a long day, and he was now starting to feel jet-lagged. He stood up and stretched out his cramped back. Then he picked up his phone to see if Benita had texted him, but she hadn't. Although he was disappointed, he decided to call her once he was on his way to her place. He yawned as he looked at the time on his phone. It was already 10:35 p.m. It was definitely time for him to go. He imagined Benita sitting on her couch drinking tea and watching some action movie before falling asleep. She had turned him on to a bunch of corny action movies on Netflix featuring actors acting as operatives.

"Why are we watching this, Benita?"
She would roll her eyes at him. "Miguel, can you just enjoy the movie? Jeez, you are so Type A."

***

He smiled when he thought about how much attitude his gorgeous lover had, and for some reason, that was something he loved about her. She was consistent with her feistiness. No matter what kind of training she got at the DTCU, she was still a stubborn Brooklynite.

"Let me tell you something, Agent Miguel Perkins. You may *think* you're the boss of me, but *I'm* the boss of me," she once screamed at him.

It didn't take much for Benita to go off on him, but he loved how passionate she got about things. He also loved the fact that she remained professional when they were surrounded by other agents. He couldn't wait to see her because he missed being around her . . . kissing her . . . caressing her soft skin . . . making sweet love to her. He was glad that they made up last night, and he was, without a doubt, going to make sure that he found her a new assignment.

Yesterday, all he could think about was getting off the plane and seeing Benita. It had been three weeks since he had laid eyes on her, and he wanted to surprise her. Unfortunately, he was the one who was surprised when she blew him off. That was all the incentive he needed to get her back to work. He sat back down at his desk, looking through a stack of potential cases. At least fifty needed to be handled, but he wanted to prioritize the right ones for his team.

Hmmm. He picked up one more folder, read through it, and smiled. *Finally.* He found the perfect case for his angry lover. *This one is going to keep her quite busy.*

Miguel answered his phone when he saw that it was from Willard. "Perkins."

"You still at the office?" Willard asked.

Miguel chuckled. "Where else would I be?"

"Oh, how could I forget? One of the hardest working agents I know. Man, you need to get a life. Or the least get some sleep. Didn't you just jump out of a plane?"

"Ha. It's been awhile since I did a mission impossible. What are you up to?"

"Well, I'm just leaving a work function representing the Bureau."

"Fun times that I don't miss. Well, listen, I think I found a case in your stack of 500 folders."

"Really? Most agents would have given up after the first 100, but I knew you wouldn't leave until you found what you were looking for," Willard joked.

"You know me so well. Thanks, man."

"Of course. Let's discuss it tomorrow."

"Sounds like a plan. Good night." Miguel hung up the phone and closed the folder, placing it in his brown leather knapsack. Just as he was about to leave, his phone rang again. He recognized the number which was associated with the Perth Amboy Police Department.

Miguel answered. "Perkins. She what?" He picked up a pen and started writing on a notepad. "Uh-huh, yeah, I got it."

He hung up, taking a deep breath. *Damn it, Benita. What happened to you staying out of trouble?*

Miguel grabbed his bag and headed out the door. If he knew Benita, she had gotten herself in a predicament that needed his immediate attention. *I'm sure this is going to be fun.* As he walked outside toward the car, he tried calling Benita, but her phone went directly to voicemail. He was annoyed thinking about the trouble she had gotten herself into.

Once he arrived at Grady's Gym, he saw several cop cars with blinking red lights flashing. He could hear Benita yelling at one of the police officers even before he exited his vehicle.

"Damn it. You've had us waiting here for over an hour. What the hell is taking so long? We've given you all the information you need. Can we go now?" Benita said.

When Evan saw Miguel approaching them, he winced. "Easy, B. Look who's here."

Benita quickly bit her tongue and braced herself for what was going to come next. Miguel was not going to be happy to see his agents arguing with the Perth Amboy Police.

"Sheriff Johnson, thanks for calling me." The two men shook hands, and Miguel put on his poker face, not letting on that he was upset with his agents.

"Of course, Agent Perkins. Once I found out who these two were, I knew that they had to be working with you or someone at the Bureau. So, I thought I would give you a heads-up." Sheriff Matthew Johnson was quite familiar with the DTCU and its agents. He had been part of many of their training sessions in the past, but tonight, when he came to investigate the drive-by shooting, the young woman had flashed her DTCU ID, and he decided to call Miguel.

"Well, I appreciate you, Sheriff Johnson."

"No problem. I'll leave you to speak to your team." Sheriff Johnson walked over to Doug, who was sitting on the sidewalk speaking to another officer.

"So, Benita? Care to explain how you and Evan ended up in a drive-by shooting?" Miguel asked.

Benita was not sure exactly how much to tell Miguel. She chose to keep her involvement to a minimum. In fact, she remained silent.

"Benita? How did you get caught up in all this?" Miguel asked again.

Benita crossed her arms and gave him a somber look. "Agent Perkins, Evan and I were leaving dinner after a much-needed workout, and just as we were about to head home, we spotted some trouble from across the street. We started investigating, and the next thing we knew, a car came barreling down the street, guns a-blazing. Isn't that right, Evan?"

Miguel turned to Evan to see if he could get a straight answer from him. "Agent Green, is that what happened? You two just *happened* to get caught up in a drive-by?"

This didn't sit too well with Benita. *How can Miguel just be so dismissive toward me?* Her blood began to boil inside, but she knew that she had to remain calm in front of Evan.

"Agent Green? Is that what happened tonight?"

"Yes. That's what happened. We witnessed two assailants assaulting that young boxer from across the street. We attempted to defuse the situation, and when Benita spotted a car speeding toward us, we took cover. She saved our lives. After that, the owner called the police."

Miguel looked over at Benita, who remained silent. "Is that right?"

"Yes, Agent Perkins. We did what we were trained to do, but unfortunately, danger comes along with that. Isn't that what you always tell us? If we hadn't intervened, then that kid over there may have been seriously hurt."

Miguel nodded in agreement. "My only concern here is that you two didn't call for backup. Next time you want to play cops and robbers, make sure you make that call. More importantly, you need to make sure that the local police handle the local crimes. That's why we work closely with them on these sorts of incidents."

Benita placed her hands on her hips but quickly dropped them to her side. "So, you're telling me if we see a local crime, then we shouldn't get involved?"

"I'm not saying that, Benita. Stop twisting my words."

"I'm sorry, Agent Perkins, but I'm just trying to understand your logic. I would hate to misinterpret what you're saying."

Miguel quickly interrupted Benita, circumventing an uncomfortable situation. "Agent Green, can you give us a minute? Why don't you check on the young man to see how he's doing? Thanks."

Evan nodded and headed over to the young boxer and the sheriff.

Miguel waited until Evan was out of earshot. "What the hell is wrong with you, Benita?"

"What's wrong with *me*? What's wrong with *you*? I was doing the job I was trained to do, and you wanna give me shade?"

"Shade? Woman, there are rules we need to follow, and you can't just put yourself in danger."

"Enough already, Miguel, with all of this 'stop putting myself in danger crap' bullshit. I told you what happened. Dangerous shit happens every damn day. What do you want me to do, huh? Hide out in my apartment, live in a bubble, and be monitored by you and all the other assholes at DTCU? Man, please. That ain't gonna happen. I put myself in danger when I signed up for this gig. Don't you remember? So don't come at me like I'm supposed to save my dangerous situations for assigned projects only. A criminal is a criminal is a criminal."

"Benita, stop wanting to be right all the time."

"But I am right, correct?"

Miguel worked to remain calm. "You know what your problem is, Benita? You don't listen, and you don't follow protocol. The key to being a successful agent is following the rules, even if you don't like them. Just because you want to jump in and be some kind of hero won't help if you end up hurt or dead. You understand what I'm saying? I need you to stop always wanting to be right all the time."

Benita paused a bit before answering.

"Well, Benita? Do you understand me?"

"Yes, Agent Perkins. I understand."

"Fine. Now go home. We'll talk about this tomorrow. Make sure that you and Evan are in the office at eight sharp. You both need to fill out paperwork and record everything that happened tonight. We need everything by the book. Do I make myself clear?"

"Yes, sir. Loud and clear," Benita mumbled back to him.

"I can't hear you."

"Yes. I will be there at 8:00 a.m.," she relented.

"Great. Now, I need to thank the sheriff for keeping me abreast of the situation surrounding my team members. Excuse me."

Benita watched Miguel as he walked away from her, heading toward the officer. She couldn't help but be impressed by a man who confidently handled his business. She knew he was right, but she had a hard time taking criticism. *Damn. Impressive.* Benita then turned her attention to Evan, who was still talking to the young fighter who looked like a scared and confused kid. She glanced over at Miguel once more before making her way over to Evan and Doug.

"Hey, there, you two. You good, Doug?"

"Tell you the truth? I'm not even sure how I'm feeling right now. I wasn't expecting almost to be a statistic tonight. But I'm glad that I'm alive . . . thanks to you two."

Evan smiled at the young man, who was clearly shaken up by tonight's events. "Doug, we're just glad that we could help avert the situation."

Benita interrupted. "Did you know those guys? I saw them at the gym earlier this week watching you, and I thought that was sort of strange."

"Seriously, I have no idea who those guys were. I mean, I leave my house early in the morning, train all day, and then go to work. A lot of these thugs just like to pick a fight for no reason whatsoever. Maybe they knew that I'm a boxer and just want to hate. But as soon as I walked out of the building, they wanted me to go with them. I refused, and that's when they tried to rough me up. And then you two came through."

"Well, listen, you're fine right now. We've given the sheriff all of the pertinent information, and they'll find those guys."

Miguel observed Benita and Evan still talking to the young man. He then yelled at his two agents. "Agent Jenkins and Agent Green, you two can go now. The sheriff will make sure the young man gets home safely."

Benita remained calm and nodded back at Miguel. "Yes, sir, Agent Perkins. We hear you loud and clear. Listen, Doug, if you think of anything or just want to talk, here's my number. Text me if you need anything. Why don't you get some sleep, and we'll talk soon? Maybe we'll see you at the gym."

"Thank you, Agent Jenkins," he replied.

Benita and Evan walked away from Doug, heading to the neighboring parking lot. She looked back at Miguel, who was talking to the sheriff. She rolled her eyes and picked up the pace, trying not to think about the conversation she just had with her boss. Most of the time, it was hard for her to compartmentalize Miguel into two categories. On the one hand, Miguel played the boss card, trying to control her every move, and on the other hand, he was her sexy lover that showed his tender side and wanted to be her protector. She started to feel that she was living a *Tale of Two Cities* life, and tonight, she had to remember that he was the boss, and she was the subordinate. This only fueled the growing animosity that she felt toward him.

Benita unlocked the doors to her Mustang, she and Evan jumped in, then she quickly drove down Smith Street toward Evan's apartment building in Livingston, New Jersey. She turned on the radio and began bopping her head to the rhythm of the music.

"What a night. Our first case. Your sixth sense really came in handy," Evan bragged.

Benita remained quiet.

"Why are you so quiet, B?"

"Oh, am I? Didn't even notice."

"Well, yeah. At first, I thought you were just joking, but then it all came together. You said something was off concerning that fighter, and it surely was. I'm just happy that we went outside when we did. You know? Things could have gone south really fast."

"Evan, do you think I'm reckless?"

"Well, yeah. That's just who you are."

"Jeez, look, I'm sorry about getting you involved in all this. I didn't mean to put you in the line of fire like that. It wasn't right."

"Hey, this is what we're trained to do. Perkins wasn't too happy, though, but then again, when is he ever?"

"Really? I guess I never noticed that."

"B, you were only looking out for that kid, and clearly, he needed our help. But did you see those body blows? Hoo-wee. He laid that fool out. If there were no guns involved, he would have probably put a real hurting on both of them. They were no match for him."

"Yeah. He's really talented. I wonder why they came for him, though."

"That's the million-dollar question. They must have thought he was an easy target. I think that he must somehow be associated with someone else," Evan replied.

"We definitely need to ask Huey to pull some info on Doug and his family. We'll speak to him after our eight o'clock meeting with Perkins tomorrow."

"Eight a.m., huh?"

"Yup. I'm ready to get our asses chewed out."

"Oh yeah. I just live for all of that. I mean, *all* of that."

As Benita sped down the quiet street, catching a string of lights, she turned up the volume on her

XM radio when she heard Trick Daddy, Trina, and The Slip-N-Slide Express, "Take It to Da House." "Damn, I love this song."

"Of course, you would love that song." Evan shook his head.

"What's not to love about this song? We are a dream team. We're gonna take this shit to the house."

They both laughed and danced to the beat while they plotted their next move.

Chapter 9

It was close to 1:30 a.m. when Sheriff Johnson pulled up in front of the Honey View Apartments Complex located on Sunny State Street. This was the first time Doug Gibson had been in a cop car and, hopefully, the last. He was trying not to feel anxious, but he was having a hard time keeping his composure. Doug had remained quiet during the entire ride home, trying to process that he had been caught up in a drive-by shooting, which could have gotten him killed. But thanks to Agents Jenkins and Green, he was still alive and was genuinely grateful.

Growing up as a young Black kid in a not-so-safe neighborhood was always a risk. Most of the Black men he knew had either landed in jail or were dead. He worked hard to stay clear of situations that would place him in the wrong place at the wrong time. *Damn it.* He wasn't sure if he would tell his grandmother because she would worry and even make him stop leaving the gym late at night. But tonight, he was shaken and won-

dered if these thugs would try to grab him again.
Why did they want me?

"We're here, safe and sound," Sheriff Johnson
commented. "You sure you're all right?"

Doug snapped out of his inner thoughts, barely
looking at the cop.

"I'm fine. Thank you for driving me home,
Sheriff."

He quickly opened the door and jumped out of
the vehicle without saying goodbye. He shut the
door and gave a slight wave as the sheriff drove
off, leaving him standing under the streetlight.
Shoving his hands deep in his front pockets, Doug
picked up the pace toward the apartment entrance.
He and his grandmother had moved into the newly
renovated three-bedroom apartment about three
months ago located in a diversified neighborhood
of Perth Amboy. With all of the recent planned
gentrification, Doug felt safe there. Convenience
was the best part of living in that area, and Doug
didn't have a problem with transportation. He
either walked, took the bus, or jumped in an Uber.
He loved the fact that he had a paved trail for his
running. However, tonight had changed things
for him. He wasn't feeling safe at all. He looked
around, checking to see if anyone was following
him. *Damn.*

Rubbing his shoulder, he walked quickly to
his apartment. It was quiet and dark. Usually, his

grandmother would have the television on, but tonight was eerily quiet. He tiptoed down the hallway toward his bedroom but made a few creaking sounds along the way. He took off his clothes and jumped into the shower. All he wanted to do was to wash away the grime and memories from a night of utter terror. He closed his eyes and let the hot water run over his muscular and bruised body.

Once he finished showering, he rubbed himself with Tiger Balm to help ease the soreness that was all over his body. He was barely able to keep his eyes open once he climbed into bed. He fought sleep because he wanted to go over the day's events to figure out just how he ended up almost getting killed.

After getting a few hours of sleep in the morning, after finishing up at Walmart stocking shelves throughout the night, he went straight to the gym where he helped Grady open for the regulars, then he trained. What caused him almost to get jumped—or kidnapped? *Does this have to do with my boxing match?*

His mind drifted to his brother, Sean. He was the only one that could bring trouble into the family. He wouldn't be surprised if Sean had something to do with what happened to him tonight. Although he hadn't seen him in a while, he remembered the last time they had spoken, and Doug had blown him off. Was this some sort of payback? He stretched one more time. Exhausted, he finally closed his eyes and was soon fast asleep.

Meanwhile, Reggie and Clay jumped out of Reggie's black Escalade and stormed inside an apartment building off Peterson Street where Sean was staying. Reggie pounded on the door. "Open the damn door, Sean."

Sean jumped off the couch when he heard the pounding. He tried unlocking three locks securely fastened to the door but had trouble with the third one. "Wait. Give me a minute. The lock—"

"Sean, man, I'ma kill you if you don't open this damn door," Reggie barked.

Finally unlocking the door, Reggie quickly grabbed Sean by the throat and pushed him back away from the entryway. Clay shut the door behind him.

"Reggie, calm the fuck down. Let go of me."

Reggie pushed Sean hard, causing him to stumble backward. He started pacing back and forth, trying to calm down from his anger. "We waited 'til your brother came out of that bullshit gym before Clay and Ace approached him. But just as we were about to snatch his little ass up, some loudmouthed bitch and her lackey friend foiled our plans."

"Fuck. This can't be happening right now. Where's my brother?"

"Who knows. Probably with the police."

"The police?"

Clay interjected. "Yeah, the police. Your brother got protection from the po po."

"Did he see you, Reggie?"

"Nah, nigga. I was in the car. That's why I let the fellas handle shit. And he ain't never seen them."

Sean sat down on the couch, clasping his hands together. "How did you guys get away?"

"We had to handle things. Loco pulled out his Glock and dropped a few caps while I drove. But that chick and her dude had guns and shit—and shot back."

"Wait, Loco shot at my brother?" Sean was now getting heated.

Clay snapped his head toward Sean. "Look, nigga, your brother fought back, and then all of a sudden, shit just went left. If Reggie and Loco didn't do what they did, we would be in jail right now. You need to fall the fuck back. This is all *your* fault, anyway. How many times did Reggie tell you to stop gambling?"

"Clay, you need to mind ya fuckin' business. You ain't got nothing to do with this shit. *I'm* gonna handle my business."

"You ain't handled shit, dog," Clay screamed.

"But you did so much better? Fuck no. All you had to do was to bring him here. But your ass couldn't even do that right. And you wanna blame *me* for you failing at *your* job? Get the fuck outta here."

"Man, I should whoop your ass right now. I'm sick of you," Clay screamed.

Sean stood face-to-face with him. "Well, I'm sick of you too."

"How are you going to pull Reggie and me into your shit? Nobody told you to borrow that money from that asshole A-Roc."

Sean glared back at Clay. "Yeah, you weren't singin' that tune when you were using that money to bet on fighters."

"Hey, Clay, man, stand down. I got this," Reggie said.

"Yeah, just like you said earlier. We ain't got nothing to show for tonight. Can't stand to look at this fool any longer. Check you lata, Reggie."

"All right. Later."

Reggie and Clay gave each other dab, and Clay made one more plea to Sean before he left the apartment. "Sean, I'm gonna tell you one more time. You betta handle this business with your brutha, ASAP. I'm not playing around with you."

"Yeah yeah yeah. Just get to steppin'," Sean replied, flicking off Clay.

Clay left the apartment without saying another word.

Then Reggie plopped down on the chair opposite Sean.

There was silence for a few minutes before Sean finally spoke. "Reggie, man, I'm sorry. This should've been easy."

"We've got one week to find that paper or get your brother to fight. I don't know 'bout you, but I wanna live to see another day."

Sean rubbed his hand over his bald head to calm himself. He knew that he made one of the worst decisions asking Reggie to kidnap his own brother. And now they had failed. If his brother ever found out that he was behind this plot, he would never forgive him. Now, he had to figure out another way to get his brother on board, or he would be dead in a week. "Reggie, I'll figure out a way to convince my brother to help for all our sakes."

Chapter 10

Benita entered her apartment and was startled when she saw Miguel sitting on her couch. She shut the door behind her. "*Seriously,* Miguel? How the hell did you get here so fast? I mean, you're a pain in my ass right now."

Approaching Benita, Miguel stood so close to her that she could smell mint on his breath and the sweet scent of his cologne. At first, she stood there stone-faced, staring back at him, but as soon as he touched her face, she melted faster than a heated ice cube. Miguel bent down, lowering his head so that their lips would almost touch.

"I'm sorry for not being around the past few months, for making you wait on a case, for giving you a hard time tonight."

Benita tried her best to remain strong, but her heart and body wouldn't let her. She slid her arms around his waist, kissing him passionately. She couldn't help but love this man, even after he acted like an ass. "Dammit, Miguel. I hate you sometimes."

He pulled her even closer, holding on to her for dear life. He kissed her forehead and gently escorted her to the bedroom, where he made sweet love to her. He thought about the times when he had desired her but tried to deny his feelings; he couldn't resist her any longer. The passion between them was undeniable, and he made sure that she knew just how much he loved her . . . every part of her. He loved touching her in all of the places on her body that made her quiver instantly with excitement. He couldn't deny how much he cared for her and would demonstrate that every chance he got.

The following day, Benita woke up to the smell of freshly brewed coffee. She slowly and deliberately stretched before getting out of bed. Taking a quick shower and brushing her teeth, she felt refreshed after an amazing love fest with her sweetie. When she saw him standing by the kitchen counter, shirtless, her heart almost dropped. *I love having this man in my life, even if it is a secret.*

"Hey," he smiled.

"Hey. What're ya doing over there?" Benita asked.

"Making my princess a power shake and coffee."

"That doesn't sound right. I don't even like coffee."

Miguel smiled and handed Benita a cup of hot herbal tea. "I know you don't. Here's your tea. The coffee's for me."

"Umm, where's Miguel? The sky must be falling 'cause he's never this damn considerate. He's always in work mode . . . serious and barking orders at people."

Miguel laughed. "Barking? I don't bark." He laughed again and pulled Benita close to him. "I bark at you?"

"Oh yeah. Like a little Chihuahua."

"Now I'm a little dog? Thanks." He went back to making shakes. He placed all the ingredients, including fruit and fresh kale, into the blender and mixed it to perfection. Then he poured the liquid into two glasses and handed one to Benita.

"Thank you."

"You're welcome. Can we switch gears a little bit? I need to talk to you about something."

"Uh-oh. I knew it was only a matter of time. He's back. What's up?"

"I thought about what you said to me last night about how we're trained to help bring down bad guys. And you're right. We can't turn our backs on people who need our help."

"Thank you for saying that. I also was thinking about what you said. I know that I allow my instincts to control my actions, but I seriously don't want to put people in danger. I promise I'll work on that."

"Good, because as much as I think you're one of the most talented agents around, you need to think before you act. You need to watch yourself."

"I hear ya, boss man. Now, what's up with my new assignment?" She playfully tapped him on the arm as she drank her smoothie.

"Well, I'm still working out a few things, but as soon as I do, you'll be the first to know."

"Okay, still no new assignment. But can I at least follow up on Doug?"

"I prefer that you stay clear of Doug and the gym for a bit. Let the local police handle things."

Benita didn't answer and continued to drink her smoothie.

"Benita, do you hear what I'm saying?"

She put down the glass and gave him a peck on the lips. "Yes, Agent Perkins." Placing her arms around her lover's neck, she kissed him deeply.

"Listen, I gotta get home, change, and head to work."

"Wow, nice transition, Miguel. At least someone has work to do."

As she loosened her grip around his neck, Miguel smiled. "Trust me, you will too. Very soon. Don't forget you need to come by the office this morning to talk about last night's incident."

"Wait, I still need to come?" she whined.

"Yes, and you will need to fill out paperwork. But I tell you what. I just got dinged for an 8:00 a.m. meeting with the director. Why don't you give Evan a call and make sure you two are there by ten?"

"Sure. I can make up for some missing hours of sleep since someone kept me up late last night."

Miguel gave Benita one more kiss. "Okay, sweetie, I gotta bounce. Don't oversleep. See you in a few hours."

"Okay."

"And don't be late."

"I won't be late, Agent Perkins."

Miguel gathered his things and walked out of the apartment, leaving Benita to think about her next move. She had no intention of listening to Miguel's orders. She still planned to check in on Doug. She texted Evan and then called Huey.

"Hey, there, Huey. It's Benita. What's happening?"

"Benita, do you know what time it is?"

"Sorry. I know it's early, but I need to ask a favor. You around later?"

"Yeah, where else would I be?"

"Great, I'll stop by after my 10:00 a.m. meeting, okay?"

Benita hung up the phone and smiled. She walked back to her bedroom and plopped on the bed to get a few more hours of sleep. She needed to make sure that she got her story right when she spoke to Huey. Evan wasn't wrong when it came to Huey. He could blow up her entire game if she didn't convince him to keep things under the radar. She would think things through once she got a few hours of sleep.

***

After filling out a ton of paperwork at the DTCU from last night's event, Benita paid a visit to her colleague, Huey Longfoot, where she planned on asking him for help. She needed him to pull any intel that he could on Doug Gibson and the owner of Grady's Gym. Huey was an excellent hacker recruited by the organization when he was arrested for hacking into the New York Metropolitan Transit Authority's intranet website. He was eventually arrested and faced many years behind bars. That was, until Miguel offered to help him stay out of prison if he came to work for the DTCU.

"Huey, what you do on your own is illegal, but if you come work for me, you can help solve a lot of cases. We need people like you to help infiltrate the dark web and bring down the bad guys."

"And if I refuse?" Huey had asked.

"Well, you can go to jail for a long-ass time. It's up to you. Think about it."

Huey quickly signed on to work for Miguel at the DTCU. Over the last five years, he had helped solve more than 100 cases and was proud of his accomplishments. Huey had learned that he was, in fact, making a difference for the greater good. However, there were times when curiosity took over, and he went back to his old ways. He once hacked into the organization's database and secretly researched all the people he had worked with.

When Benita started at the organization, he became curious about her. She wasn't the typical DTCU agent recruited out of the military or college. In fact, she did a stint in prison just like him. When she chose to leave prison, she had to leave her family and friends behind. Huey secretly had a connection to her, and whenever she asked for his help, he couldn't say no. He always felt compelled to assist her.

Benita strolled into Huey's office as he worked his magic on his supercomputer system, zooming through loads of data in the blink of an eye. It amazed her just how talented he was at researching and uncovering secrets on the dark web. He was also great at creating new identities for the DTCU agents when they went undercover.

Huey glanced at Benita, giving her an awkward smile. "What's going on, pretty lady?"

"Hey, there, Huey. Sorry that I called you so early this morning, but I wanted to catch you before you left for the office."

"It's all good, but I'm not a morning person."

"I know. Roaming the dangerous dark web."

Huey chuckled and nodded in agreement. "Yup. That's what I do when I'm supposed to be off work, though I'm really not off work. So, what are you up to?"

"Well, I had to fill out some paperwork on a case that I found myself a part of, and I'm still waiting for my next assignment."

"Really? I heard you created your own case."

"What? No. Where'd you hear that news? Did you speak to Agent Perkins?"

Huey laughed while he pounded on the keyboard. "Big Brother knows everything."

"Big Brother, huh?"

"Yep."

"Anyway, I was hoping that you could help me out with something."

"And that is?"

"I need you to do some research for me on a young boxer friend of mine. His name is Doug Gibson."

"No can do, Benita. The last time I helped you, I got my ass chewed out."

"Oh, come on, Huey. All you need to do is to see if he has any priors and where he lives. That's all."

"Why?"

"Why what?" She seemed surprised by his question.

"Yeah. Why do you need this information? And how is he your friend?"

"Dang, man. Why can't you do me this favor?"

"As I said, I am not supposed to be doing any kind of research except for projects that I'm assigned to at the DTCU. That's why. But if you're telling me he is someone that is on the agency's radar, then I *may* be able to help you out."

"Well, he's definitely on my radar, but not for reasons that you think. He's a good dude that may be in danger. You see, last night, some thugs came for him, and I just want to make sure that he finds his way out of whatever situation he finds himself in. I want to make sure he's all right."

Benita walked behind Huey and started massaging his shoulders. He looked intensely at the screen, trying to ignore the sweet-smelling perfume radiating from Benita. *Damn, I can't resist her charm.*

"Come on, Huey. Please? It'll take you like three minutes, five minutes tops."

"Benita, this is against regulations. Haven't you heard about the Me Too Movement? No touching colleagues."

"Oh, come on. Loosen up, man. Listen, you are the king when it comes to decoding highly classified information. It's not like you have to break into any illegal databases or something. I just want us to do something good other than going undercover and be someone we are not. Right now, you and I can do something good in the world. And it will only take a few keystrokes to do it. If you get any blowback, you can blame me. I got you."

Huey looked up at Benita with his doe eyes. "Promise?"

Benita held up one of her pinkies and placed it in Huey's face. "Pinky swear."

"Fine. But I need you to stand over there next to the door. Your massages are distracting."

Benita kissed him on the cheek and started backing away from him with her arms held up high. As Huey worked his magic, she noticed a file on another desk with a Ted "T-Bone" Taylor label on it. She flipped through it, and her eyes became cold when she saw a photo of the brother of her ex-best friend, Nikki. Benita was still angry that not only had he tried to kill her, but he also ended up helping to set her up for conspiracy to commit murder. She tried to suppress her outrage, but once she saw his face, everything came flooding back. No way would she ever let this go, and one day, she would make him pay for what he did. She scanned the contents looking for an address but found nothing.

A few minutes later, Huey let Benita know that he retrieved information on Doug. After he jotted down something on a small pad before closing the web page on his computer screen, he ripped off the page and handed it to Benita. "Here ya go."

She took the information and quickly scanned over it. "Thank you, my friend."

"Now, if anyone asks you where you got that information . . ."

"It never came from you. My lips are sealed."

"Good. Okay. I gotta get back to work. Have a nice day. And stay out of trouble, will ya?" He turned back to his computer screen when he heard a few notification bells sounding off. He instantly became distracted by whatever appeared on his screen.

"Thank you, Huey." As Benita turned to leave, she grabbed the T-Bone folder while Huey wasn't looking and headed out the door. She would copy the information and return it to the office before Huey knew it was missing.

Chapter 11

Benita parked her car in the parking lot close to Grady's Gym. Looking down at the folder on the passenger seat, she couldn't resist picking it up and reviewing the contents one more time. *T-Fucking-Bone.* If it weren't for this asshole, she wouldn't have ended up in prison. He had lied to cover his ass when he said that she was behind the shooting at Ray's Place, the same night her ex-boyfriend, Joe, had gotten shot. She blamed herself for getting Joe hurt, especially since he was at the pub early to meet with her to discuss who was behind her cousin Deon's assault.

Not a day went by without her feeling guilty about Joe. If only she had listened to him and helped get him out of there . . . but she had to know what was going on with Ted. *This is all your fault, Ted.* She shook her head in disgust when she thought about how T-Bone was responsible for so much hurt and pain for her family, as well as the rift between Benita and his sister Nikki who had been her best friend since grade school. She planned on finding him and making him pay for all of the problems he caused—especially when it came to Joe.

A single tear fell down Benita's face when she thought about how much she missed Joe. Her grandmother had kept in touch with Joe's aunt to find out about his prognosis while Benita was in prison, but once she had gone to work at the DTCU, she could no longer communicate with her grandmother. She made a mental note to ask Wes if he had updates about Joe.

Closing the folder, she finally got out of the car and headed to the gym. She was dressed in black leggings, a yellow and black oversized T-shirt, and a black jean jacket. When she walked into the gym, she looked around to see if Doug was there. She spotted his trainer yelling at another boxer, so she walked over to him.

"Manny, get your hands up. You're leaning on the left side. Block that punch. Block it."

"Looks like you gotta winner on your hands," Benita commented.

The gray-haired man didn't look Benita's way but knew she was beside him. "Yeah. Maybe if he can follow directions."

"So, just how many guys do you currently train?"

"Let's see. I have five right now. Ones that I consider contenders."

"Impressive. Are there any I should keep my eyes open for? You know, for upcoming fights?"

"A few. Manny, how many times do I have to tell ya? Keep that right hand up."

"I was wondering if you also trained women."

"Who's askin'?"

"I am."

The old man turned to Benita and gave her a once-over. "Come on. What's a pretty little thing like you wanna get in the ring and get all bruised up for?"

"Hey, there's a few pretty ladies out there who can fight like the men. I mean, if Laila Ali can do it or Ronda Rousey, then why not me?"

"You gotta point, but I don't train girls."

"Oh, okay," Benita responded.

After a few minutes of silence, the coach started talking again. "What's your name, sweetheart?"

"Benita."

"Benita, I'm Jerry. You look familiar. You been here before?"

"Yes, sir. I have been here with my father, Leroy Jones."

"You don't say."

"Yup."

"Leroy never told me that he had a daughter. Son of a gun. You know what? I've been training here for more than twenty years, and this is the first time I came in contact with a beauty queen. Maybe you should concentrate on another profession."

"Well, actually, I was thinking more like mixed martial arts."

"Oh, that's even better," he said sarcastically.

Benita wanted to jump inside the ring and show the man that she was no lightweight, but she refrained. "I'm not sure you're the right trainer anyway. Maybe I should ask Doug. Are you his trainer?"

"Doug Gibson? That kid's got talent. Nah, that's Lenny. He's his trainer. But he's not here today."

"Oh, okay. Do you think they'll be here later on?"

"Nah. Neither one of them are here today. Grady said that Doug called in earlier. He won't be coming in. Maybe tomorrow. What's weird is that Doug never misses a day at the gym. The kid practically lives here."

"Oh, I see. You ever see any bad eggs roaming around here?"

"I'm sure there are good ones and bad ones that frequent this establishment. Who knows? Manny, don't you ever listen?" Jerry yelled back at the boxer.

"Okay, thank you for your time."

Just as she was about to walk away, Jerry stopped her.

"Hey, the next time you come here with your father, let's see what you got going on."

"Will do, sir." Benita smiled and then left the gym. She pulled out her phone when she received a call from Evan.

"Hey, what's up? Where you at?"

"Oh, I'm at the gym."

"Really? You working out?"

"No, I decided to find Doug, but he's not here."

"I'm sure he's traumatized right now. Did you speak to Huey?"

"Yeah. Talked him into giving me Doug's address. I think I'll pay him a visit later."

"What? Weren't you supposed to lie low for a bit?"

"Yes, Evan, I am. But after speaking to one of the trainers who knows Doug, I'm worried about him."

"You don't even know him, Benita."

"I know I don't know him, but I feel like he needs a friend. Someone he can talk to about what happened to him."

Evan knew that it was a waste of time to argue. "Well, listen. Just be careful, please?"

"Of course. Do you think that I'm just going to put myself in danger?"

"Of course not, B. Why would I *ever* think that?" Evan chuckled.

"I'll call you later," she said.

They ended the conversation, and Benita walked back to her car. Just as her mind went to Doug, a sense of panic and anxiety came over her. She knew that her intuition was kicking in, and it was telling her that something terrible was about to happen. Of the many times that she had experienced these feelings in the past, she was usually right. Her grandmother also could sense when things were wrong, and she would often tell Benita that it was essential to listen to her spirit. God was speaking to her, and she shouldn't ignore those feelings.

Benita remembered her grandmother telling her that when she got a strong urge or a sense in her core, that was her purest intuition telling her that she should never go against her initial thoughts. *"Benita, once you veer from your gut, you miss your calling. You make unnecessary mistakes. Learn to listen to your intuition and take action. Your intuition will never steer you wrong."*

A feeling of sadness came over her when she thought about her grandmother. She looked down at her phone and was about to call her, but she knew better. *I can't. I can't. I made a promise not to contact you. I need to keep you safe. I miss you so much, Grams.* The more Benita thought about her grandmother, the more she wanted to see her. How could Miguel make her promise to stay away from her family? Her grandmother was everything to her, and she didn't know how much longer she could keep up the charade of being okay with her decision to choose to be an agent over her family.

Benita was never going to give up seeing her grandmother. She began to take deep breaths to control her emotions, but she had a hard time holding back the grief that she was feeling. Pulling out a locket that her grandmother had given her, she looked at the photo inside and eventually made a fist, holding on to the locket for dear life. She placed the locket back into her bag and decided to call her father.

"Dad, can you meet me at Los Mintos? I need you," she said.

Chapter 12

Benita crossed her arms as she waited for her father. He was in full workout gear, but he knew that something was wrong when he saw her face. His smile was not reciprocated, and he became concerned with his daughter's behavior. She wasn't the cheerful, funny, and engaging woman that he had seen the week before. Something was seriously wrong. He gave her a big hug, and she held on to him for dear life. Tears began flowing down her cheek, and she couldn't stop herself from having a minibreakdown.

"It's all right, sweetheart. It's all right. Let it out. Just let it out."

She cried for a few more minutes, and then Leroy wiped the tears from her eyes.

"Listen, why don't we grab something to eat, and you can tell me what's going on with you, okay?"

Benita nodded in agreement. She was a wreck, and she knew it. One minute she was planning on seeing Doug, but her attention went to her grand-mother in an instant. All she could think about was how much she missed her Grams and brother. But the one thing that she was grateful for was to have her father in her life as a mentor. He was the only one she could talk to about the pain that she was feeling.

Leroy placed his arm around Benita's shoulder as they walked into the Mexican restaurant. They headed to the back and found an area where that they could speak privately. After the waitress dropped off a bowl of chips and salsa, the two ordered a pitcher of margaritas. Leroy then placed his hands over Benita's trembling fingers. "Now, what's going on with you, Benita? I've never seen you this upset before."

"I don't know if I can do this, working on future cases while not seeing my family. It's just too much."

"What happened? Tell me."

"There's this guy Doug, who was with his grandmother at the gym earlier this week. They were so cute together. Well, it's a long story, but I ended up saving his life last night."

"Wait, you saved his life?" Leroy asked.

"Yeah, but that's not the point."

"What *is* the point, Benita? You can't just tell me something like that and gloss over things."

Benita poured herself a margarita and took a few sips. "Evan and I stopped two thugs from beating up Doug, the boxer from the gym. And before we knew it, a car came by shooting at us. It's all good, though. Everything's okay."

Leroy shook his head in disbelief. He too poured himself a margarita and drank it like a shot. "Benita, what happened to you being careful?"

"Dad, I was doing what I was trained to do. As soon as we saw the speeding car, we took cover. But that's not what this is about."

"Then what *is* it, Benita? *Tell* me." Leroy poured himself a fresh drink.

"Just when I thought I had things figured out, I started thinking about what Grams is doing without me. I realized just how much I miss her and Wes. This is harder than I thought, and it's not fair that I can't be with them. I don't want to be without them anymore. I was so scared of going to jail that I sold my soul to this place. Now, I have to live my life as if they don't exist. How can I do that? I'm losing a piece of me every day."

Benita started crying, and Leroy tried his best to console her. "Benita, don't cry. Everything is going to be okay."

"It's not okay, Dad. That's the problem. I can't be this secret agent and lie to myself. I can't. I just can't live without my family."

After a few minutes of Benita crying, Leroy finally spoke. "Maybe you don't have to."

Benita used her napkin to wipe away her tears. "Well, Miguel threatened to send me back to jail if I didn't stay away from my family."

"You let me work on that, but in the meantime, you have me. *I* am your family, and *I* will always be there to comfort you when times get rough. When I was just starting at the Agency, I definitely did what I had to do once I went undercover, and that included having a relationship with your mother. If I hadn't done that, then you wouldn't have been born. I know that she kept that secret from you, but I am so glad that I didn't follow the rules because I have the best damn daughter in the whole wide world."

. Benita was so happy to have her father in her life. Her mother had never spoken of him, and after a while, Benita had stopped asking. But as an adult, she understood how hurt her mother must have been to have the man she loved ghost her. Leroy had tried everything in his power to make up for the lost time, and she was so thankful, so very thankful, especially since she had no one else to turn to.

"Sometimes we just have to break the rules," Leroy said in between eating some chips.

"What exactly are you saying, Dad?"

Leroy waited until after the waitress dropped off some more drinks and walked away.

"What I'm saying is that if you're careful and don't get caught, then you should do what you have to do to survive this job. But I'm warning you right now . . . You will not last another day if you allow yourself to become emotional. That leads to mistakes, and you will end up putting your life and others around you in danger. So, I'll help you see your family, but you need to promise me to do what I say and not deviate from what I say going forward. Can you do that?"

"Yes, of course, I can do that. Anything to see my family."

"Good, so you'll start by making sure that no one at the Agency, and I mean *no one,* not Evan or Luciana or Huey, knows what you're planning to do. Because you must avoid putting anyone in a compromising situation."

"Okay, I can keep all plans to myself."

Leroy gave his daughter a stern look. "Benita, this is a dangerous game you're about to play, and if you make one wrong move, you'll lose everything. Do you hear me?"

"Yes, Sensei Leroy. I hear you, and I understand the danger."

"Good, because if this meeting is to work, then I need you to follow every instruction to a T, and we do all things in secret. Because as much as you're learning the ropes at the DTCU, some people there will turn on you at the drop of a dime. None of those people are to be trusted. They will bring you down as quickly as they bring down the bad guys."

For the next few hours, Benita listened intensely to her father, who was dropping knowledge on the inner workings of the DTCU. The more she listened to him, the more she knew she could never share secrets with Miguel, or any of her colleagues, for that matter. She would never give up her family, and Leroy would ensure that she covered her tracks so as not to place her family in danger. For the first time in the past three months, she felt optimistic about her future.

Chapter 13

Elsie had awakened when she heard her grandson come into the house. She groggily turned to her alarm clock and saw that it was after 1:30 a.m. She wasn't surprised at the time because she knew he was either at the gym or at his job at Walmart, where he worked as a stock boy. His hours changed every week, but most of the time, he put in about five hours each day to help pay for his training. She was proud of how disciplined he was.

She remembered when he first told her that he wanted to pursue a career in boxing after graduating from high school. Although she encouraged him to attend the community college, he had no desire to go that route since his passion was boxing. He worked, trained, and stayed out of trouble, unlike his older brother Sean, who was the complete opposite.

Finally falling back asleep, Elsie woke up at six o'clock to get ready for work. She was the executive director at the Perth Amboy Richmond Nursing Home Facility and was responsible for the general administration. She managed a staff of twenty people and made sure that all rules and regulations related to patients' health care and safety were adhered to. She loved her job, especially helping people. She may not always agree with the CEO, who oversaw over twenty locations, but she respected his policies and made sure their patients were number one.

After taking her shower and getting dressed, Elsie peeked into Doug's bedroom, who was sound asleep. Then she ate her breakfast and left a note on the counter for Doug when he got up. *Your breakfast is in the refrigerator. Just heat it when you're ready.* She cut off the light, exited the kitchen, and walked to her car that was parked outside the apartment building.

It was a beautiful day with a clear blue sky, and Elsie enjoyed the quiet time before she got to the facility. She knew that she had a long day ahead of her and wasn't going to get home until late that evening. There was an annual budget meeting that was coming up with the board in less than a month, and she and the chief operating officer had to gather all of the information from the departments to help craft the approved budget. Traffic was pretty light at that time of the morning, so her thirty-minute drive moved at an average pace.

Oh, I forgot to let Doug know that I was going to be late tonight. I'll call him when I get to the office. She finally arrived and pulled into her assigned parking spot. Then she gathered her things and got out of the car. After clicking the alarm, she walked toward the building. She noticed a black SUV parked across the street, and uneasiness came over her. She looked around to see if anyone else was around her, but there was no one else at that time of the morning. Never taking her eyes off the car, she watched as the vehicle sped off. She breathed a sigh of relief and continued on her way.

It was 10:00 a.m. when Doug finally woke up. He couldn't remember the last time he had slept in that late. He would normally have been up already and out the door, either running the neighboring trail or off to the gym. But not this morning. He woke up to a massive headache. It took him a few minutes before slowly getting out of bed. Passing his grandmother's bedroom, he noticed that she had made her bed, and her room was tidy. Her room was always neat. She would tell him that three places should always be clean: the bedroom, the bathroom, and the kitchen.

His grandmother had always pressed for him and his brother to be disciplined and consistent with their actions. *"Boys, I won't always be around, and you need to make sure that you can take care of yourselves."* He smiled when he thought about how she always looked out for him and his brother.

Doug slowly made his way to the bathroom and splashed water on his face. *Damn it; my head is killing me.* He opened the medicine cabinet looking for some aspirin. He didn't find anything, but Doug knew his Nana had other places around the apartment that she may have housed the meds.

As he made his way to the kitchen, he heard his phone ring. He walked back to his room to answer his phone. He saw that it was his grandmother calling. "Hey, Nana."

"Hey, my dear. How are you doing?"

"I woke up to a headache. Do you know if we have any aspirin?"

"Did you check the medicine cabinet in the bathroom?"

"Yeah, but I didn't see any."

"There should be some in the kitchen. Check the top drawer near the refrigerator."

As Doug walked to the kitchen, he continued to listen to his grandmother.

"Doug, I hate that you are working so hard. You gotta get some rest, son."

"Grams, I'll be okay. You worry too much."

"What am I supposed to do but worry? You going to the gym today?"

"No, I think I'm going to hang out at home. Like you said, get some rest. It's been a long month, and I'm tired."

"I understand. Did you have to work late last night?"

Doug wasn't sure what to say next because he didn't want to tell her the truth and get her upset. "Yeah. I got called in to help out last minute."

"Okay, well, there's food in the refrigerator. Did you find the aspirin?"

Doug went through the drawer and found a single pack of aspirin. "Yes, ma'am. I'm good."

"Great. Hey, have you spoken to your brother lately?"

"No. It's been a minute. Why do you ask?"

"Oh, I was just thinking about him this morning. I saw that he called me but didn't leave a message. When I tried calling him back, it went straight to voicemail. Maybe I'll call him later."

Doug didn't answer her because he hated speaking about Sean. Whenever he spoke ill of him, his grandmother would make him feel guilty. She would tell him that they only have each other and need to squash any issues they had. Because no matter what, they were family, and, in the end, family was all you got in this world.

"Okay, Nana. I'm going to go back to bed."

"All right, baby. You do that. Look, I got a late meeting tonight. I should be home after 7:00 p.m. So, order you some food for dinner, okay?"

"Gotcha. Be safe, and I'll see you tonight."

"Bye, sweetie." Elsie hung up the phone.

He poured himself a glass of water and took his aspirin before heading back to bed. He texted Lenny letting him know that he wasn't coming by the gym today. He was in no shape, mentally or physically, to train. All he could think about was resting up before he got back into the groove. He lay back down and quickly fell asleep.

It was dark by the time Doug woke up from his nap. He looked at the time on his phone, and it read six o'clock. He was shocked by how long he had slept, but he knew that he needed the rest. Happy that his headache had disappeared, he took a much-needed shower. The hot water eased his stiff joints, and he thought about how hungry he was since he slept through breakfast, lunch, and dinner. He decided to grab a few slices at his favorite pizza joint. He had earned it with all of the training that he had been doing.

While he got dressed in a pair of gray sweats and a black T-shirt, he thought about calling his grandmother to see if she wanted some pizza, but he decided just to pick her up a few slices since she would be hungry after finishing up her meetings.

He walked to the restaurant, where he enjoyed sitting outside looking out at the water. After finishing his food, he walked back to the apartment building, where he saw Sean waiting outside. He reached into his pocket for his keys while ignoring his older brother.

"Hey, baby bro. What's going on with you? You good?"

"Yeah, I'm good. You?"

"Things are good. Real good," Sean replied.

"What do you want, Sean?"

"Why do I have to want something? Can't I just come by to visit my fam? I buzzed, but nobody was home."

"That's because we work around here. You know what? Maybe you should try it sometime."

"I know she got a job, Doug. I thought she would be home by now. It's after seven, and she's not home yet."

"Grams had to work late. Why the hell do you care?" Doug barked.

"I wanna see her. She's my grandmother too. Why don't we go inside and wait for her?" Sean asked.

"Nah, son. You ain't welcome inside, remember?"

"Damn. Can't you be civil for once?"

"Sean, I ain't got time for this bullshit. I'll tell Nana you came by. Now, you need to bounce."

"Come on, Doug. I need to look you both in the eyes and tell you how sorry I am for what happened in the past."

"Why don't you just call her cell? She'll let you know when she's coming home. 'Cause I'm not letting you inside without her saying that it's okay."

Sean pulled out his phone and tried calling her. "She's not picking up."

"Then you should just leave a message."

"Hey, Nana. It's Sean. I'm out here in front of the building with Doug waiting for you. Yeah, see you soon. Love you." He hung up the phone and continued to look over at Doug.

"Well, I suggest that you need to bounce, brutha. Nana will call you when she gets home."

"Why don't I just hang out here?"

Doug shrugged his shoulders. "If that's what you wanna do, but you can keep your ass outside because you're definitely *not* coming in."

"I heard what happened last night. You good?"

Doug stopped dead in his tracks and stared directly at his brother. "What did you just say?"

"Word gets out, man."

"Nah, nah. Word just doesn't 'get out.' What do you know?"

"I heard that somebody tried to rob you."

"Really? And where did you hear that from?"

"Around the block. News travels fast. That's one of the reasons why I came by to make sure you were a'ight."

"For some reason, I just don't believe you."

"Why would I lie?"

"Because that's what you do. You lie. You cheat. You steal."

"I'm not lying."

"Yeah, whatever, because if I find out you had anything to do with me getting jumped, I will *definitely* beat your ass."

Just then, Doug's phone rang. It was his grandmother calling him. He quickly answered. "Hey, Nana. You on your way home?"

"Yes, sir. It has been a long day. Did you eat?"

"Yes, ma'am, and I picked up some pizza for you."

"Fantastic. I'm starving. Hey, I got a text from your brother earlier. He still there?"

"Yeah, he's here."

"Oh, okay. Nice. Can you please keep him company until I get there? I should be home in about thirty minutes. Wait. Hold on for a minute."

"Okay."

Doug was confused when all of a sudden, the phone went dead. "Hello? Nana?" He tried calling back, but the phone went straight to voicemail.

"What's going on? What happened?" Sean asked his brother.

"I don't know. She told me to hold on a minute, but the phone went dead."

Chapter 14

It had been a long day for Elsie when she finally packed up her things to head home. Just when she was about to leave her office, her phone rang. She looked down to see Darwin Hayes's name. Elsie smiled and picked it up. "Mr. Hayes."

"Oh, you're still here."

"Well, where else would I be? I mean, we just finished our meeting about five minutes ago."

There was a hearty laugh that came through the phone. "I guess you're right. Glad that I caught you then."

"What can I do for you, Darwin?"

"Well, I was thinking since we still have a lot more work do on the budget, maybe we can finish up tonight. How about you join me for dinner? I'm ordering now."

"Oh, that would be lovely, but unfortunately, I need to get home and check on my grandson. He wasn't feeling well today."

"Okay, no worries. Rain check?"

"Sure, that would be great."

"Have a nice evening, Elsie. We'll pick up where we left off tomorrow."

"Good night, Darwin."

Elsie hung up the phone, and a huge grin filled her face. She knew that this wasn't an ordinary call. She and Darwin, who she secretly referred to as the "Silver Fox," had been working together for the past six months. There was an attraction between the two of them, but she knew better than to assume anything, especially since they worked together. It had been a long time since she had a crush on someone, and she definitely thought about him as more than just a colleague. *What am I gonna do about you, Mr. Hayes?*

She cut off the light and headed out the door. Looking at her watch, she saw that it was now 7:00 p.m., and she couldn't wait to get home. The hallway was desolate since all of the people who reported to her had already left for the day. Only the nurses who attended the elderly remained, and they were located in the adjacent building. Maybe she would walk past Darwin's office to say good night, but she didn't want to be too obvious since his office was in the opposite direction. *Tomorrow, Mr. Hayes.*

As she continued to walk down the hallway, she thought about both of her grandsons. She saw that Sean had tried calling her earlier, but she had missed it. A part of her felt hurt and disappointed by Sean's actions, especially since he had not done right by her or Doug. She hated kicking him out of the apartment, but she had no choice after he had stolen from her. In fact, he had gotten them thrown out of the apartment that she had lived in for over twenty years. Thank goodness her friend Margaret had helped her move into an even better apartment that was cheaper and in a better neighborhood. In the end, she had to choose between her two grandsons, and it had to be Doug. He was a good kid who always looked out for the family.

Once she got outside, she called Doug, letting him know that she was headed home. As she continued walking to her car, she noticed a similar van to the one parked on the street earlier. She didn't think much of it and continued focusing on her call with her grandson. Just when she asked Doug to hold on a minute because she needed to open the car door, two guys came out of nowhere and grabbed her. One of the goons placed a cloth filled with chloroform over her mouth, and she instantly passed out. Her phone fell to the ground, and the other guy picked it up, turning it off. Then he put the phone in his back pocket, and they placed Elsie in the back of their van.

As the van barreled down the street, A-Roc sat in the passenger seat and took a long drag from his cigarette. Elsie's phone kept ringing, but DeAndre kept hitting the decline button.

"What the fuck, man?" A-Roc screamed. "DeAndre, hand me the damn phone."

DeAndre handed the phone to his boss. A-Roc looked at the name and saw that it was Elsie's grandson, Doug, calling.

"Ah, look who's calling. Doug Gibson." A-Roc looked back at Elsie, who was sound asleep. "So, Grams, should I call your grandson, Doug, back?"

Elsie didn't wake.

"I got a betta idea. I'll text your other grandson. You know, the trifling one." He texted Sean from his phone. Sean, I got your grandmother. Where you at?

Sean texted him back. I'm with my brother, Doug. What do you mean you got my grandmother?

A-Roc looked over at Snake, who was almost too big to fit behind the driver's seat.

"Damn this traffic. A-Roc, we not gonna get to the safe house for at least another thirty minutes."

A-Roc took another drag. "It's all good." He turned around and looked at DeAndre and Red. "Just make sure that she stays asleep before we take her out of the van."

DeAndre looked at Simon, who remained silent. They both focused on watching Elsie, who was fast asleep.

Snake smirked and continued driving through the traffic.

Elsie's phone rang again, and this time, A-Roc answered. "Hello?"

Doug took the phone from his ear and looked down at the number. "Hello, who is this?"

"Why don't you ask your brother?"

"What the hell are you talking about? Put my grandmother on the phone," Doug demanded.

"You see, that's going to be really hard since she's sleeping right now."

Doug looked over at his brother with both confusion and anger. "Listen, I don't know what type of sick game you playing right now—"

The deep voice on the other end started laughing. "Man, does it sound like I'm playing a damn game? All you need to know is that I got your family, and if you don't do what we say, we're gonna put the old lady down. You feel me?"

"What do you want?"

"Your brother owes me a lot of money, and if you don't pay up in three days . . . Well, now, you understand what I'm saying?"

Doug glared at his brother. "I have nothing to do with my brother's debts."

Sean looked horrified. He took a few steps back.

"Well, unfortunately, since he can't pay up, then it is up to you."

"How much does he owe you?"

"Twenty grand. He's got three days to get my money, or I'm gonna use your grandmother as a down payment."

"I don't have that kind of money," Doug pleaded.

"But you got the skills, right? I hear you're an up-and-coming prizefighter. I can use someone like you."

"What do you mean 'someone like me'?"

"We can make a lot of money together, homie. Talk it over with your brother. I'll be in touch. Peace."

The phone went dead, and Doug was fuming. He started walking toward his brother as Sean put up his hands to calm him down. "What the hell did you do, Sean?"

"Doug, man, let me explain."

"Who took Nana?"

Before Sean could answer, Doug punched his brother in the face so hard that blood exploded from his mouth. Sean backed up a few steps, touching his jaw, then charged at Doug, who quickly moved out of the way. Doug pushed his brother to the ground, and then he kicked him in the side, making Sean cry out in pain.

Sean rolled out of the way before Doug kicked him again. He jumped to feet and swept Doug's leg, causing him to fall to the ground. Doug hopped up and rammed his body into Sean's chest, causing them both to hit the ground hard. They began rolling on the ground just as Benita drove up to the scene. She observed the young boxer in a full-on fight. *What the hell is going on here?*

She quickly put the car in park and jumped out to break up the fight between Doug and a guy who was clearly getting beat up on the sidewalk.

"Doug, get off of him! Stop it right now." Benita dragged Doug off the bloody body that was crawling away.

"Let go of me. Let go."

"Not until you calm down," Benita yelled. She looked over at the other guy, who was slowly standing up. Waiting for Doug to calm down, she got ready to release him; however, he geared up to jump back on the guy. This time, Benita grabbed his arm and twirled him around, causing him to fall on his butt. "Doug, stop."

Doug's shock turned to anger, and just as he was about to respond, he changed his mind and remained quiet while catching his breath. He stood up and wiped the dirt from his hands. Just as the other guy got up, Benita stood in front of Doug, who was heading back toward him. She directly blocked Doug's path. "I'm sorry, Doug, but I can't let you hurt this dude."

"Who the hell are you anyway? And how do you know my brother?" Sean barked back at Benita.

She swung her head around and stared at the bruised man. "Who the hell am I? *I'm* the person who just saved your life. Because if I hadn't stepped in, brutha, you would definitely not be around much longer."

Sean touched the side of his face and winced in pain. "Bruh, I don't know who this chick is, but you and me need to work things out—alone."

"Muthafucka, I ain't got shit to say to you," Doug yelled.

"Doug, man, we're family. We gotta get Nana back."

"Oh, now you wanna get her back? This is all *your* fault. If it weren't for you, Nana would be safe right now. Get the hell out of here."

"I can't leave, man. We gotta work together to get her back."

"How the hell are we gonna do that? You got twenty thousand to get her back? You know what, you suck ass? You a piece of shit."

"I know. I know. And I wish to God that I didn't cause all of this. But it's too late now."

"I think you should give Doug some space," Benita suggested.

"And why should I listen to you?"

"Well, since I have a third-degree black belt, and I own a gun, I seriously would hate to use either one on you."

Sean looked over at his brother, who had now slid down the wall. He watched as Doug placed his head on his crossed arms and rocked back and forth in silence. He needed to get through to Doug before something terrible happened to their grandmother. He spoke to his brother one more time, "Doug, I'm sorry. I didn't mean for anything like this to happen. I'm gonna let you cool down. We need to figure this out."

Doug didn't even pick up his head to acknowledge what Sean was saying. He was having a hard time comprehending the recent events. First, he was a part of a drive-by shooting, and now, his grandmother was kidnapped. *How in the world am I going to get her back?*

"Just leave, Sean. Go."

"Okay. I'm leaving. Call me when you're ready to talk." He finally walked away and headed north down the street.

After watching Sean leave, Benita sat down next to Doug.

"How did you find me?"

"It wasn't that hard. You know I'm an agent, right?"

"Yeah. Yeah. An agent with a gun."

"Listen, I came by to check on you since you weren't at the gym. And it's a good thing I did because you were doing some serious damage to that guy. You almost beat him to a pulp."

"He deserved it after what he did."

"What did he do exactly?"

Doug looked at Benita but didn't know how much to tell her. "Why should I talk? I don't even know you."

"Well, I would have thought since I saved your life last night that you would see I'm not the enemy."

He placed his chin on his folded arms and remained silent as he looked in the opposite direction, avoiding Benita's gaze.

"Doug, whatever it is, I'm sure we can work out a solution." Benita touched his knee. "Tell me what's going on with you. Who was that guy?"

"My no-good brother."

"Okay. And what does he have to do with all of this?"

Looking over at Benita, he realized that she might be the only one who could help him. "It's a long story."

"I got nothing but time. Why don't we go inside, and you can tell me all about it?" Benita replied to a distraught Doug. She stood up, dusted off her butt, and reached out for Doug's hand. He grabbed it, and she pulled him up from the ground. "All right, Doug. Let's go."

The apartment was eerily quiet when the two of them entered the kitchen. Benita poured water into the tea kettle and placed it on the stove. She found a box of tea bags and took out two cups from the cabinet. "You know, my grandmother and

I used to drink a cup of tea every night before we went to bed. Really calmed us down."

"My Nana loves tea. Whatever free time we both have, we just sit in the kitchen, talking things through over a cup of tea as well."

Benita smiled when she thought about her grandmother. "It's a grandma thing."

After the kettle whistled, she poured the hot water into the cups with the tea bags and placed them on the table. "Here you go, Doug."

"Thank you."

Benita sat down across from him, holding on to her hot tea. "Now, you wanna tell me what's going on between you and your brother?"

"Sean is a complete fuckup. No matter what he touches, it turns to shit. I will never forgive him for what he's done to this family. Not in a million years."

"What exactly has he done?"

He began to tell Benita how Sean had robbed his own family to pay back a huge gambling debt. One night, Doug had come home early after finishing up a boxing match at the gym. That's when he saw Sean rummaging through his grandmother's drawers, looking for money. After he counted the money, Sean put it back in the envelope and placed it into his back pocket. Doug and his grandmother were blocking his path, not letting Sean leave the bedroom.

"Nana looked at my brother with tears running down her face. She couldn't believe that her own flesh and blood would steal from her. He then lied about it, telling her that it wasn't what she thought. She was so upset. I mean, I'd never seen my grandmother that upset before. She had taken us in when we were very young and had given us the best life she could. Neither one of our parents was around. And for her to see her grandson steal from her? It really changed her. She kicked him out of the apartment."

"I'm sorry, Doug." Benita hid the pity in her eyes by taking another sip of tea.

"My brother is a gambler. He needed the money to pay off some debt. He said that if he didn't pay up, then he would get hurt."

Benita took another sip of her tea. "So what happened next? Did he get to keep the money?"

Doug's demeanor changed, and he pounded his closed fist on the table. "I was so pissed that I punched him in the face. Then I gave my brother a beating that landed him in the hospital. I broke his jaw and a few ribs. My grandmother was horrified. She gave him the money to pay off his debts, and she made him move out of the apartment."

Benita felt Doug's pain that was masked under his anger. Especially when it came to the treatment of his grandmother. She thought about her own family and how much they meant to her. But if her

brother Wes had ever done something that trifling to harm their grandma, Grace, he wouldn't be
alive to talk about it. There was never a reason to
steal from the one person who has loved and cared
for you. "I'm sorry, Doug. That is so horrible."

Doug looked sorrowfully at her. "And now, Sean
has done it again. But this time, his actions have
put my grandmother in grave danger. She's been
kidnapped, and if we don't come up with twenty
grand, the man who took her will harm her. This
can't be happening right now. If anything happens
to my grandmother, I promise you I will kill him.
I swear to God, I will kill him and the men who
kidnapped her."

"What if I told you that I could help get your
Nana back?"

"Why would you want to do that? I mean, you
don't know me or my family."

"That's because it's the right thing to do."

"I don't know." He shook his head in disbelief.

"We're going to get your grandmother back. I
promise you that."

"How you gonna make a promise you can't keep?"

"Watch me." Benita whipped out her cell phone
and called Evan. "Hey, Evan. I'm sitting here with
Doug Gibson from last night. Listen, some things
have come up, and Doug needs our help. Can you
reach out to Huey and find us a safe house to lock
down? Yeah. I'll explain later. Evan, time is of the
essence. We're gonna have to act fast."

She hung up and stood, looking at Doug. "Do you believe me now? All you have to do is come with me. Will you let me help you?"

Doug placed his head down on the table, not knowing what to do.

Chapter 15

As Sean quickly walked down the street, he tried calling A-Roc, but the call went straight to voicemail. *Dammit, A-Roc.* When he finally made it to the corner of Sunny and Wagner Avenues, he called an Uber and waited at the nearest bus stop. He was horrified at the thought of anything happening to his grandmother. *Nana, I'm so sorry.* He knew that A-Roc had given him two weeks to come up with the money, or he would be sorry, but he never thought the bookie would kidnap his grandmother. He didn't want to think about what this crazy man would do to his grandmother if he didn't deliver the money.

He called Reggie, but that call went straight to voicemail as well. *Reggie, man, where the hell are you?* He winced when he shifted his weight because his side was sore from Doug's kick. It had been a long time since he had seen that much hate in his brother's eyes. Sean had promised to do better, but he just couldn't keep it. He knew that if anything ever happened to his grandmother, Doug would definitely kill him.

Sean tried A-Roc one more time in hopes that he would finally pick up.

"Yeah?" A-Roc answered.

"A-Roc, what the fuck, man? Where's my grandmother?"

"Oh, she's fine . . . for now. Your brother told you my demands?"

"Why did you have to get my grandmother involved?"

"Nigga, why you think? I know you ain't got the cash, but your brother's got the hands."

Frustrated, Sean rubbed his head and looked up at the sky. He wasn't sure what to say next. "A-Roc, I'll get you your money, but you gotta let my grandmother go."

"Sean, you know I ain't gonna let your grandmother go until I get what I want. I suggest you talk to your brother and make shit happen. You feel me? By the way, you need to get better friends. Tell Clay I said, what's up."

Before Sean could answer, A-Roc hung up the phone, leaving him speechless. He tried calling Reggie once more, but the call kept going to voicemail. *Reggie, where are you?* Sean jumped into the backseat of his Uber, placing his head on the headrest and massaging his aching temples. He'd never in a million years thought that he would put his grandmother's life in danger. He looked at his brother's number, but he closed his eyes. He needed to let Doug calm down before he pleaded his case.

After A-Roc hung up on Sean, he looked over at Snake, turning up the music in the van. They finally pulled up to a boarded-up building located on the opposite side of town, off of Cramer Street. This was one of the worst neighborhoods in Perth Amboy, and A-Roc liked it that way. No one would come and bother them, especially since he was about to have a middle-aged woman locked up in the basement of the apartment building. A-Roc looked at DeAndre when he heard a groggy Elsie starting to stir. DeAndre quickly covered her mouth again with chloroform, making her fall back asleep.

"Good job, DeAndre. And I didn't even have to tell you what to do this time. Simon, you're in charge of cleaning out the van, making sure that there ain't nothing left tying us to this little kidnapping. Let's move her into the basement," A-Roc ordered his minions.

Snake slowly put the van in reverse and moved it to the back of the building. DeAndre and Simon carried Elsie to the basement, where they laid her on a cot. Simon took a blanket located on the dresser and placed it over Elsie as she continued to sleep.

"Sweet dreams, Granny," Simon whispered to her.

Simon and DeAndre left the basement with DeAndre locking the door behind them. They remained silent as they walked back upstairs because they knew they were working for a dangerous man who would just as easily kill them if they even thought about ratting him out. They did their jobs and remained silent for both of their sakes. As they walked into A-Roc's office, their boss was already leaning back in his office chair.

"All set, boss," DeAndre stated.

"Good. Now, all we have to do is wait for that fool Sean to come by with either my money or his brother fighting on his behalf. Snake, go grab us some fish and chips from the seafood spot down the street. I've worked up an appetite."

"You got it, boss." Snake, DeAndre, and Simon left A-Roc alone, smiling from the day's events.

Meanwhile, Sean finally got to the apartment that he shared with Reggie, where he found Reggie and Clay going at it on the PlayStation.

"Hey, man. You speak to your brother?" Reggie landed a killer punch combination on Clay's avatar.

Sean went directly to Clay and started punching him.

"What the fuck, man?" Reggie said as he pulled Sean off of Clay.

"This muthafucka been running his mouth to A-Roc. Got my grandmother kidnapped."

Reggie, who was still holding on to Sean, looked over at Clay. "Clay, man, what did you do?"

"Shit, yeah. I just told A-Roc about Sean's brother, and if he wanted his money, he needed to figure out a way to get him to fight in A-Roc's underground club. Shit, Reggie, you the one who told me that the kid lives and breathes for his grandmother. So, I told him that he just needed to have a little talk with her."

"You muthafucka. You don't fucking speak for me. How you gonna even form your lips to speak about her? You know how crazy that dude is? I swear to God, I'm gonna kill you!"

"I didn't tell A-Roc to grab your grams, Sean."

"But he did, didn't he? You put that shit in his head."

"I'm sorry, but you brought this all on yourself," Clay pleaded.

"Clay, man, why don't you leave? I'll call you later," Reggie promised.

"I'm sorry, man. I didn't know he was going to go that extreme." Clay left, leaving Reggie and Sean alone in the apartment.

Reggie grabbed two bottles of beer from the refrigerator and handed one to Sean.

"This shit has gotten out of hand, Sean. Your brother would solve everything for us—"

"I know . . . It's either the money or my brother. And if I don't give A-Roc what he wants in three days, well, I don't want to even think about what he would do to my grandmother," Sean cried.

"Did you speak to your brother?"

"Yeah, and he's pissed the fuck off. If it wasn't for this girl who came by earlier, I would probably be dead."

"Wait. What girl?"

"Some badass chick that broke up a fight between me and Doug."

"Word? Damn, man. It might be the same girl from last night. I told you that there was this girl who interfered in us grabbing Doug."

Sean took a long swig of his beer.

"Who the hell is she, and how is she involved with your brother? Whoever she is, she's causing all kinds of problems for us. You need to talk to your brother like ASAP and get him to fight."

"I know. I know. I'll call him tomorrow. He needs to cool off."

"All right, listen. I gotta head out for a bit to handle some business. Get some rest and let's strategize for tomorrow, okay?"

Sean bobbed his head in agreement and then made his way to the spare bedroom that Reggie was letting him crash in. He pulled out a towel and washcloth and headed to the bathroom to shower. Reggie was right. He just needed a good night's sleep and would come up with a plan to work things out with his brother tomorrow.

As Reggie watched his best friend walk away, he grabbed his keys on the table and left the apartment. He was mortified when Sean discovered that Clay had talked to A-Roc about his grandmother. And now, she was in danger. There was no telling what A-Roc would do to Ms. Gibson if he didn't get his money. If he could have turned back the hands of time, he would have never shared what he knew about Sean and Doug's relationship with their grandmother. Guilt overtook him when he thought about his last conversation with Clay.

"Reggie, how you let that fucking Sean convince you to bet on one of those fights? Don't you know how crazy that A-Roc is? He will kill you for a few pennies. It's the principle with him." Clay finished his Hennessey as he looked at his friend, who was staring into his vodka tonic. *"So, whatchu gonna do about it?"*

Reggie looked at Clay and shook his head. "I don't even know, man. Sean thinks that he can convince his brother to fight."

Clay laughed. "Man, you know that ain't gonna happen. Didn't you tell me that Sean's brother ain't spoken to him in a minute, ever since Sean stole money from him and his grandmother? Get the fuck outta here with that nonsense."

"Sean ain't got a choice. He's gonna have to get his little bro to pony up."

"And just how you think he's gonna do that?" Clay asked before throwing back his beer.

"I told him that we would grab the little nigga and get him on board."

Clay took another swig of his beer. "I'm good with that. Anything to get you out of this shit show."

"Good looking out, my man. Appreciate that."

"Whateva you need. You know I got you. And if that means to rough up that dude a little bit, let's do it. Because this shit ain't no joke."

Little did Reggie know that Clay's actions had just complicated things even more. He was now on a mission to find Sean's grandmother before things got out of hand. And he knew just exactly who to contact to get some answers.

Chapter 16

Benita looked over at the young boxer sleeping peacefully while she drove to one of the DTCU safe houses located about an hour and a half from Perth Amboy. She had finally convinced him to come with her after promising that she would use all of her company's resources to find his grandmother. As soon as Doug got into her car, he fell fast asleep. Poor thing was exhausted after everything that had transpired over the past twenty-four hours. Feeling how hopeless he felt, she knew that it was the right thing to do to help him.

As she continued driving up S-206 North, she was soon surrounded by farmland country. Growing up in Brooklyn, she rarely traveled out of the city limits and only went to New Jersey or Upstate New York when she and her family went apple picking. She never imagined living in New Jersey, let alone driving all over the most obscure areas throughout the state.

Once she had spoken to Evan, they had agreed to set up shop at the Black Creek Hills in Newton, New Jersey, which was located two hours north of

Philadelphia. She remembered the first time that she had visited the sprawling estate, reminding her of a scene out of *Gone with the Wind*. A long road led to a beautifully restored mansion. Miguel had brought the entire team here to recuperate after their last assignment.

Since the 1960s, the DTCU had purchased several of the larger, midsized estates as a way to operate in complete privacy. Black Creek Hills was built in 1908 and was located in front of the Kittatinny Mountains. It was an estate that offered total seclusion, which was a prerequisite for any property owned by the DTCU. This property sat on ten acres of land and included beautiful green pastures, wooded havens with many trails, open fields, and streams. Black Creek Hills was charming with its barns and the thoroughbred horses running around the pastures.

Benita fell in love with the property the first time she set foot on it. It was tranquil, which was what she needed after completing her first assignment a few months ago. It was the first time she had ever visited a place that she could only describe as heaven. Growing up in Brooklyn, she was surrounded by the concrete jungle, and the only time she could get anything close to this serenity was at Prospect Park. But even then, there were millions of people always in her line of vision. When she saw that Black Creek was immediately available, she knew this was the perfect place for

Doug. Hopefully, it would offer him the peace that he so needed right now to think things through.

Benita wasn't ready to talk to Miguel about her plans just yet. She decided she would call him once she got settled at the Hills. Even feeling a little guilty about not keeping her promise to him, she knew she'd made the right choice to find Doug. Because if she hadn't, then she wouldn't have found out about his grandmother being kidnapped. She knew that Miguel would be pissed off at her, but he would get over it once they brought back Doug's grandmother safe and sound. She had thought things through and made up her mind to save someone's life, and that trumped any protocol currently in place.

She finally passed a sign reading Black Creek Hills. It was now pitch dark, and she barely could see the entrance leading down a narrow-paved lane. Once she turned off the main road, she drove up to a large, six-foot-high gate. She punched in a four-digit code, and the gate automatically opened. Doug suddenly woke up and saw that Benita was driving slowly toward a huge house.

"Where are we?"

"At one of my company's properties."

"Really? What kind of company is this? I thought you were like a detective or something."

"Or something. Let's just say the organization I work for specializes in taking down big criminals.

I thought it would be the best place for you to meet my team."

"Benita, I don't understand any of this. It's like you're this superhero chick that just walked out of a magazine or something. I mean, you're gorgeous. You drive a cool car. You carry a gun. You fight like a guy. I've never met anyone like you before. Tell me, what the hell is going on here? Who are you really? Are you a spy? What exactly do you get out of helping me and my family?"

Benita looked at him with a serious expression. "Doug, I'm no one special. I'm just an average girl who happens to work at an amazing place. In fact, I'm more like you than you know."

"No. Nope. You're nothin' like me. I work at Walmart stocking shelves, and I train to one day make it as a boxer. You ain't like me at all."

Benita knew that this all came as a shock for Doug. Hell, when she thought about it, it sounded pretty crazy to her as well. *Who would ever believe that a Brooklyn girl would turn secret agent?* "Look, I used to be a hairstylist. And I mean, I loved doing hair. However, I made a mistake trying to protect a family member, and my circumstances abruptly changed. I'm not only in a position to help others, but I can also help you now. You feel me?"

"Yeah, I feel ya. I guess I'm lucky, huh?"

Benita chuckled. "Yeah, very lucky . . . for sure."

Just as she pulled into the U-shaped driveway, her phone buzzed. She waited until she parked the car in front of the sprawling manor before reaching for it. "Dang, it's my father. I'll be right back." Benita got out of the car, leaving Doug inside. She redialed the number, connecting to her dad.

"Hey, sunshine. I've been trying to call you all day. What's going on with you?"

"Hey, Leroy. Sorry, I've been kind of tied up."

"You working a case?"

"Something like that."

Leroy, who was cleaning up from the last class, stopped what he was doing and paid close attention to the conversation. "And what exactly does that mean, 'something like that'?"

Benita remained silent.

"Well? Benita? What does 'something like that' mean?"

Benita looked inside the car and saw that Doug had his eyes closed. "Well, okay. Remember when we were working out at the gym, and I mentioned that I was concerned about a few shady guys watching the two boxers?"

"Yeah. What about them?"

"Well, I was right. Last night I ended up stopping an assault on one of the young boxers there."

"Really? And you're just now telling me that news?"

"Wait, before you go off on me, let me explain what happened."

Leroy took a deep breath and let his daughter describe the past twenty-four hours. Although he was not surprised by her good deeds, he also knew that she would probably get serious blowback from her decision to pursue this situation. "Benita, you know you could get in serious trouble for this."

"I know, Dad, but I just couldn't sit back and do nothing, could I? Listen, we just got to one of the safe houses, and as soon as I get him settled, I'll call you back."

"Make sure you call Miguel first and explain everything to him."

"I promise. He's next on the list."

"Do you need my help? Send me the address, and I'll be there in a few hours."

"No, Dad. I can handle this. I'll let you know if I need your help."

"You sure?" he asked.

"Yeah, I'm sure. I'll call you later." Benita hung up the phone and tapped on the passenger-door window. Doug was startled but got out of the car, grabbing his overnight bag. As they walked toward the front door, her friend and fellow agent, Luciana Rodriguez, greeted them. Benita gave Luciana a big hug. "Girl, when did you get back in town?"

"This morning. And while I was in the office, I ran into Evan, who filled me in on what was happening in your world."

"Yup. A lot is going on right now. I'm happy that you came to help." Benita looked at Doug, who was quietly standing on the side while the two women caught up. "Doug, this is Agent Luciana Rodriguez."

"Hey," he nervously shifted on his feet. "You an agent too?"

Luciana smiled at the young man. "Yup, I certainly am."

"This makes no sense to me. Seriously, do all the agents look like you two?"

"You mean looking like badasses? 'Cause, ah, yeah," Benita teased.

"Okay. If you say so. I mean, I just haven't seen female agents before. That's all."

"Well, we do come in all shapes and sizes," Luciana responded.

"And I promise you, Doug, Agent Rodriguez and my other colleagues are the best in the business, and we're all going to do everything in our power to bring your grandmother home."

Just then, Evan walked out of the door to greet Benita and Doug. "Hey, Doug. How ya feeling?"

"Under the circumstances, I guess I'm all right," he answered.

"Good. I'm glad. You gotta stay positive, my man. Benita, can I have a word with you?"

"Sure." Benita looked at Doug and Luciana. "Luciana, can you take Doug inside? We'll be right in."

"Sure. Doug, come on. Let's get you settled. You hungry?"

"Yeah, I can eat something."

The two of them walked inside the house, leaving Benita and Evan in front of the mansion.

Benita observed a nervous look on Evan's face. "What's up?"

"Did you speak to Miguel yet?"

"No. I wanted to get Doug here before dealing with him. Wait, did you?"

"No, but I did talk to Huey, who tracked the grandmother's cell phone number. It seems Doug's grandmother is being held in an area known as the Black Hole."

"The Black Hole?"

"The area is currently on DTCU's radar. A lot of illegal underground fighting over there. Benita, that place is extremely dangerous. According to Huey, there are many boarded-up buildings and tunnels. It's going to be tough to find her."

"Jeez. Doug told me earlier that his brother Sean was into gambling. Do we know who's running the boxing ring?"

"There seems to be some kind of consortium. I'm not sure who the head person is. We need to get more intel."

"How in the world did we go from protecting this guy from an attempted kidnapping, an attempted murder, to an actual kidnapping, and now he's somehow linked to an illegal boxing club?"

"I have no idea, but I guess we can thank your gut. It definitely didn't steer you wrong."

"Evan, we need a plan."

"Well, who can better help us but Miguel? You gotta call him before we go any further. We need him to bless this case. Plus, Huey isn't willing to do any more digging for us until he gets an official greenlight."

Benita bit her lip because she wasn't ready to explain herself to Miguel. "Of course, let's go and check in on Doug first. I'll call Miguel in a bit."

"Okay, we can do that," he agreed.

They walked inside to find Luciana and Doug in the dining room. Doug looked up at the two agents as he ate a slice of pizza. "This place is fire. I mean, you got vending machines and food stations twenty-four seven. This is seriously bananas."

"Well, there are definitely perks working for the Agency," Benita said as she sat down next to Doug. "Hey, have you ever heard about something called the Black Hole?"

"Hmmmm. It's some kind of local underground fighting club."

"Have you ever participated?" Evan joined them at the table.

Doug looked at the agents with utter confusion. "Nah, my grandmother would kill me. Shoot, that would kill any chance I had to fight in a legitimate boxing match. Wait, why are you asking about the Black Hole?"

"Well, we think your grandmother is being held somewhere near the fight club," Evan responded.

"Wait. Please tell me that my asshole brother hasn't been betting on those fights? That is suicide, man. Those people are no joke. I've heard some of the dudes talking about it at the gym, and many of them have gotten seriously injured there. I even heard one story about somebody dying. Is *this* why my grandmother got snatched up over his dumb ass? Oh, I get it now. He needs *me* to fix *his* gambling debt by fighting for him."

Benita tried to calm Doug, who was becoming unhinged. "We don't know that for sure."

"We don't? It seems pretty obvious to me," he barked.

"Has your brother ever done anything like this before?"

"My brother has done a lot of shitty things, but this takes the cake," Doug answered Benita. "His addiction has now put my Nana's life in danger. She could be seriously hurt right now, and there's nothing I can do about it."

Benita looked at Evan and Luciana while rubbing Doug's back. "We gotta get his grandmother back. I don't care what we gotta do. We gotta make it happen."

Chapter 17

It was so dark when Elsie finally opened her eyes. She was extremely groggy and confused about where she was. Her head was pounding, and her mouth felt full of cotton. She lay there on the cot for a few more minutes trying to get her bearings straight. Then, slowly, she sat up with a flood of questions going through her head. *Where am I? Who are these guys? What do they want?* Trying to stand was more of a difficult task. She felt woozy and slipped back on the small cot. A few attempts later, she finally stood up.

Finding a light switch next to the door, Elsie flicked it on. She attempted to open the metal door, but it was locked from the outside. *Maybe I can find something to pry it open.* Scanning the room for tools, she saw nothing she could use. It had a small bathroom with only a tiny sink and toilet in the corner. Some worn furniture, including a table and chairs, a small refrigerator, and an oversized cushioned chair were there. Her eyes moved to a small window with bars on it. She looked outside, searching for anyone walking down the street. The only thing she could make out were a few boarded-up buildings since the street was practically black due to the lack of streetlights.

Where the hell am I? Think, Elsie, think. What do these thugs want? Why did they target me? Her heart began racing, faster by the moment. *Calm down, Elsie.* She was racking her brain, thinking about how she became a target. Who would want to kidnap her? She instantly thought of Sean. *Did you cause this?* She hadn't heard from her grandson in months, not since she kicked him out of the apartment. Suddenly, things started to make sense. Why would he just show up at her place unexpectedly earlier today? Why was he waiting to talk to her?

Her mind quickly went to Doug. She remembered talking to him before everything went blank. *My poor Doug. He's probably worried sick. I gotta get out of here.* Hearing a clicking sound coming from outside the door, she backed up and pressed her body against the wall as a way to brace herself from the unknown kidnapper. Maybe she could find something to arm herself with, but the only thing near her was an empty crate next to the cot.

The door slowly opened, and DeAndre walked in holding a plastic bag filled with Fish and Chips.

"Hey, Grams. I see you're awake."

"My name is Elise Gibson, not Grams. And, yes, I'm awake. And you are?"

"I brought you some dinner." The young thug placed the plastic bag on top of the refrigerator located near the door.

"Thank you, son."

"You're welcome."

"Can you tell me why I'm here?"

The young kid smirked at Elsie. "You need to ask your grandson."

"My grandson? Which one? Sean?"

DeAndre could not hold his poker face, making it clear that Sean was the cause of her kidnapping. However, he remained silent because he was ordered not to communicate too much information. "I gotta go. Enjoy your meal."

Before Elsie could ask any more questions, he shut the door, locking it behind him. Elsie ran to the door and started banging on it. "Wait. Don't go. Please. Hey, please don't leave me here. Let me out. Please." Elsie continued yelling, but the youngster was long gone. She was disappointed and hurt by Sean's actions. *Oh, how could you let this happen?* She lay back down on the cot and curled up in a fetal position, eventually crying herself to sleep. Maybe tomorrow, someone would tell her exactly what kind of trouble her grandson had gotten into.

Meanwhile, as A-Roc and Snake finished up their dinner, DeAndre walked into the office.

"You delivered the old lady's food?" A-Roc asked.

"Yeah."

"She still sleeping?"

"Nah. She awake now."

"Well, I guess that's a good thing. You weren't thinking she was dead, were you?" A-Roc teased.

"No. No. But she was sleeping for a long time."

"That's what we wanted, right? Didn't want her waking up knowing where she was. Well, D, why don't you get on home, and we'll pick this back up tomorrow."

DeAndre nodded in agreement. "Okay, I can do that."

A-Roc reached in his pocket and pulled out some cash. "Here's three hundies. Try not to spend it all in one place, okay?"

DeAndre took the money and quickly jetted out of the building. He had done many errands for A-Roc, but this was the first time he was ordered to kidnap a woman in broad daylight. He was scared of A-Roc and wasn't sure what the crazy man would do to her. When it came to his boss, he made sure he stayed on his good side. He couldn't wait to get back to his place and shower. Most of the days, he was okay with A-Roc's demands, but today was different. DeAndre felt guilt when it came to Sean's grandmother. She didn't deserve to be brought into this mess. As he walked down the dark street, a black Escalade stopped in front of him. He immediately recognized the vehicle, seeing that it was Reggie.

"Get in, man. Let me holla atcha for a minute," Reggie said.

DeAndre looked around to make sure no one was watching him before he jumped into the passenger seat. Reggie placed his foot on the pedal, and the car zoomed down toward the highway. "So, y'all took the grandmother? Is she all right?"

"Yeah, she good for now. What's Sean saying?"

"This got him fucked up. I swear I didn't know you guys were going to grab the ol' lady."

"Whatchu think was going to happen when you told Clay? You think that nigga wasn't gonna run and tell A-Roc? Sean doesn't know that it was you who did this shit?"

Reggie shook his head and took a deep breath. "I just wanted A-Roc to scare Doug into fighting. Never thought that fool would kidnap her."

"Well, it's too late now. I hate to tell you, but A-Roc may not let her go. That dude ain't wrapped very tight. He can go from hot to cold in a drop of a hat. Anything can set him off," DeAndre warned his cousin.

"Well, listen, D, it's up to you to make sure that don't happen. I would feel some kind of way if anything happened to Mrs. Gibson. She has always looked out for me."

"I'll try, but all I can say is you better work on your boy because time is definitely of the essence, and that nigga is trying to fill out all kinds of slots for the next set of fights. You feel me? Work on your friend before everything goes to shit."

Reggie pulled up in front of the Rose Towers where DeAndre lived. He watched as his cousin headed toward the building with both of his hands pushed into his front pockets. He was glad that DeAndre had given him a heads-up on what was going down, but he kept the news to himself. No way was he going to tell Sean his part in what was going down.

One day when he and Clay were at a local car wash, A-Roc and Snake accosted both of them by pushing them against the wall, asking where A-Roc's money was. When Reggie told him that Sean was working on getting his brother Doug to fight, that's when Clay mentioned that the best way to do that was to scare the grandmother. That suggestion put A-Roc's plan in motion.

I'm sorry, Sean. Now, Reggie planned on pushing Sean to keep his end of the bargain, because as DeAndre had mentioned, A-Roc was a dangerous man, and he would hurt anyone who didn't pay him back his money, including Mrs. Gibson. Reggie stopped by the liquor store and picked up some Tito's and tonic water. He absolutely needed a drink if he was going to make it through the night.

Chapter 18

"Hey, you. Hope you enjoyed your day. I think we're close to getting your next assignment. Give me a call when you get this message." Miguel followed up the message with a text, then went back to reviewing cases that his other teams were working on. He was exhausted. Between meetings and calls, he barely had time to grab something to eat.

He opened up an email from the DTCU Safe House Department requesting his approval for the use of Black Creek Hills. When he read through the request, he immediately saw Agent Benita Renee Jenkins and Agent Evan Green's names. *What the . . .?* He placed a call to the director of Safe Housing, who picked up on the first ring. "Maggie Burns."

"Hey, Maggie, it's Miguel Perkins."

"Hello, Agent Perkins. Long time, sir. How can I help you?"

"Well, I see that there was a request for one of our safe houses from Benita Renee Jenkins."

"Yes, Huey requested the space on her behalf."

"Really? Oh, okay."

"Is there a problem?"

"No, no problem. I don't see who they plan on housing there. Did Huey give you any additional information?"

"No. I didn't get any specifics."

"I'll follow up with Huey. Thanks for the update. Expect confirmation from me shortly."

"Thank you, Agent Perkins. You know I just like to make sure I stay on top of all my requests. We have to follow company policy if we get a request less than twenty-four hours in advance. We need to get approval from the manager of the team. Thank you so much for confirming. I can now close out this request."

"No problem, Maggie. Thank you."

"Have a good evening, Agent Perkins."

Miguel hung up the phone and rubbed his chin. He was angry that Benita had not only lied to him about staying low-key, but she also tried to set up things behind his back. On top of that, she had gotten Evan and Huey involved in her plans. He was highly disappointed in how none of these agents followed company rules, and he now had to punish them. He first called Huey to find out what Benita was up to.

"Cyber Unit," Huey answered.

"Huey, it's Miguel."

"Agent Perkins. You're working late. How can I help you?"

"I just received a request for the use of the Black Creek Hills. What the hell's going on with you, Evan, and Benita?"

"Oh, she didn't tell you?"

"What do you mean, 'she didn't tell me'? Why didn't *you* call me and tell me?"

Huey, who didn't want to get himself in trouble, tried to downplay his involvement. "Well, Evan told me they needed a place to house someone who was a part of a drive-by shooting last night. I did some research and provided them with an available location to keep the witness safe."

Miguel worked to keep his cool. "At Black Creek?"

"Yes, sir."

"I suggest the next time you get a request from any of my team members, you call *me* first before making moves. Understand?"

"Yes, sir."

"Good. Do you know who else is there?"

Huey checked the online form he submitted. "It looks like Agent Rodriguez is also there."

"Got it. The three musketeers."

"Anything else, sir?"

"For now, send me over any information that you've collected about this so-called case. And get your ass ready to meet me there."

"Yes, sir."

Miguel heard a ping from his computer and opened up a report that Huey just sent regarding the incident involving Benita and Evan. After reading the incident report, he reviewed the photo of Doug Gibson, who was a part of last night's drive-by shooting. While reading the document, he noticed Doug's occupation. *"So, Doug Gibson. You're a boxer."*

Suddenly, Miguel remembered seeing a case that caught his eye earlier that day, and he had put it to the side to discuss with Willard. He began flipping through his stack of folders and found the one he was looking for. It was labeled "The Black Hole." As he scanned through the documents in the folder, he couldn't help thinking about how much of a coincidence it was between Willard's open case and Benita's involvement with the young boxer from the gym. *Hmmm.*

Miguel called Willard, who immediately picked up.

"Hey, Perkins. What's happening?"

"Well, I'm curious about one of our cases—the Black Hole."

"It's an illegal boxing ring that we've been trying to shut down for a while now but haven't been able to infiltrate the group. The last agent couldn't move on anything. I had to pull him off the case and move him out of the country. We need an agent who can get inside."

"Why haven't you been able to shut it down?"

"It's a real moving target. There've been fighters who have ended up crippled or even dead. The sad part is that no one is talking," Willard replied.

"And hard to pin down the culprits. Well, I think this may be a great case for Agent Jenkins."

"Okay, when do I meet this Agent Jenkins?"

"I'm headed up to Black Creek to meet with her and a few of my other agents. I'll call you once I get settled."

"No problem. We'll speak soon."

Miguel hung up the phone and reviewed the file again. *Well, isn't it funny how things just fall into place?*

He closed the folder, grabbed his laptop, and headed to the safe house to find out what trouble Benita had gotten herself into now.

Chapter 19

Benita was in the dining room with Doug and her other team members when she received a message from Miguel. *Damn*. She knew she needed to call him back but wanted to get Doug settled into his room. As they walked through the property, Doug soaked in the beautifully decorated mansion painted in a rustic-brown color, trimmed in beige and black walnut. There was a sense of warmth and sophistication exuding throughout the estate. He looked up at the ten-foot-high wood-beamed ceilings and perfectly stained wide-planked hardwood floors. The living room had a Gettysburg marble mantel fireplace and built-in window seats. The bay windows extended from one side of the living room to the other, allowing in a huge amount of light. The scenic canvas wallpaper panels with panoramic views depicted the mountains, lakes, and valleys. The tone was set for family gatherings and elegant events.

The walls throughout the house contained built-in bookshelves and French doors connecting the numerous conference rooms. Each conference room had different themed galleries, including photos of former presidents, DTCU directors and agents, plus books and paintings. The custom-tiled bathrooms were accented in wainscoting and vintage black-and-white tile floors. A back office was situated past the main conference room and adjoining bathroom.

Doug had never been to a place like this before and still couldn't wrap his head around how he ended up here. This estate was the perfect place to recalibrate his life. Under different circumstances, he might be able to enjoy it, but he was too focused on finding his grandmother.

"So, what do you think?"

"I've never seen anything like this in my life. This place is phenomenal."

"Yeah, I was pretty blown away the first time I visited. I love how it's in the middle of nowhere. It really serves as a place to relax and think things through."

Doug nodded in agreement. "So, where am I gonna sleep?"

"I'm about to show you. Follow me."

The two of them walked through the back door and saw a row of rustic-colored cottages, all perfectly aligned with individual sidewalks and shrubbery surrounding each bungalow.

"This is insane. I get to stay in one of these tonight?"

"Of course, Doug."

Benita unlocked the door to Bungalow #5 and flipped on the light. "As you can see, it's not that big, but the beds are comfy. And there's a shower in the bathroom." Benita opened the door to the bathroom. "If you need anything, you can call or text me. I just sent you my information. Get some rest, and we can discuss our plan in the morning, okay?"

"Thanks."

Benita left Doug in the cottage. He sat on the bed and picked up the remote lying on the nightstand. Doug decided to watch a little television to relax. Then hearing his phone buzz, he picked it up and read a text from Sean. Bro, I'm sorry for everything that I put you through. Call me so we can figure shit out. We gotta work together to get Grams back.

Suddenly, the young boxer became nauseated and felt the urge to throw up. He ran to the bathroom and barfed up all of the past twenty-four hours' toxicity that had filled his body. He was having an anxiety attack and ended up crying on the bathroom floor. He had no choice but to trust a stranger who had unexpectedly come into his life. Whatever it took, he was going to work to get his grandmother back. All he could do at that moment was pray for a miracle. He hoped she was safe.

Benita looked back at the cottage as she walked toward the manor. Knowing that she had pushed

Doug into trusting her, she now felt responsible for his well-being as well as getting his grandmother back safely. *Damn that brother, Sean. How could he have done this to his family?* Family was everything to her, even if she couldn't see hers. They were always top of her mind. In fact, they would always be her number one concern. She knew that the young boxer was ill-equipped to handle this situation on his own. His brother had put him and his grandmother in grave danger, and she was going to make sure that everything was going to turn out right. She was willing to put her life on the line if that meant finding Doug's grandmother. Now, she would just have to convince Miguel that it was the right thing to do.

Benita sat down on a bench and finally called her boss. She knew that he wasn't going to be happy with her decision to help Doug, but she wasn't going to back down. She knew she was doing the right thing. Wasn't that what a good agent was supposed to do? Sometimes, you just had to make the best decisions on the fly. *Okay, Benita. You can do this.*

As the phone rang, her right leg started bouncing up and down. Finally, her lover answered. "Perkins speaking."

"Hi. It's Benita."

There was silence on the other end of the phone.

"Hello? Miguel? You there?"

"Yeah, I'm here."

"Oh, okay. Well, I'm returning your call from earlier." Benita tried to keep the conversation light, but there was major tension between them.

"Is there something you want to tell me?"

"Actually, yes. Well, remember the guy from last night? I visited him at his place today, and a lot of bad things went down, so I had to move him to one of the safe houses in New Jersey. His life was in danger."

There was silence on the other line. Again, Benita was surprised that Miguel remained quiet.

"Miguel, are you still on the line?"

"Yes. I'm just listening. Please, continue with your story."

"Okay, Well, Doug's grandmother was kidnapped. His brother owes some criminals a lot of money and is responsible for this mess. I thought it was my duty as an agent to help him. So I made a few calls to see what we could do to get her back."

By this time, Miguel had utterly lost his patience and could no longer hold back his temper. "How many times have I told you that you can't just do things on your own? What's it going to take for you to understand that?"

"I know, Miguel, but—"

"But *what*, Benita? I don't want to hear anything else you have to say. I'm on my way to Black Creek Hill right now, and when I get there, you and I need to have a real come-to-Jesus talk. Do you understand me?"

This time, Benita was speechless.

"Do you understand me?" he screamed.

"Yes, Miguel."

"That's Agent Perkins to you. I'm not going to sit back and watch you get others hurt because you decided to take matters into your own hands. I gotta go. I'll see you and your Rambo team in a few hours."

Benita knew Miguel might be annoyed, but she had never heard him get *that* angry before. Had she finally crossed the line with him? What would this mean for the two of them and their secret love affair? There was something very different in his voice. Closing her eyes, she reflected on the past twenty-four hours. Maybe Miguel was right. Perhaps she had gone too far this time. She wasn't sure what to do next to fix things. All she could do right now was to pray he understood where she was coming from and allow her to find Doug's grandmother.

After licking her wounds, Benita found Evan and Luciana in one of the studies, located on the west wing of the building. The room was filled with traditional paintings and a whole wall of books. It offered tranquility for the agents to come together and devise a plan of action. Benita closed the door and sat across from her fellow agents on the black leather couch.

"Is Doug settled in for the night?"

"Yeah, he's good," Benita answered Evan. "I'm worried about him, though. I think I heard him crying."

"It's understandable. I can't imagine what he's feeling right now. The worst of it is that he can't do anything about it but pray and wait. You know what I'm saying?" The other two agreed with Luciana's observation.

"I know, but it doesn't make sense. How could this happen to a guy who is just trying to make it as a boxer?"

Evan watched Benita silently pet one of the lush down pillows on the couch before it hit him. "You haven't called Perkins yet, have you?"

"I spoke to him," she shrugged.

"What did he say?"

Benita laughed nervously at Evan's question and then smirked. "Well, let's just say that the call didn't go well. I think I may have finally crossed the line this time."

Luciana walked over to a small cabinet and poured herself a cup of tea. "Well, what exactly did you expect, Benita? Roses? You guys want some tea? Or is coffee better?"

Benita shook her head. "I thought he'd understand why this is important."

"Well then, you'll need to convince him because we all know if we don't have Perkin's support, we're screwed. I've worked with him for a long time, and he can be an asshole if he wants to. I mean, a real bona fide asshole. He'll block everything, and we'll be back to square one. He thinks he's the only one who can do anything worth a damn." Luciana sat down with the cup of steaming tea.

"Look, Benita, we're both behind you 100 percent, and we are just as much in this as you are. But Luciana is right. If we can't convince Miguel to move forward, we're stuck. And how is *that* going to help Doug?"

Benita smiled back at the two agents. "You two are amazing. I don't understand why you would put your careers on the line for me. You could just have walked away, but you didn't."

"Listen, we do this because we believe in the cause. We know that you have a heart of gold and passion to match despite your unconventional ways. We know you wouldn't intentionally put us in danger. Plus, what person wouldn't want to help find someone's grandmother? It's just insane how many heartless people there are in the world, and I, for one, am not going to let some no-good thug get away with kidnapping a woman off the street like that." Luciana delicately sipped her tea.

"I couldn't agree with you more, Luciana. Well said," Evan nodded.

Benita was touched by their faith. "I promise you I would never put either one of you in danger on purpose."

"You need tea to think." Luciana retrieved another cup and brought it to Benita. "You don't have to worry about that. We can handle ourselves in these streets. We completely support you. We always got your back."

"Well, I appreciate you guys, but trust me, when Miguel gets here, it'll definitely *not* be pretty. He has warned me that he and I are going to have a long talk about my actions." Evan held up an imaginary cup as if to make a toast. Benita and Luciana followed suit with their own. "Ladies, let's toast. There's no time like the present to go down fighting for the cause. Here's to us getting Doug's grandmother back."

Luciana seconded, "Let the games begin."

Chapter 20

Just as the agents were heading to their respective rooms, Miguel walked through the front door.

"Miguel, you're here already?"

"Are you surprised?" he asked Benita.

"Well, yeah, I didn't expect to see you until the morning."

"So, I see it's the three amigos all located under one roof. And none of you thought it was important to tell me what you were up to. Very interesting."

"It's not like that, Miguel," Luciana protested.

"Save it, Luciana. I had no idea after all of these years working together that you would go off the reservation. If anyone knew better, I thought it would be you."

"*Really*, Miguel?"

"Yeah, *really*, Luciana."

Evan tried to defuse the situation. "Agent Perkins, we were trained—"

"None of you have the authority to make decisions about an important case. You see, that's why

I'm the boss, *not* any of you. But that doesn't matter, does it? Here you are, booking safe houses and making plans. I guess you all think you're the shit, don't you? Did you ever think about bringing in agents who *specialize* in kidnappings? Huh? Of course not. Why would you, since you all have things handled?" Miguel's scathing tone made all three of them look down in discomfort. "What do you have to say for yourselves?"

Benita, Luciana, and Evan remained silent as Miguel stared.

"Fine. I've made some calls to find out more about Doug's grandmother's kidnapping. I expect you to be downstairs at six o'clock tomorrow morning. We've got a lot of work to do. Now, good night, everyone." Miguel stormed off, leaving the three agents to recognize their precarious situations.

Benita tried to find the words to apologize to her friends, shrugged helplessly, and then ran after Miguel, who was halfway to his bedroom on the second floor. "Miguel, please wait. Let me explain."

"Benita, I'm not interested in hearing any more of your bullshit tonight."

"Is that what you think I'm doing? Bullshit? Look, I admit that I shouldn't have gone over to Doug's place, but it was a good thing that I did because I would never have found out his grandmother was kidnapped. *Kidnapped,* Miguel. He didn't know what to do next. So, I did what I was trained to do. And that's to help Doug get his grandmother back and keep him safe. You know what I'm saying? I had to protect him."

Miguel stood in silence.

"Well?"

"You know what I find most interesting? It's your lack of respect for law and order. You have gone through countless hours of mental and physical training, but the one thing you can't seem to figure out is you cannot go off and make your own decisions. I'm tired of having the same damn conversation with you about how you don't follow protocol. There's a code that we must follow. A code that will make sure we do what's necessary to work these cases. All you talk about is how you're trained to protect people. Well, that is *not* all you're trained to do."

"Miguel, I'm sorry you feel that way," Benita whispered.

"I'm sorry . . . Look, I want you to think about what you're doing because I'm tired of you justifying your every move. I need you to start learning how to follow orders, or you'll end up in a place where there is no coming back from."

"Meaning what?"

"Meaning you'll end up on the other side of the world fending for yourself—without the support of the team you've learned to work with right here. So

I'm warning you right now. If you don't stop going off the reservation, I will not protect you from the consequences. Do you understand what I'm telling you right now?"

Benita remained silent.

"You know what I did this morning? I reviewed about a thousand cases to find you the perfect assignment. All I asked from you was to be patient and remain low. But what did you do? You lied to me. Lied about contacting Doug. You broke every damn rule in the book. You found your own assignment. Recruited your fellow agents. Why couldn't you just trust me?"

"But I had a good reason—"

"Do you think I give a damn about your good reason? I ordered you not to get involved."

"I know, but—"

"You know what? I'm done talking to you. You're gonna find yourself on the street because if I have to continue to cover your ass, you'll have one less person who believes in you."

Benita blinked a couple of times. Miguel's words stung more than she cared to admit. *I knew he'd be mad, but not like this kind of mad.* In truth, his words frightened her. She didn't want him to lose trust in her. "Miguel . . . I'm sorry."

"Yeah yeah yeah. Always sorry with you. You think it's so easy to get over on me? Well, I have a surprise for you. Tomorrow, you'll work with

Agent Willard Cole. He heads up the Perth Amboy Gang Task Force, and it seems your assignment fits right into his world. So you and your cohorts can brief him on the kidnapping. I'm done."

"Miguel—"

Miguel opened the door to his bedroom and shut it in Benita's face. She stood there in silence for a few minutes. Then she walked back downstairs, where she found Evan and Luciana in the kitchen.

"So, he's really pissed at us, huh?" Luciana questioned her friend.

They glanced at Benita with concerned looks on their faces.

"How can anyone be that much of a prick?" Evan muttered.

Benita knew she had to be careful how she responded to her colleagues because she didn't want them to know about her secret love affair with Miguel. "Sorry for pulling you guys in on this case. Honestly, I am."

Evan touched her hand. "No worries, B. Your heart was in the right place. I mean, there's a missing person, for God's sake. Can't the man have a little bit of empathy? It would be nice for him to understand that a part of this job is to let us do our jobs. And that means we need to be willing to help anyone who needs us."

"Look, guys, I'm sorry to have to tell you this, but Miguel is right. I know your heart is in the right

place, Benita, and this is why I'm here to help, but
we still have rules to follow. I've been working at
this job for a long time. Longer than the two of you,
and I know that Miguel expects us to use our intelligence wisely. His expectations are high, but he
will always have your back. We just have to think
about using our skills within the confines of the
agency. We have all been trained to use our keen
observation, intuitiveness, the ability to assume
false identities, secretiveness, and specialized
skills to solve these cases. Maybe we need to take
a minute and think about what our next steps are."

"Wow, Luciana, you really know how to bring a
brutha down."

Luciana shrugged her shoulders. "I'm sorry,
Evan. But I'm only speaking the truth. You just
need to start thinking things through because the
one thing that matters working at this agency is
following protocol. Benita, are you okay?"

Benita looked at both of them with defeat in
her eyes. "I hear what you're saying. I know I
may have been the cause of the friction between
Miguel and the team, but I promise you I'll fix this.
I understand I need Miguel's blessing if we are to
work on finding Doug's grandmother."

"I think that's a great idea, my friend. Because
anything other than that is a losing battle with
Miguel," Luciana said.

"I remember Director Bolden once telling me
that the agency prides itself on doing things a

certain way and that if we are to be respected as superior agents, then we have to learn to be on top of our game. No matter what we do, we can't always do what our hearts tell us to. We have to do what is best for the organization."

"You're right, Evan. And so are you, Luciana. I appreciate both of you so much. And I'm sorry that I put you both in a compromising situation."

"Look, we all know what we got ourselves into, and now we have to make sure we do the right thing for Doug without compromising rules," Luciana replied.

"Oh, have either one of you heard of an Agent Willard Cole?"

"That guy is a nut job," Luciana answered her. "I've heard nothing but horror stories about him. I've seen Cole push a few agents over the edge with his dumb shit. Why do you ask?"

"Miguel told me we're going to be working with him on a gang-related task force."

"Fantastic. That dude is one of the meanest agents in the organization. I worked on a case with him one time, and that was one time too many. So, Miguel is truly pissed off if he has turned things over to him. I cannot believe we'll be working with him. I seriously need a drink right now." Luciana poured herself a glass of wine.

"Well, I'm not worried. No one's going to intimidate me. We've got a grandmother to find.

Hopefully, this Agent Cole guy will let us do our job."

"We can all hope." Luciana downed the rest of her wine.

Benita also hoped that Miguel calmed down fast because she didn't want him to stay mad at her.

Meanwhile, Miguel had lost his cool, and he didn't care who knew it. He'd always tried to remain cool, calm, and collected around his team, but tonight was different. He didn't appreciate Benita deciding to do what she wanted and not respecting boundaries. He was steaming mad the entire ride to Black Creek Hills and finally made that call to Willard.

"Hey, Perkins. How are things?"

"Look, I need for you to come to Black Creek Hills tomorrow morning. We need to move forward with the underground fighting case."

"No problem. But, brutha, you seem stressed. What's happened to make you want to move on this case?"

"You know one of the worst things that could happen is when an agent defies all rules and orders to stand down. I need for you to take over this team since they want to go rogue on a case that happens to be tied to our case."

"Really? Is this Agent Jenkins that you mentioned earlier to me?"

"Ah, yeah. The one and only. Plus, two other agents that have decided to join her in her pursuit for justice."

"I see. So, you really want me to rein these folks in? 'Cause I'm down for it."

Miguel spent another forty-five minutes briefing Willard on the case. He explained in great detail how these agents took it upon themselves to step out on their own. Willard agreed to meet him in the morning at Black Creek Hills and promised he would whip these subordinates into shape. He also told Miguel to get a good night's sleep because he would handle everything. Miguel finally got off the phone prepared for bed. He would deal with Benita tomorrow. It was time she was taught some tough lessons when it came to following orders. She wasn't going to be able to run over Willard like she was doing to him.

Miguel was mad at himself for allowing Benita to control his emotions. It was becoming a task to separate what he felt for her. *Dammit, Benita.* He crawled into bed and finally closed his eyes. Before he knew it, he was fast asleep.

Chapter 21

It was 5:45 a.m. when the agents entered the conference room. The kitchen staff had brought in an assortment of crudités and various dipping sauces, as well as croissants, muffins, and Danish strategically located in the back of the room. There was also a fresh pot of coffee and assorted teas.

Benita was the last one to arrive. She walked directly to the back of the room to grab a small blueberry muffin and a cup of green tea. "Morning, everyone. How did everyone sleep?"

Luciana sat down next to Huey, who was already there working on his computer. She was sipping on her cup of coffee and rubbed the side of her temple. "Is it a good morning? I couldn't tell. I closed my eyes, and before I knew it, the alarm was going off," Luciana whined.

"Don't mind her. She really isn't a morning person," Huey chuckled.

"And how would *you* know that, Huey?"

"Oh, Huey knows everything." Huey smiled at Luciana, who smirked at him.

"Whatever, man. Six o'clock in the damn morning is way too early to deal with Agent Cole. We're in for an extremely long day. I'm not looking forward to seeing him—or working with him, for that matter." Luciana turned her face back to the comfort of her coffee.

Benita sat across from Evan, who was looking down at his phone. He definitely wasn't in a good mood either. "Evan, are you okay?"

"As good as I can be expected. It just kills me that we can't do anything good without it being sanctioned by Perkins."

She felt guilty because she had dragged everyone down a rabbit hole with her. If she could turn back the clock, she would have kept them out of this case. Hopefully, Agent Cole wouldn't be as bad as everyone made him out to be. She then turned to Huey, who was deep into his laptop. She wondered if he ever went anywhere without it. "Huey, I didn't know you were coming out this morning. What time did you get here, anyway?".

Yawning, Huey stretched out his back. "Around four in the morning. When the boss man requests your presence, you come."

"Of course, that's what we do, right? Agent Perkins gets what he wants anytime he wants. You know what I think? He loves seeing us all jump through hoops. And we're supposed to simply say thank you for all you do," Evan muttered.

"It could always be worse."

"You don't know just how bad it can get, Benita. But I'm sure we'll all see when Agent Cole gets here," Luciana spoke with a voice of doom.

Evan made his way over to the food and looked back at the team. "Again, all roads lead back to Perkins."

Although Evan always complained about Miguel, Benita trod lightly when it came to her boss and lover. She hadn't slept well knowing that Miguel was mad at her, and now she had to deal with an agent who no one liked. She thought about Doug and needed to check on him in a few hours. She tried to stay focused. Just when she was going to comment about Miguel, he walked into the conference room with Agent Willard Cole.

"Good morning, team. Hope you all had a few good hours of sleep. Wanted you all to meet Agent Willard Cole. You've been assigned to work on the Black Hole task force. It seems your case is related to his. Agent Cole, meet Agents Benita Renee Jenkins, Evan Green, and you know Luciana Rodriguez and Huey Longfoot."

Cole didn't bother catering to any pleasantries. "Agent Perkins assigned you to my task force because it seems you've taken it upon yourselves to work independently on a case that you weren't authorized to do."

"Yes, but—" Benita tried to answer, but Cole immediately cut her off.

"Don't ever interrupt me, Agent Jenkins, when I'm talking. I hate when people interrupt me. What I expect from all of you is to follow orders. I will not tolerate any kind of insubordination on my team. You will follow my rules or get booted off the case. Do you understand?"

Benita was taken aback by Agent Cole's attitude. "Sure. Okay." Agent Cole was nothing like she had expected. The man couldn't be more than five feet tall, and as he stood next to Miguel, who was way over six feet, he looked more like Miguel's child than his colleague. Benita couldn't believe this guy was in charge of a major crime division. He was rude, loud, and obnoxious. As she glanced over at her fellow agents who were looking directly at Agent Cole, she winced every time he barked orders.

"Now, I want to meet the young man you brought to the safe house. Where is he right now?"

Everyone remained silent ever since Agent Cole yelled for them all to be quiet.

"Well, can *anyone* here tell me where the man is? Agent Green?"

"He's sleeping, sir."

"Sleeping? Why is he still sleeping?" Cole asked.

"Because it's early. It's been a hard few days for him. I was hoping he could get some rest before we share the game plan," Benita answered.

Cole stared at the young agent with a look of disdain on his face. Then he started laughing while looking over at Miguel. "Perkins, you got a live one here. She was hoping to come up with a game plan, I see. So, maybe you would like to take the lead on the case since you have all of the answers, Agent Jenkins?"

"I never said that I had all of the answers—"

"Well, that's good to know, Agent Jenkins, because as far as I'm concerned, you need to shut up, listen, and learn some things. Understood?"

Benita was about to respond, but Miguel gave her a stern look. She quickly backed down and remained silent.

"Now, where was I?" Cole walked over to the coffee station and poured himself a cup. He looked back over at the team and continued to yell at Benita. "So, Agent Jenkins, why do you ever think that it's okay to go out on your own and find yourself a damn case?"

Dang, man. That voice. He was so loud it caused a vibration in the room. *How can one little man be so annoying?* Every time he opened up his mouth, Benita wanted to punch him in the throat. She tried to remain focused, but between the yelling and his tone, she was losing steam. He even made her cringe. She wasn't sure how much more she could take from this pocket-sized man before going off on him. But when she looked at Miguel, she continued to hold her tongue. It was one thing to go off on Miguel, but another to go off on this agent who also had the power to destroy her and clearly would use it in ways she felt Miguel never would.

Miguel was sitting at the end of the table watching Agent Cole without any facial expression. She knew he was enjoying this tirade. It was nothing more than a spectacle and a way for him to get back at her for not following his lead. *Damn you, Miguel. Well played, sir. Well played.* All she wanted to do was drink some tea and pray that this little man would shut up for a bit. She had never heard a person who didn't breathe between sentences. She just wanted to tune him out because his voice was becoming whinier by the minute. He might easily be one of the most annoying persons she had ever met.

Although she didn't like the fact that Cole insulted people, she tried to see beyond the exterior. She wondered if he ever smiled. That was one of her pet peeves. She didn't like it when people were 100 percent serious. There was always at least one reason to smile. She realized Agent Cole didn't, and that bothered her. Maybe he didn't want people to see him in any other way but to be seen as an authoritative asshole.

Agent Cole stood in front of Benita and bent down close to her face. "Hello? Earth to Agent Jenkins. Are you paying attention? Did you hear what I asked you? Who do you think you are?"

"Yes, yes, sir. I hear every word. Every single word."

Benita and her fellow agents—Evan, Luciana, and Huey—remained silent as the little man with the big mouth continued ranting. Although he would constantly ask them questions, he never stopped long enough for them to answer any of them. In fact, if there were any objections, Agent Cole would simply yell even louder. After Agent Cole finally finished up lecturing the team, he dramatically plopped down in the oversized chair, exhausted. He looked among the team and asked, "Well?"

"Ah, Agent Cole, you okay? You look like you're about to pass out."

"Agent Jenkins, don't get me started with you again. Now, tell me about this young boxer and how he's related to my case."

Just as she was about to answer, Agent Cole cut her off. Again. "No. Second thought. Just tell me how you were planning on helping this kid. Or did you even think about the next steps?"

Agent Cole looked over at Evan, waiting for him to respond. "Well, Agent Green? Do you have an answer?"

Right before Evan was about to respond, Agent Cole waved him off. "You're all seriously no damned help."

"Well, since we got that lecture out of the way, why don't we grab some breakfast and discuss the next steps with the case?"

"Good idea, Miguel. I'm starving. And Agent Jenkins, please bring the young boxer here for breakfast. I think it's time that I have a heart-to-heart with him since you claim that he needs our help."

Agent Cole and Miguel walked out of the conference room, leaving Benita and her team behind.

"I swear to God, if I had my gun on me, I would shoot that mutha right between the eyes. I cannot believe he spent two freaking hours ranting and raving like a damn madman. I just think he loves to hear himself talk," Luciana commented.

"I'm right there with you, sis. That dude has a few screws loose, for sure," Benita said.

"Yes, ma'am, he certainly does. He makes Miguel look like a pussycat." Huey actually looked up from his laptop.

Evan shook his head as they walked to breakfast. "That went well."

"Exceptionally well, Agent Evans," Luciana chuckled.

"It's been a long day already, and it's only a little after eight. Well, let me check on Doug. I'll see you guys in the dining room." Benita walked toward the back of the house.

"Don't take too long. We wouldn't want the little leprechaun to stomp on you with his magical cane," Evan chuckled.

"Oh, that's a good one, Evan," Luciana remarked as they walked toward the dining room.

Chapter 22

Doug tossed and turned all night worrying about his grandmother. He was staring at the ceiling when he heard his phone buzz. It was a text message from Sean. Bro, you ready to talk to me? We really need to figure this shit out. I need you to call me.

Doug sat up in the bed and texted back. Nigga, all I wanna know is where's Nana. Where is she?

He reached for a bottle of water located on an end table next to his bed. After gulping it down, he went to the bathroom to shower, brush his teeth, then changed into a black T-shirt and jeans. It took everything in him not to lose control of his emotions. He spent the night crying out for his grandmother. He was so scared that something terrible would happen to her. What if he never saw her again? This was all Sean's fault. *Fuck you, Sean.*

After making the bed, he sat down on the corner, contemplating his next steps. He continued to wipe the tears coming from his eyes. He picked up his phone and pulled up a selfie of him and his grandmother. She was one of the most amazing women that he knew. She was truly his best friend, and ever since he was a young boy, he loved hanging out with her. She would often tease him that he needed to hang out with people his own age, but he told her that he didn't need anyone else, just her. He so desperately wanted to talk to her, and he would do anything to get her back.

The knock broke his reverie on the past. Doug opened the door to find Benita standing on the other side.

"Hey." Benita noticed that Doug looked somber. "Can I come in?"

He moved out of the way, letting her enter the room.

"I see you're dressed. Perfect timing. I wanted to invite you to breakfast to meet the head of the task force who'll be handling your grandmother's case."

"So, you're not in charge?" Doug asked as he sat down on the bed.

"No, but I'm a part of the team. Like I told you last night, I promised that we would do everything in our power to bring your Nana home. And I'm going to keep that promise." Benita sat beside the young man and rubbed his back. "Doug, it's going to be okay. We're going to find her."

"I'm scared. I'm scared for my grandmother. She didn't deserve this. She's a hardworking woman who raised two young boys. And this is how she's repaid?"

"Sometimes bad things happen to good people. There was nothing you could have done to stop this from happening. It's not your fault."

"No, but it's my brother's fault. Maybe I should have killed him when I had a chance. Then none of this would have happened."

"Please, don't say that."

"Oh, it's true. Can we go?" He stood up, avoiding Benita's eyes.

"Sure. Let's go meet the rest of the team."

They walked out the door and headed to the house. Before they were about to enter, Doug realized he forgot his phone. "Damn, give me a minute. I need to get my cell. Be right back." He took off back to the cottage.

"Sure. I'll just take a seat on the bench. Take your time. But not really. I so need to stop talking to myself," Benita chuckled.

Doug opened the door to the cottage and picked up his phone. Just when he was about to leave the room, his cell rang. It was his brother Sean calling. "Hello?"

"Hey, li'l brutha. Did you get my texts?"

"Yeah, I got them. I see you didn't respond to the last one. Who is this nigga that got Nana?"

There was a brief silence before Sean answered. "His name is A-Roc."

"How in the hell did you let this happen?"

"Does it really matter how? I fucked up, all right? Listen, I'm headed over to the apartment now, and we can talk then."

"I'm not there," Doug answered.

"Where are you? At the gym? Work?"

"Don't worry about where I am. It's none of your damn business."

"Sure. Fine. Don't tell me, but I'm telling you right now, you need to put your anger aside and do what you gotta do to get Nana back." Sean calmly spoke to his brother.

Doug was so pissed off that he wanted to go through the phone and beat his ass. Sean was the only one that could bridge the gap to make sure his grandmother was going to be okay. *Nigga, I hate you so much.* "Fine, muthafucka. What am I supposed to do?"

"I need for you to stay by your damn phone and be ready for instructions. Understood?"

"Instructions. Yeah, yeah. I hear you."

"Good. I'm going to see about Nana. I suggest you keep all of this shit to yourself because the only thing you would be doing is to put her life in danger. I gotta go."

Sean hung up the phone, and Doug sat on the bed in silence. He finally stormed out of the cottage. When he saw Benita waiting on the bench, he had a look of desperation on his face.

"What's wrong? What happened?"

"I just spoke to my brother."

"Sean? And what did he have to say?"

Doug started hyperventilating and was having a hard time breathing. "I can't breathe. I can't . . ."

"Whoa, man. Calm down," Benita said anxiously. "It'll be all right. You're getting yourself all worked up. Please, sit down. What good are you gonna be for your grandmother like this?"

Doug sat down on the bench, and Benita looked around to see if she could get him something to drink. "Hold tight. I'll be right back. You just sit there and breathe."

Benita hurried into the mansion and made a beeline toward the kitchen, where she got a bottle of water and a banana. She headed back outside, where she found Doug still sitting on the bench staring at the cottage. Benita handed him the bottled water and the piece of fruit. "Here you go. This should help calm you."

"Thank you." Doug opened the bottle and took several gulps before peeling the banana.

"Now, let's take a deep breath and try this again. What exactly did your brother say?"

Doug looked at her and remained silent.

"Come on now. You can tell me." She touched his arm, letting him know that she was there to listen. He finally spoke.

"Take me home."

"But you just got here. This place is for your own protection."

"I don't need protection. I need to find my grandmother, and you ain't doing shit to help."

"Whoa, you need to calm down."

"No. You need to fall back and let me handle things. This is family business, and you ain't family."

"Doug, I know I'm not your family, but I'm your best chance of getting your grandmother back. What? Do you think your brother can bring her home safely?"

Doug took a deep breath and closed his eyes. He now looked defeated. "I don't know what to do. All I know is that I want my Nana back."

"Doug, do you remember when we first met? I walked over to you and tried to start a conversation? You basically told me to fall back because you didn't spar with girls. Do you remember that? Well, that didn't stop me from being there for you when those guys tried to grab you. I know you may not believe me, but you and me, we were destined to meet. And I'm going to do everything in my power to get your grandmother back home."

Benita saw Miguel out of the corner of her eye standing by the back door, listening to the conversation she was currently having with Doug. "You see, awhile back, I got into some real trouble, and there was someone who believed in me. He said

I was destined for greatness, but I didn't believe him. Why would I? I didn't know him. I blamed myself for getting involved in the wrong things. Even when he tried to ease my mind, I still fought him every step of the way. But you know what? He never gave up on me, and I'm asking you right now. Don't give up on me. Let me help you."

"Benita," Miguel interrupted.

Benita looked up to see Miguel was now standing next to her. "Doug, you remember Agent Miguel Perkins from the other night? Agent Perkins, I was just telling him that there is a team of agents here to help him get his grandmother back."

"Doug, Benita's right. We're gonna do everything in our power to bring her home. Benita, may I speak with you for a moment?"

"Sure. Be right back, Doug."

The two of them walked away from the boxer, who was sitting on the bench with his eyes closed.

"We were wondering what happened to you," Miguel said.

"Sorry. I was trying to calm him down. He's having a hard time processing what's going on in his life right now."

"I understand. Well, it's clear that you care about his well-being. Why don't we bring him inside to introduce him to Agent Cole?"

Benita nodded, and they walked back over to Doug. "Why don't we go inside?"

As he entered the mansion with Benita and Miguel, all Doug could think about was his grandmother. He was so scared for her. He knew he couldn't handle this dreadful situation by himself, so maybe Benita was right. They were destined to meet and work together.

After breakfast, Doug and the agents discussed how they needed him to speak to his brother about the necessary steps needed to find his grandmother. Doug called several times to get in touch with Sean, but no answer.

"Try again, Doug," Benita suggested.

He hit the redial button, and Sean finally answered. "Hello?"

"Damn it, Sean, where have you been?"

"Trying to find Nana."

"Well, did you?"

"Not yet, but I have an idea where she is."

"Sean, don't fucking play with me. Where do you think she is?"

"Calm down, little brother. You need to fall back. That's what *you* need to do."

"Man, just tell me what you know," Doug yelled.

Benita crossed her arms and watched Doug as he got more irritated.

"Sean . . . Sean . . . You still there?"

"Yeah. I'm still here. I ain't going nowhere."

"Well? Tell me what you know."

Sean took an audible breath before he continued. "All right. Like I told you this morning, his name is A-Roc. He is a part of the Ortez gang, and I owe them a lot of money."

"I already know that. Twenty grand. That's what the dude said when he called me from Nana's phone. How you gonna get that money and get our grandmother back?"

"Well, that's where *you* come in. All you gotta do is participate in a fight," Sean replied.

"What did you just say to me?" Doug balled up his fist and slammed his hand on the table.

"A-Roc runs underground fights. He told me a few weeks ago that if I got you to fight for him, then my debt would be cleared. And now that he's got Nana, I really need for you to fight."

Now, Doug was shaking with anger. "You're a real piece of shit. You know that? Do you even care that if I fight for him, I can never fight professionally?"

Benita wrote on a yellow pad and slid it over to Doug. He took a beat to read it as his jawline tensed. She whispered in Doug's ear to ask his brother when the fight was happening.

"I'm sorry, man. I really am. I guess I never thought about that. I'll make it up to you," Sean whined.

Doug took a deep breath and balled up the note. "When is the freakin' fight goin' down?"

Sean sighed. "I don't know yet. I'm going to meet up with A-Roc and will let you know when I get the update. Can I count on you to fight?"

"Just call me with the info. But, Sean . . . If anything happens to Nana, I swear I'll kill you. Believe that."

"Yeah, I know. You've told me that a million times. Maybe one day you'll get your wish. Call you back in about an hour. I gotta go."

"Yeah, you just do that." Doug ended the call. He was so angry he threw his phone across the room. Then he stormed out.

Benita was going to follow, but Luciana stopped her. "Let him go. He needs a minute to cool down."

Benita relented and nodded. "You're right. Location?"

Huey was sitting in front of a computer tracking a multicolored map filled with red dots. "You see that moving blip? Well, that looks like it's Doug's brother traveling east on Smith Street. And the time we were tracking Mrs. Gibson's phone was where that green dot is. Unfortunately, the tracker was disconnected, and I'm not sure if she's still there."

"Wait, Sean's dot is walking toward the last location where his grandmother was?"

"It appears that way."

"So, this is how you handle conflict, Agent Jenkins? You let Doug just walk away?"

Benita turned around to find Agent Cole standing at the door. "Just what was I supposed to do, Agent Cole? Please enlighten me."

Agent Cole walked into the study and sat down across from the team. "Well, first of all, you needed to do a better job of prepping Doug on how he was supposed to deal with his brother. You just let him go off the rails, similar to the way that you seem to do. Second, Agent Jenkins, if you weren't sure how to proceed, then it would have been best to come to me so that I could have a conversation with the young man. Does *that* help to enlighten you?"

"Yes, sir," Benita commented.

"Good. Now, I'll go find young Gibson and talk him off the ledge. We're gonna need him to be on his game tonight if we're to bring these guys down. Excuse me." Agent Cole left his fellow agents in the study, with Benita and the others brooding.

"That's guy's an ass," Luciana said.

"Yeah, but he's right. I let Doug lose his cool. I need to learn how to handle situations like this better."

"It's not your fault. You're handling things the best way you can," Evan consoled her.

"Well, currently, that's not good enough. Because at the end of the day, *I'm* responsible for this guy. I brought him here to help get his grandmother back, and I need to make sure that he's on board with the next steps."

"Well, he's in good hands with you, Benita." Luciana smiled at her.

"I hope you're right because I'm going to do everything in my power to see this case to the end."

Chapter 23

Reggie drove down Smith Street, listening to Sean apologizing to his brother and explaining how they can work to get their grandmother released. After Sean hung up the phone, he placed his head against the seat headrest. A few minutes later, Reggie turned up the music to lighten up the mood. "Sean, you good?"

"Yeah. He finally agreed to fight."

"Cool. Really cool, man. Now, we can put all of this behind us."

Sean gave him a half smile. "Reggie, man, thank you so much for not giving up on me. Most dudes would just have left me in the cold. But you have been there with me all the way, and I appreciate you, brutha."

Reggie wanted to tell him that he had talked to his cousin DeAndre about Sean's grandmother, but he was scared that Sean would retaliate against him. He just wanted to get out of this situation because A-Roc would make *him* pay for introducing Sean to him. "Man, listen. You know I got you.

We're in this together. If you go down, then I go down too."

"I need to make sure that my Nana is good, though. Did you speak to your people?"

"Yeah, nobody knows anything about your grand-mother."

"Damn. I know *somebody* knows something. I just need to know that she's okay."

"I'm sure she is. I mean, A-Roc ain't gonna do anything as long as you and your brother keep your word." Reggie turned on to Cedar Grove Street, and Sean directed him to pull over. "You sure you don't want me to come with you?"

"Nah, I'm good. It's better if I handle this alone. Just hang out here until I get back. Cool?" Sean jumped out of the SUV before he answered and walked about two blocks down to 809 Cedar Grove Street. He knocked on the door of a boarded-up building and started rocking back and forth as he waited for someone to let him in. Finally, Snake grunted when he opened the door and saw the small, scrawny guy staring back at him.

"I need to speak to A-Roc." Sean nervously looked around.

Snake smirked and barely crossed his muscled arms. "Man, watchu want with A-Roc?"

"Tell him Sean Gibson got his guarantee for the money that I owe him."

"Wait here." Snake shut the door, leaving Sean outside, who was looking around at the other empty houses. He glanced up and down the street, seeing if he saw anything suspicious happening, but he saw nothing. Stuffing his hands into pockets, Sean felt his cell vibrating but ignored it. He felt guilty for dragging his grandmother into his troubles, and now he was going to fix the problem with his brother's help. He prayed that after the fight, their grandmother would be released.

The door swung open, and Snake stepped aside, letting Sean enter the building. "Walk straight back to the last door on the left."

"It's not like I ain't been here before," Sean grumbled at the bouncer.

"Just shut the hell up and keep it moving," Snake grunted.

Sean walked down the dark hallway toward a metal door. He passed several men sitting on a dirty, worn-out gold couch playing video games on a sixty-inch-screen television. He heard Snake's deep voice shouting at him. "Keep it moving, will ya? A-Roc ain't got all day."

He picked up the pace and made his way to the back of the building. The hallway was filled with trash and empty beer bottles scattered over the floor. It was nothing more than a cesspool. He frowned when he saw a tiny mouse trying to break free from a glue trap. It was squealing, but no one paid it any mind. Sean could relate to the little mouse's pain because he was feeling that way right now. He felt trapped by his current circumstances, but he knew that he could make it all right after tonight's fight. He noticed Simon and DeAndre standing outside the door, and when Sean approached them, DeAndre spoke. "What up, Sean?"

"Hey, DeAndre. You good?"

"Yeah. You?"

"Yeah, I'm good now. Hope to wrap up things, you know what I'm saying?"

Simon rolled his eyes. He turned around and beat on the metal door. "Boss, you got a visitor. Sean's here to see you."

A voice from behind the door yelled out, "Pat him down first. I don't want no funny business coming from that nigga. After that, send him in."

Simon pushed Sean against the concrete wall and frisked him, checking for weapons. "A'ight. You clean. You can go in."

Sean straightened up his black jacket and rolled his eyes at these wannabe thug bouncers. "Can you move out of the way so I can get through?"

After a long pause, Simon moved out of the way, allowing Sean to walk past him. As Sean entered the room, a pair of hands grabbed his shoulders and forced him down in a chair facing A-Roc. "It's about damn time you found your way to this place. Either you got my paper or my next fighter."

"Where's my grandmother?" Sean's voice cracked as he mustered up the courage to speak for himself.

A-Roc placed his fat fingers behind his head as he leaned back in his black swivel chair, which looked like it was about to break under all that weight. A-Roc nodded at one of his crew, who backhanded Sean across the face. Sean touched his jaw, wondering if it were broken. He remained silent as he looked down at the dirty floor, knowing that he shouldn't make any eye contact.

"Now, let's try this again. My paper or my fighter?"

"Fighter."

"Your brother came through, I presume?"

"Yeah."

A-Roc flipped through his spiral notebook and pointed to something on the page. "Let me see. You owe me 20K. I pay my fighters five thousand for each fight. So he owes me four fights."

"Four? I thought he just needed to fight once."

"Sean, that's the problem with you. You don't think about the big picture. What can one fight do for me? I'm doing you a favor with a guarantee of four fights to pay off your shit. Of course, there's also interest, and you've racked up a bunch of interest."

"How is this fight, I mean fights, supposed to go down? Will this happen all in one night?"

"What are you, his manager now? He'll fight as long as it takes."

"What about my grandmother?"

"What about her?"

"Where is she? Can I see her? When will you let her go?"

"Whoa, Sean. You're asking too many questions. All you need to worry about is the fight. Make sure your brother's ready when I call you. Now, get the hell out of here. I got business to conduct."

"A-Roc, please, let me see her at least. I gotta know that you haven't hurt her."

A-Roc stared at the skinny weakling and sneered. "What kind of man do you think I am? Do you really think that I would hurt a grandmother? Hell, I got a grandmother too. I mean, I *had* a grandmother before I killed her. I'm just fucking with you, Sean. You just make sure your brother comes tonight, and nothing will happen to your grandmother. Understood?"

"But—"

"It's over, Sean. Time to go."

A-Roc nodded to his soldiers to get rid of him. Benny, one of A-Roc's protectors, grabbed Sean by his jacket and pulled him up from the chair. "Come on, let's go. A-Roc got things to do."

"All right, all right. You ain't gotta be so rough," Sean whined.

"Stop being such a punk ass and move it. A-Roc said he's got things to do, and you holding him up from doing his business," Benny barked.

Benny threw Sean out of the office, causing him to slide onto the concrete floor until he crashed into a wall. He then slammed the door behind him.

Sean stood up and brushed himself off. As he rubbed his hands together to wipe the dirt from his clothes, his phone buzzed. He looked down and saw that it was his brother calling. He placed the phone back into his pocket and looked over at Simon and DeAndre, who remained motionless. He smirked at them. "See you guys tonight."

As he began walking away from them, he prayed that A-Roc kept his word and didn't hurt his grandmother. Just as Sean was about to make it to the front door, he heard Benny yelling to DeAndre. "Hey, DeAndre, bring your ass in here. A-Roc wants ta know how the old lady is doing." Sean stopped dead in his tracks and turned around to see DeAndre walking into Λ-Roc's office. He was pissed because he knew that Reggie had lied to him about his cousin DeAndre not knowing anything about his grandmother's kidnapping. Once he got outside, he walked quickly to the end of the street where Reggie was waiting for him. Reggie saw a look of anger on Sean's face and jumped out of the car. "Hey, Sean. What's up?"

Sean clocked Reggie in the face, causing Reggie to drop. Then he continued to pounce on him, yelling about how he was lying to him about his grandmother until Reggie pushed him off.

"So, you lying to me now?" Sean screamed at him.

"What the fuck is wrong with you?" Reggie asked.

"You looked me dead in my face and told me that your people didn't know anything about my grandmother—and guess what? Your cousin DeAndre knew all along where she was. In fact, he seems to be keeping tabs on her."

"Sean, I didn't know."

"You lying. You knew because he told you. Don't you think I know how close you two are? That little nigga looks up to you and ain't gonna keep anything from you."

Reggie took a deep breath and tried to calm down his friend. "Sean, my cousin works for one of the most dangerous dudes in the area. He's only going to share so much with me."

"Look me in the eye and tell me that you didn't know about my grandmother's whereabouts."

Reggie turned away, not making eye contact.

"I thought so. You can't even look me in the eye, can you? *Can you?* Well, you betta talk to him because if I find out that anything happens to her and he had something to do with it, I'm going to wring his little fucking neck. Believe that."

Sean's phone buzzed again, and he pulled it out of his front pocket to see that Doug was calling.

"Is that your brother?" Reggie asked.

"Don't worry if that's my brother. I need you to find out about my grandmother." Sean started walking away from Reggie. He needed to find a quiet place to speak to his brother.

"Where you going?" Reggie yelled after his angry friend.

"Talk to your cousin, Reggie. Like *now*." Sean kept walking away, leaving Reggie standing by his black Escalade.

Reggie took a deep breath and texted his cousin. Call me when you get a chance. Reggie.

Meanwhile, DeAndre stood in A-Roc's office talking to A-Roc when his phone buzzed. However, he wouldn't dare answer any phone calls when he was in with his crazy boss. "What's up, boss?" DeAndre asked.

"How's the old lady doing? Did you check on her this morning?"

"Yeah, I did. She was sleeping when I left her food."

A-Roc tapped his fingers on the desk as he reviewed the boxers that he had fighting later that night. Then he slid a phone over to DeAndre. "Good. Now, take this phone to Granny. Have her call her grandson, Doug, letting him know that she's alive and well. We need to keep him in check so that he won't back out of tonight's fight."

DeAndre took the phone and walked out of the office past Simon, who was still guarding the door. As he headed to the basement, DeAndre checked his phone and saw a message from Reggie. *Damn*. He stopped at the top of the stairwell and called his cousin. The phone rang several times before Reggie picked up. "What up, cuz? I'm calling you back. Whatchu know good?"

"Nigga, how did Sean find out that you knew about his grandmother?" Reggie answered.

"He must have overheard Benny yelling for me to speak to A-Roc about Mrs. Gibson. Damn, is he mad?"

"Nigga, whatchu think? Of course, Sean's mad, and you're now on his shit list. I would stay clear of him if I were you. I mean, I ain't ever seen him so angry."

"Well, he better chill with that shit 'cause A-Roc ain't having none of that drama tonight."

"So, is Ms. Gibson all right?"

"Yeah, she good. I'm actually headed to the basement to see her now. A-Roc wants me to get her to call Doug so that he knows she okay."

"Cool. I'll let Sean know what's up."

"Man, you can't do that. You wanna get me killed? You know I ain't supposed to be snitching."

"Okay. But I gotta tell him something. You know what I'm saying?"

"Yup. All right, son. I gotta bounce. Will hit you up later." DeAndre hung up the phone and visited Elsie in the basement. Before entering, he knocked on the door and saw Elsie in a chair reading a book that he had been nice enough to bring her earlier. He was also happy that she had finally eaten something since she hadn't touched the food from the night before.

"Hello, dear," Elsie greeted him.

"Hi. Did you have a good night's sleep, Mrs. Gibson?"

"As well as could be expected. It's hard to get comfortable on a small cot. Please, come in and have a seat."

"Okay, just for a little bit." DeAndre sat down on the edge of the cot and nervously looked at the middle-aged woman who was unexpectedly calm. He felt bad that she was used as a pawn to get Doug to fight in the underground club, but it wasn't his decision to kidnap her. He just did what he was told to do.

"So, can you tell me what's going on? I've been here for almost two days now, and I still don't know why . . . or when I'm getting out of this dungeon."

DeAndre reluctantly gave her updates because he didn't want to keep secrets from her anymore. It was too hard for him to continue to remain silent. "Well, it looks like your grandson Doug is going to be working for my boss."

"What kind of business is your boss in? And why does he need to drag my grandson into his nonsense? Tell me, son, what's going on?"

"My boss is a very dangerous man who is forcing Doug to fight in one of his matches."

"But why has he targeted Doug? He would never get mixed up with any dangerous people, including your boss."

"But Sean would. And now Sean owes my boss a lot of money, and the only way for him to pay off his debt is to get Doug to fight."

"And what happens if Doug doesn't want to fight?"

"Well, that's why you're here. To make sure that he does." DeAndre pulled out her phone and handed it to Elsie.

"Wait. That's my phone."

"Yes, ma'am, it is. And now my very dangerous boss wants you to call Doug to let him know that you're okay."

"And if I refuse?"

"I think you know what would happen if you don't do what I ask. Please, Mrs. Gibson, make the call."

Chapter 24

Benita looked out the window as she watched Agent Cole speaking to Doug. She was surprised to see how caring he was toward the young boxer. Doug was having a hard time dealing with the last conversation he had with his brother, and, in turn, he completely shut down, not speaking to anyone. Earlier, Doug was outside practicing his boxing moves when Agent Cole approached him. Somehow, Agent Cole eased Doug's fears and made him trust him. Something clicked for her, and she started to realize that not only did Agent Cole operate by the rules set forth at the DTCU, but he also had this uncanny ability to reach Doug in a way that she hadn't been able to do so far. She wondered if there were things about being an agent that she needed to learn to improve her job.

Benita remembered when she didn't trust anyone at the DTCU until she met Agent Samantha DeVreau. Benita recalled the first time that she met this amazing, beautiful, and well-put-together agent who automatically eased her concerns about working at the agency. Samantha knew just the right words to say to Benita to calm her down as a criminal psychologist. Even though she had trained the worst of the worst, Benita became her biggest challenge, and she instantly fell in love with the round-the-way girl with a big attitude.

In another lifetime, Agent DeVreau was one of the top experts in psychology and specialized in post-traumatic stress disorder cases, focusing on ex-military soldiers. She had a calm demeanor about her, but she never allowed anyone to break her spirit, not even Benita. Once, she told Benita that she knew Benita was special and that she only needed a little nudge to get her to a place of greatness. She just needed to figure out how to ground herself and channel her stubbornness into something that would work for the greater good.

Benita chuckled to herself when she remembered that one of the first things that Samantha gave her was a book on anger management and said, "If you are to survive here at the DTCU, you first need to control your temper. I know this is hard for you to believe, but you aren't alone. These agents here, especially the ones that you work closely with, are your new family. It's time to prepare yourself for your new life. Today is the first day of the rest of your life. Now, sit back and enjoy the ride."

Benita walked to the front of the mansion and called Samantha.

"Well, hello, my dear Benita. How are things?"

"Oh, you know. Things are going. I'm on a new case." Benita looked down at her feet and started kicking the grass.

"And how do you feel about it?"

Benita wasn't sure how much she should tell her, knowing she had really messed up by not following the rules.

"Benita, are you there?"

"Yes, I'm here."

"Well?"

"I think I messed up with Agent Perkins, and he was so mad that he assigned me to work with Agent Willard Cole."

"I see. Agent Cole. He's a bit of a handful, isn't he? And how's it going working with him?"

"Very hard. I mean, all he does is yell and scream at the team. I didn't expect all of this drama from a senior team leader."

Samantha laughed on the other side of the phone. "Unfortunately, leaders come in all shapes and sizes. I'm sure you'll be able to handle yourself. Remember some of the techniques that we talked about?"

"Yeah, I remember, and I also know that you really always helped me see the bigger picture."

"Benita, trust me, you're not going to get things right every time, but as I often told you, when you do something wrong, you first need to own it, and then you need to address it. So, maybe you can have a conversation with Agent Cole, letting him know you're open to criticism and you're there to learn. Because, my dear Benita, believe it or not, Agent Cole is one of the best agents at DTCU. As an agent, you need to look beyond the surface."

This is why Benita respected her so much because she always was straightforward in a loving and respectful way. She so appreciated that about her. "Thank you, Agent DeVreau, for your honesty."

"Anytime, my dear. Call me if you need to talk. You know I'm always here for you."

Benita ended the call and thought about how much trouble she was in. She acted first and thought about things later. She wasn't sure if she would ever conform to DTCU's rules. But Samantha was right. She was always right. She needed to own her mistakes and apologize to Miguel. Then she would talk to Agent Cole.

As she turned around, headed back into the house, she ran into Miguel, who was waiting for her at the top of the stairs. She bit her lip, thinking about what she would say to her pissed-off lover.

"Hey, there, Agent Perkins."

"Hey, yourself. I was looking for you."

"Really? I was just getting some fresh air," she replied.

Miguel chuckled. "If I didn't any know better, I would have thought you were staying clear of Agent Cole."

"If it were only that easy. You really outdid yourself this time, assigning me to Agent Cole."

Both of them remained quiet, and the silence was deafening. Benita was the first one to speak. "Miguel, I know I crossed the line with you, and I'm sorry. I don't know what to do to fix this between us. I just wanted to help Doug and his family. I know that I didn't follow the rules, but it's just hard for me to sit back and do nothing."

"Benita, when you go off on your own, you not only put your life in danger but also those of your fellow agents around you. How can you become a good agent if you don't listen to those who have lived and breathed this life forever? Just because you see a problem doesn't mean that you have to follow up on that problem. There are better ways of handling things. It's not in your best interest or your colleagues to go off on your own. It'll get you hurt or killed. Do you understand what I'm saying?"

"Yes, I understand. And, yes, I was wrong. I own that. But, Miguel, you don't have to teach me a lesson all the time. I know that you assigned me to Agent Cole for that very reason. You knew he's a little bully who thinks that barking at people will get him what he wants. I mean, he's mean, and he rules by fear—not cool."

Miguel stared at her. "Benita, you're not in any position to question a superior officer's tactics. Agent Cole is very good at what he does, barking and all. You may not like him, but I suggest you put your bruised ego aside and learn a few things from him."

Evan ran to the door and yelled out to the agents. "Benita, Doug's brother is on the phone. Get in here quick."

"Excuse me. I've got a case to solve." Benita ran past Miguel and headed to the conference room where the listening device was set up.

Doug was trying hard to hold back his frustrations surrounding his brother, and the more he spoke to Sean, the more he was reaching a boiling point. "Sean. Sean. Stop talking in circles. I don't need to know why we got here. We're here now. So, all you need to do is to tell me if Nana is okay."

"Look, I'm trying to tell you that she'll be okay after you do what you gotta do to help bring her home."

"I seriously don't understand you at all. You act like this a game."

"Little brother, if there were any other way that I could make this right, I would. But this is the *only* way."

"What the fuck, Sean? You better hope nothing happens to Nana. I will *never* forgive you."

Benita noticed Doug was about to lose control and took the phone from him, placing it on mute. "You're doing good, Doug. Take a deep breath and remain calm."

Doug relaxed and took the phone back. He unmuted the call to speak to his brother. "Okay, Sean. When is this fight going to happen?"

"I don't know yet. I'll text you the time and place. Just need for you to be ready to fight later."

Doug hung up on his brother and paced back and forth. Benita stood beside him, trying to comfort him. "I know this is hard for you, but it's going to be okay."

He began to rub his temples and remained quiet.

"Talk to me. I can't—" Benita looked at Evan, Luciana, and Huey. "We can't help you unless you tell us how you're feeling."

"No matter how hard I try to play by the rules, my brother always has a way of messing things up for my grandmother and me. I used to look up to him. You know, he was on his way to be this incredible big hip-hop star? But when he got arrested for drug and weapons possession, everything changed. He had a hard time keeping a job and ended up hanging out with the wrong crowd. I don't think he realizes how much damage he caused his family." Suddenly, Doug's phone vibrated. "Oh my God, it's my Nana's number."

Chapter 25

Doug quickly answered the phone while Huey began to record the call.

"Hello, Nana?"

"Doug, baby. It's me."

"Where are you? Are you okay? I've been worried about you."

"I'm fine, son."

Doug took a deep breath. "Nana, what's going on? Talk to me."

"I just wanted to tell you that I'm okay and that I'm proud of you."

"Nana, I don't . . . don't understand."

"I don't want you to worry about me. I'll see you soon."

"Can you tell me where you are?"

All of a sudden, the phone went silent, and a male's voice started speaking. "Yo, Doug. You need to make sure that you win your fights if you want to see your grandmother again."

"Who is this? When I find you, I'm gonna kill you. You hear me?"

The caller hung up the phone, and when Doug tried to call back, it went straight to voicemail.

All of a sudden, he threw his phone across the room and snapped. He started pacing back and forth. "I gotta go find my Nana. Like *now*."

Benita tried to comfort Doug, but he wasn't having any of it. "Doug, calm down."

"I know you're trying to help, but it ain't working. I need to go."

Agent Cole came running into the room after he heard Doug arguing with Benita. "Gibson, pull yourself together right now and tell us what the hell is happening."

Doug plopped down in a chair. "First, my brother tells me that I'm on the hook for four fights. *Four* fights. Once I step into that ring, they're gonna own me. That freakin' gang is gonna own me. And the last call? Some asshole threatened me. If I don't win, they're going to hurt my grandmother. How can I save Nana if I lose?"

"Listen to me, youngblood. Ain't nobody gonna own your ass but you. Understand? You see all these people around you? Do you think they're putting themselves in danger to let somebody own you? Hell nah. Now, you gonna stop your fucking crying and act like a man with some damn sense. You hear me?"

Doug couldn't hold back the tears. Agent Cole yanked him out of the chair and hugged him hard, not letting him go until he stopped crying. The other agents in the conference room looked on in silence. Agent Cole finally released Doug from his grip. "Now, you and I are going to go outside and get some fresh air. Give me a second to speak to Agent Jenkins, and I'll meet you in the hallway."

Doug nodded and walked out of the conference room.

Agent Cole turned to Benita and her team. "Agent Jenkins, this is where the rubber hits the road. You're going to be the lead on this case. What I need for you to do is first find that brother so we can talk to him. He can fill us in on just how his grandmother got caught up in this dangerous web. It's time we break up the fucking underground fight club. Do you understand?"

Benita looked around the room and was shocked by Agent Cole's request. She saw Miguel standing by the door. "*My* team, sir?"

"Are you hard of hearing? Yes, *your* team. Now, hop to it. Like *now*, damn it." Agent Cole walked of the room, leaving the team speechless. Miguel gave Benita one last look and followed him.

"Wow. I can't believe it. Agent Cole released the reins for a quick second and allowed you to be the lead on this case. I'm shocked," Luciana said.

"I can't believe it either," Benita responded.

"Well, you heard the man. We need to find Sean. What do you want us to do?" Evan asked.

"Right. Huey, can you ping Sean's phone and find out where he is?"

Huey pulled the phone number on his screen, finally seeing a green light pop up. "Yup," he confirmed for Benita. "Sean is located near downtown Perth Amboy."

"Good. Good. Listen, Evan and I will head up to Perth Amboy and have a little chat with him. Luciana, can you work with Huey to pull any information that you can find on the Black Hole? This way, by the time we get back, we'll have a better understanding just who we're working with."

"You got it, boss lady," Luciana answered.

"I can't lie. I love that. I'm exactly that. A boss lady secret agent. Evan, you ready to rock and roll?"

"Ready when you are."

"Benita, I think it would be best if you took the company car instead of your little sports car. It would look more official that way," Luciana suggested.

"Oh, right. And just how do I go about doing that on such short notice?"

"Oh, I can take care of that for you. There's a fleet of cars less than a mile away from here. I'll order one for you right now. Any preference on make and model?"

"Surprise me, Huey. Thank you, sir. Okay, let me change my outfit and get more prepared for the field. Can't have anybody see me looking like this. Evan, why don't we meet back here in thirty minutes. That will give me time to change and speak to Agent Cole and Doug. I want to let them know that we'll be leaving soon."

"Sounds like a plan." Evan nodded in agreement.

He and Benita headed to their rooms, and after a quick change, Benita found Miguel and Doug sitting across from Agent Cole, who was being extremely animated as he was telling a story. "Agent Cole? I just wanted to let you know that Evan and I are headed to Perth Amboy to speak to Doug's brother, Sean. We're hoping to get as much information as possible about where Doug's grandmother is, as well as when the next fight is going to take place."

"Do you want me to come with you?"

"No, we got this handled, Doug," Benita responded.

She looked at Miguel, who continued to remain quiet, waiting to see what she would say next.

"Well, Agent Jenkins, good luck with your questioning. I suggest that you think about a plan B in case he's not so open to having a conversation with you. Understood?"

"Yes, sir. I clearly understand what you mean," Benita said.

"Okay. What are you waiting for?"

Just as Benita was headed back inside the mansion, Miguel stood up and called out to her. "Benita, let's talk for a minute. I want to make sure you're clear about your orders."

"Sure. Do you mind if we walk and talk? Evan is waiting at the car, and I need to get my stuff from the room."

Miguel nodded and excused himself from Agent Cole and Doug.

"So, do you think you're prepared to meet with Doug's brother?"

"Not sure if you heard Agent Cole, but he *did* say that time was of the essence, and we need to move things forward. Wait. I'm confused right now. Do you *not* think I'm prepared?"

"Well, I just want to make sure that you think things through. This is a big deal, and I don't want you to walk into a situation you're not ready for. Plus, you are partnering with Evan, who is just as green as you are."

Benita tried her best to keep her cool with Miguel, but he made it extremely tough for her to do that. "Wow, Miguel. You're unbelievable. I mean, you don't believe that I can do this without messing things up, do you?"

"I never said that," he quickly snapped back at her.

"You didn't have to say that. But, wait. This has *nothing* to do with my skills, does it? You're jealous. Jealous that you're not in the field with me. Well, listen, Evan and I plan on reviewing our questions before we meet up with Sean. You don't have to worry about things. I mean, Agent Cole has confidence in me, and I also know what I need to do if things don't go smoothly."

Miguel felt flustered by his lover, but more importantly, he felt hurt by her attitude. He knew that the more he talked to her, the more she was getting irritated by him. He finally decided to let things go. "Okay, Benita."

"Okay, what?"

"Just be careful, and make sure that you play by the book. It's important we get the answers we need to help close this case," Miguel said.

"Sure, Agent Perkins. I'll most definitely play by your rules. You have nothing to worry about. Now, if you would excuse me, I need to head to Perth Amboy to speak to Doug's brother. I'll definitely keep you in the loop."

Benita stared at Miguel one last time before walking away from him as she headed to the front door. She was getting more annoyed with Miguel and found herself not wanting to think about how he was starting to stifle her. It didn't sit too well with her. The more he invaded her space, the more she wanted to run away from him. She wasn't sure how she would handle him going forward, but at least she was able to spend time away from him.

She saw Evan waiting for her at their freshly cleaned SUV, standing by the driver's side. With her hand out, she smiled at him. "Keys, please."

Handing them over, he started walking to the other side of the car. "Why do you have to drive?"

"Because I'm a better driver."

"Yeah yeah yeah. You're lucky that I like you."

"I know you do. Plus, I need you to work your magic with the computer so that we can prepare for our conversation with Sean."

Evan nodded in agreement because he knew she was right. They were a good team, and he had no problem following Benita's lead . . . even though sometimes she led them down the wrong path. But, today, he felt confident that they were on their way to helping find Elsie Gibson. And if Benita wanted to lead, then he was sure to follow.

Chapter 26

DeAndre took the phone back from Elsie and placed it into his pocket. She was sitting in her chair, rocking back and forth with tears streaming down her face. "What are you young men expecting from my grandson?"

DeAndre was about to leave but sat back down. "Ms. Gibson, Doug just needs to show up, fight his fights, and everything will be fine."

Elsie wiped away her tears and bit her lip. She was so disappointed in Sean and couldn't understand how he could do this to his family. She needed to hold on and pray that she got out of this dungeon soon.

"Listen, I'll get you something else to eat. Is there anything that you're craving? Like fried chicken? Or Chinese food?"

"No, whatever you want to bring me, that's fine. Thank you."

"Okay. Well, I'll be back. But in the meantime, don't worry. Doug's gonna come through for you. I know he will. Hopefully, you can go home soon."

"Thank you, son."

DeAndre walked out of the room, leaving Elsie there to lament over the dangerous situation that she and her grandson were in. Although she was not sure what to do next, she definitely prayed for a miracle.

Chapter 27

Sean packed up his stuff that was currently in Reggie's apartment. He planned on crashing at his friend Jamie's house until he figured out a way to get back into good graces with his family. He couldn't believe that Reggie tried to downplay his cousin's involvement in his grandmother's kidnapping. The more he thought about it, the angrier he became. He had known Reggie more than half of his life, and they had been closer than brothers. Now, their friendship was over. In a short week, he had lost two family members and a best friend. All he could do now is try to keep his blood safe, even if they couldn't find a way ever to forgive him.

After receiving information for tonight's fight, he forwarded it to Doug, who was none too pleased to talk with him. Doug knew that this was the final straw and that their relationship was over and done. Doug vowed never to help or speak to him again. How could they have once been so close, but now, they were practically strangers? Sean's selfish ways had ruined their relationship, and the outcome saddened him. He missed his younger brother and wished they could be close again. Just as he was about to walk out of the apartment, he bumped into Reggie.

"Hey, bruh. Where you going?"

Sean clenched his teeth to keep from cursing him. "I'm out."

"Listen, I'm sorry that I didn't tell you about DeAndre."

"Cut the crap, Reggie. I know now that it was you who set all of this shit in motion. For real? You got my Nana involved in this shit?"

"I don't know what you're talking about."

"Man . . . I spoke to Clay, who told me you were bitching and moaning about how I had caused issues with you and A-Roc and that it would be great to get my brother to fight. But if that didn't work, maybe he should speak to the grandmother."

"Look, on my honor, I never thought he would kidnap your grandmother," Reggie pleaded.

"Why would you even bring up my family in the first place? I told you I was going to talk to my brother."

"Yeah, and how did that work out for you? I mean, you didn't seem to mind if Clay and I roughed up your brother or threatened him to get him to fight. I did that for you, man, because I didn't want you to get hurt."

Sean took one look at Reggie and picked up his bag. "I gotta go. I'll pick up the rest of my stuff later."

"Let me take you."

"I don't want you to take me anywhere—ever again. As far as I'm concerned, we're done. Hopefully, my brother will win all of those damn fights, and A-Roc will let my grandmother go—no thanks to you."

Reggie smirked at his friend. "Sean, you and I both know that Doug will fight but never be free of A-Roc. He's got both of you in his back pocket. That kid is never going to get out of this situation."

Sean knew in his heart that Reggie was right. His stomach churned from despair. As he started to walk toward the door, Reggie blocked his path. "Where you gonna go, Sean?"

"Anywhere but here. Now, get out of my way."

Reggie raised his hands and moved out of the way as Sean left the apartment. He had always talked a bunch of smack to his friend, even threatened him on many occasions, but they had each other's back . . . until now. He felt horrible that he had crossed that line with Sean, and if he could do it all over again, he would have never told Clay about Sean's money situation. He prayed that Sean would understand that he only vented to Clay because he was scared. And now, he had lost the only best friend he had ever had.

As Sean walked outside, he started worrying about his family. He decided to call DeAndre to see if he would reveal where his grandmother was located. Just as he was about to hang up the phone, DeAndre surprisingly picked up.

"Hello?"

"Hey, DeAndre. It's Sean Gibson, Reggie's friend."

"Whatchu want, man?"

"Look, Reggie told me that you know where my grandmother is. Can you get her on the phone so that I can speak to her? I just wanna make sure she's okay."

There was silence on the phone. Finally, DeAndre answered. "Nah, I can't do that. But I can tell you that she's okay."

"You sure? DeAndre, where is she?"

"Sean, all I can say is that she's good."

"Okay, that's all I need to know."

"I gotta go. Don't call again." DeAndre hung up.

Sean felt that he heard the worst news of his life. Had he just set up a death sentence for his grandmother and his brother? He didn't realize that there was a voicemail message which he began to play. To his surprise, the message was from A-Roc. "Sean, my man. Hope you got the info that you needed. The time has finally come for you to pay up or shut the fuck up. I want you to know that not only do I expect your brother to fight as if his life depended on it, but if he doesn't, then there will also be a whole lot of broken necks. See you tonight."

After he hung up the phone, Sean's body went limp. He sat down on the grass and wrapped his arms around his legs, rocking himself back and forth. *I'm sorry, li'l brother. I'm so sorry.* He was scared for his family because he knew that A-Roc meant business. Pulling out his phone, he checked the time. He had a few more hours before his brother's first fight. *Please, forgive me, Doug. Please.*

Sean called an Uber and waited patiently until the car arrived. Then he stood up, grabbed his bag, and jumped in the vehicle. He decided to stop by his favorite Chinese place to enjoy his last meal. He sent one more text trying to find his brother, who had been MIA, but he had kept that information from him. All he wanted was for his brother to forgive him. He closed his eyes, praying that all would end well.

Chapter 28

Benita and Evan slowly pulled up in front of The Wonton Restaurant, located five blocks from Perth Amboy's historic waterfront that had a view of the Raritan Bay and the New York borough of Staten Island. Benita looked out the window of her white 2017 St. Regis Dodge Charger while surveying the area for Sean.

As Evan looked down at his computer, he pulled up a mug shot of Sean Gibson and read, "Sean Gibson. Age 26. Incarcerated twice for petty crimes. Spent six months in jail for petty theft and trespassing."

Benita frowned when she thought how this guy went down the wrong path while his brother went in a whole other direction. "Evan, you ever wonder how people who grow up in the same household can take different roads?"

"I stopped thinking a long time ago why people do what they do. No matter how much you think about things, you will never get a clear answer."

"Yeah, you're right. I'm just amazed how Doug is focused on his boxing while his brother focused on committing crimes."

Evan saw Sean sitting alone at a picnic table eating. "Hey, look over there to your left. I think that might be Doug's brother."

Benita pulled out her binoculars to get a closer look at the guy, and she confirmed that it was their target. "Okay, let's go talk to him."

"I'm with you, boss lady."

They got out of the car and headed toward the picnic table. Sean didn't see them walk up to him since his back was to them. He looked down at his phone and was about to text Doug again, but he changed his mind. That's when Benita and Evan interrupted his meal.

"Sean Gibson? Can we have a word with you?"

Sean was surprised when he recognized the female voice and didn't turn around. Instead, he continued to eat his scallion pancake. After he finished swallowing his last bite, he turned halfway, looking at Benita and Evan from the side. "So, what are you doing here? Aren't you supposed to be with my brother?"

Benita looked around the area. Only a few people stood around waiting for their food. Then she grabbed Sean's arm and swung him around to face her. "Listen, I am not in the mood to hear your sarcasm."

Sean stood up and stood extremely close to her, but he backed down when he saw Evan moving closer.

"Hey, I think you need to back up, buddy, before you get yourself hurt," Evan growled.

"What the hell do you want?"

"We need you to come with us. We want to ask you some questions about the disappearance of your grandmother."

"I'm confused right now. Who the hell are you? And why are you here? Look, I don't know you, and I got nothing to say."

Benita looked around and smiled back at Sean. She stood next to him and knuckled him in his stomach while Evan blocked the view from the other patrons. "Listen here, asshole. I'm not here to play any games with you. My name is Agent Jenkins, and this here is Agent Green. Now, you need to get it in your thick skull that we are not your fucking enemy. We're here to help find your grandmother. So, I suggest you walk with us and stop with all of your bullshit."

Sean coughed and nodded in agreement.

"Good. Now, we're going to walk slowly to my car and go for a little ride. Away from the crowd. Do you understand?"

Sean looked sheepishly at Benita as he dug his hands in his pockets. "So, you're a fucking cop?"

"You will find out all you need to know when we get a chance to talk. Okay?"

Sean started shaking his head. "Ah, you know what? I'm good. We don't need to talk."

Benita stood close to him again. "This *isn't* a request, Sean. Either you come with us willingly, or we will drag you in front of all of these people. Which is it going to be?"

Sean stared back at Benita and then looked over at Evan. However, this time, he realized he had no choice. "I hope you're enjoying yourself right now. I still don't know why you're all up in our family business since the last time I checked . . . You ain't family."

"Okay, let's go, Sean. Like right now."

Just as they got close to the car, Sean again had second thoughts. "Where are you taking me?"

"Sean, just get in the car, and we'll discuss it," Benita said.

"Nah. Nah. I'm not getting in your fancy-ass car. Not even a real cop car," he argued.

"We're not cops, Sean," Evan reminded him.

"Then, what the hell are you? FBI?"

Benita glanced at Evan as she popped the trunk. "You know what, Evan? I'm not going to listen to this fool talk anymore. Sean, get in the trunk."

"Are you out of your damn mind? I'm not getting in your damn trunk," he yelled at Benita.

"You're a pain in my ass—a real piece of work. We're here right now because of your involvement with some very bad people, and now, your family is in danger. How does that make you feel right now? Big man?"

"You need to back off me. You don't know what the hell I've been through."

Benita jabbed Sean in his kidney, and this time, he buckled from the pain.

"Well, I don't care what the hell *you've* been through. I only care about your brother and helping to get your grandmother back. Do you understand what I'm saying?"

Benita's powerhouse hit Sean in his stomach. "I am sick of you and your badass attitude. You listen to me, and you listen to me good. One, if you don't do exactly what I say, then I can't help you. Two, if anything happens to your grandmother or your brother, I'll kill you myself. But more importantly, three, the people I work for will probably arrest you for illegal gambling, robbery, and conspiracy to kidnap. So, I'm warning you one last time . . . If you don't follow the damn rules, you will truly be sorry. 'Cause, baby, you don't know who you're talking to. Do *not* play with me, Sean. We clear?"

Sean remained silent as he stood up straight. Shocked by her bluntness, he finally realized that she meant business. He slowly nodded his head.

"Now, get in that damn trunk before I *make* you get in."

Sean looked around the area one more time and slowly climbed into the trunk. Benita slammed the top down and headed to the driver's side of the car while Evan opened the door to the passenger side. Once they both got situated, they headed south toward the end of the street and finally made their way toward Interstate 85.

"You know what, Evan? I can see why Doug hates that dude. He's too busy doing the wrong things and not looking at the bigger picture here. His grandmother has been kidnapped, and he doesn't even seem to care."

"Yeah, I definitely peeped that, B. But you gotta understand he doesn't know us, and he's only protecting himself."

"I understand that, but if somebody is trying to help, sometimes, you need just to put your ego aside and accept it."

The screen on the dashboard lit up with the name Willard Cole.

"Wait, Agent Cole's first name is Willard? Who names their child 'Willard'?"

Evan shook his head at Benita. "Gurl, answer the phone and stop playing around."

Benita rolled her eyes at him and pushed the button located on her steering wheel. "Hello? This is Benita."

Agent Cole's voice came through the car speakers. "Agent Jenkins, this is Agent Cole."

"Yes, Agent Cole. How may I help you?"

"Did you speak to Sean Gibson?"

"Yes, sir. We found him to be quite hostile toward us and thought it best if we brought him back to the estate for us to interrogate him and extract the information that we need."

"Not surprising. Where is he now?"

"He's in the trunk, sir. Didn't want him to see where we're bringing him."

"I see you learned something in your training. What's your ETA?"

Benita looked over at Evan, who mouthed the words *forty-five minutes*. "We'll be there in under an hour."

"Good. Right before you get to the main entrance leading to the mansion, you'll see a second road that will lead you to a barn. Drive to that location, and I'll meet you there."

"Second entrance. Barn. Understood."

"Looking forward to meeting the young man who is the center of all this mess. See you soon." Agent Cole hung up.

Benita pressed the button on her steering wheel and heard sounds coming from her trunk.

"Maybe we should pull over and allow him to stretch. That dude is pretty tall, and he's now rolled up like he's in a cocoon," Evan suggested.

Benita rolled her eyes and cocked her head to the side while she tapped her finely manicured fingers on the steering wheel. She thought about what she should do next. On the one hand, Sean had created this situation for himself, and she wanted him to suffer. On the other hand, she wanted him to feel what it must have been like for his grandmother to be taken away. But after Evan had mentioned that Sean was cooped up in a very small space and to let him stretch out a bit, she reluctantly agreed with him.

"Fine. I'll pull over at one of the backward-ass rest stops. But I'm telling you, if that dude gives me trouble, I'll just knock him out. And then he won't have to worry about being uncomfortable."

Evan smiled at her and looked out of the window. "Did you ever think that we would be doing all kinds of shit to solve these cases?"

"Actually, Evan, I don't really know what I thought when I agreed to come work for the organization."

Her mind wandered back to when she decided to take the deal and relinquish all contact with her family. Every day she regretted that choice and struggled with keeping her promise not to contact her family. She had already defied the Agency by communicating with her brother, but she justified her decision by keeping tabs on her grandmother through her brother. She wished she could share her feelings with Evan and Luciana, but Leroy had warned her not to tell anyone about her plans. Because in the end, no one at that place could be trusted. So, for now, she consciously hid her desires and plans from her coworkers. It terrified her, thinking about what might happen if she got caught.

Then her mind went to Doug. From day one, she felt a connection to him. She remembered being impressed with his boxing skills and how he was working hard to perfect his craft. She couldn't get him out of her mind, and that bothered her. She didn't know when, but she knew that he would eventually need her help. However, in the beginning, Doug didn't want her assistance. He was focused. He was real, and he was honest. He didn't want to be bothered. Ironically, those were some of the qualities that made her feel like she was dealing with a man who brought some normalcy to her life.

More importantly, when she saw Doug with his grandmother, she wanted to get to know him. Even after a few quick glances, Benita knew he was very close to her. Their relationship reminded her of the relationship that her Grams had with Wes. She needed to know more. She wanted to see more interaction between the two of them. And she was committed to getting them back together.

Benita pulled into an abandoned rest stop and let Sean out of the trunk. He slowly pulled his stiff limbs from the compartment. Once he got out, he gave himself a much-needed stretch.

"What the fuck, man? Where are we?" he asked.

"What does it look like?"

Before an argument ensued, Evan tried to keep the peace between Benita and Sean. "Thought it would be good for you to stretch before we made it to the final destination."

Sean looked around and had no idea where they were. "This is some crazy shit. Why you gotta take me to some undisclosed location? You trying to kill me or something?"

"I wish it were that easy, but, nah. You ain't ready to die just yet. Not until we get the information that we need to know from you," Benita answered.

"Look, I don't have any information to give you."

"We'll see about that," Benita said.

Benita couldn't believe that Sean and Doug were so different. This guy lacked compassion and was extremely selfish. Not once did he think about his family, and that definitely bothered her.

"Okay, you good? Time to get back into the trunk."

"Please, don't make me do that. I'll keep quiet. Just let me sit in the backseat." Sean had a look of desperation on his face.

"Sure, we can accommodate that. Benita, you good with that?" Evan replied as he watched Benita remain silent.

Without saying another word, Sean climbed into the back of the car, and the three of them drove away. Evan pulled out a bottle of water and handed it to him. "I thought you might be thirsty."

"Yeah. I could use a drink."

Sean took the bottle. After a few gulps, he slumped over, fast asleep.

"That should keep him quiet until we make it back to the estate." Evan smiled at Benita, who did not return his enthusiasm.

Benita was feeling nostalgic and just wanted to rewind her life and start all over. She longed for her family. She longed to be working with Deon at his hair salon. She longed just to be a woman out there running the streets. She regretted ever coming to work for an organization that controlled her every move. She never imagined that her life would change so drastically in such a short period, and now, she would risk her limited freedom to keep some level of control over her life. Since her father had volunteered to be the conduit between her and her grandmother and brother, she needed to continue to keep her wits about her and keep everyone at arm's length. No one could ever know that she was attempting to spend time with her family. She hated the fact that Miguel demanded complete control over her life, and that didn't sit too well with her, either.

"Benita, why are you so quiet? You know that concerns me when you drift off to another place."

"Sometimes, Evan, quiet is a good time to listen to what the universe is trying to say to us. I learned a long time ago that when you're centered and focused, you gather insights necessary to guide you each day."

"So, you were connecting with the universe?" He looked at her with skepticism.

"Every chance I get. It's the one thing that has been the most consistent thing in my life. Right now, I need all the help I can get to navigate through this crazy world we live in."

Chapter 29

Thirty minutes later, when Sean woke up, it was dark. He noticed a large barn with lights shining to be the only light illumination in the area. He was centered in a secluded wooded area. Neither Benita nor Evan was in the car. He was left alone. Panic set in because he didn't know where he was and didn't trust these people who had brought him to this nondisclosed place.

What the fuck is going on here? He looked for his phone, but he didn't have it on him. *Damn. I must have left it in the truck.* He opened the door and got out of the car to stretch. Just when he was finishing bending down to touch his toes as a way to stretch out his back, he saw Benita walking toward him with a small man wearing a very serious look on his face.

"Sean Gibson? Agent Cole. Domestic Terrorism Crime Unit. Follow me, please," Agent Cole barked and turned around and walked back toward the building with Benita. Sean followed closely behind. With a confused look on his face, Sean whispered to Benita. "So, who is he?"

Benita turned to him and said, "Your worst nightmare, my friend. You're going to wish you never had to deal with him. Believe that."

They finally walked through the door, and Evan, who was sitting at a desk reviewing notes on a computer, nodded toward a corner. Before Sean knew it, two agents dressed in all black grabbed him and escorted him to an empty chair. Sean gazed over at the group of people and suddenly became concerned. "What's going on here?"

Agent Cole stood very close to his face. "Man, I need for you to shut the hell up and let *me* ask the questions. First things first. Where's your grandmother?"

"I don't . . . know."

Agent Cole slapped him across the face. "Wrong answer. Try again. Where the hell is she?"

Sean screamed out in pain. "I just said that I don't know, man."

"But you know who has her, right?"

This time Sean remained silent.

"Well, *do* you know who has her?"

Just when Agent Cole was about to hit him again, Benita interrupted. "Ah, sir, can I speak to you for a moment?"

Agent Cole thought about Benita's request and took a deep breath. "Sure, let's step outside."

They walked out, and Agent Cole entered Benita's space. "Now, what was so important that you needed to interrupt my interrogation?"

"Well, sir, I thought maybe we could start with how he got involved with the Black Hole circle and—"

"Oh, you thought? Well, Benita, I didn't ask you to think, did I?"

"No, sir, you didn't. But you did tell me that I would be running point."

"Would you like to ask the questions since you think that I don't know how to get the information?"

"Well, I would like very much to take a swing at him . . . if you don't mind," Benita answered.

Agent Cole smirked and moved out of the way to let Benita pass. "Then, by all means, Agent Jenkins. Please, take a crack at him."

"Thank you, sir."

The two agents walked back into the room as Sean sat in the chair, too nervous to look at anyone or anything other than his own feet.

Benita moved an empty chair and placed it in front of him. Before she began, she saw Miguel enter the barn out of the corner of her eye. "So, Sean, how you doing tonight?"

Sean began to bite his fingernails while his right leg began to shake. "I'm curious about why I'm here."

"You're here because you have answers that we need to find your grandmother. Did you forget that she's missing?"

Sean looked around at the different people in the barn and still remained silent.

"Okay, let's try this again. So, why don't you tell me about A-Roc."

"Who? A-Roc? I don't know no guy by the name of A-Roc."

Benita shook her head and looked over at Agent Cole and Miguel as they watched her intensely. "A-Roc is the leader of the Ortez gang. And I know for a fact that you owe him a lot of money. And *that's* why you need your brother to fight to save your ass."

Sean perked up when Benita mentioned his brother. "Do you know where Doug is right now? I haven't seen him since you came around."

"Yeah, and I saved your ass from getting a beat-down too. Look, Sean, I'm trying to help you. You see those men over there? They'll be a lot harder on you than I am, so I suggest that you tell me what I need to know so that we can put an end to all of this. You see, we all want the same thing, and that is to find your grandmother."

"Like, I said, I don't know no A-Roc."

Agent Cole rolled up his sleeves. "So, you wanna play with us? Do you think we're that stupid, son?"

Sean looked over at Agent Cole. "Nah, I don't think you're stupid. I'm just saying—"

Cole moved at lightning speed and grabbed Sean's jacket collar, shaking him uncontrollably.

"Now, you betta start talking, or you will regret fucking with us. Do you hear me? I'm not gonna ask you again. And if you don't tell us what we wanna know, I'm going to personally drag your sorry ass to prison and throw you in with some of the most dangerous criminals I can find. We're not here for our health, son. We're trying to find your kidnapped grandmother."

"Don't you think I know that? I know it's my fault. I need my brother to fight for me. But it all went south. I had no idea that they would snatch up my grandmother. That wasn't my fault. That *wasn't* my fault."

Benita watched as Sean started crying, and she knew that he was telling the truth. At that moment, she felt sorry for him because he didn't understand the magnitude of the situation or how his actions had caused all of this chaos. He now had to face the fact that his family could be hurt. "Agent Cole, it's okay. You can let him go now. I can take it from here."

Agent Cole released Sean and walked back over to Miguel. He crossed his arms and turned his focus back to Benita.

"Sean, I know that this is hard, but I need you to tell me everything you know about A-Roc and his gang. Because if you ever want to see your grandmother again, we need to find her. And we can't do that without your help."

Sean nodded in agreement as he finally acquiesced to answering all of the questions thrown at him. He discussed how he first got involved with A-Roc as a gambler and how his addiction ended up betting on illegal boxing matches. He later discussed A-Roc's other partner, Jermaine Thomas, and how he was the mastermind behind the fight clubs situated across New Jersey. Benita finally saw a bigger picture than what she initially thought. She listened to every word that came out of Sean's mouth because it was clear that A-Roc and his crew needed to be shut down for good.

Chapter 30

Grace Jenkins was washing dishes when her doorbell rang. She wasn't expecting any visitors, and she thought that it was somebody for Wes.

"Wes, darling, can you get the door, please?"

Wes, who was sitting in the living room watching basketball, went to the door to find Leroy standing outside. "Sensei Leroy, what's up? What's going on? Come on in."

"Thank you." Leroy followed Wes into the living room.

"Grams, it's Sensei Leroy." Then turning to Leroy, who was looking at the pictures of Benita and the rest of the family, he asked the older man if he wanted something to drink.

"No, I'm fine, Wes. You coming to class this week?"

Wes gave him a big, toothy grin. "Yes, sir. I wouldn't miss it. I should have been taking those classes the same time Benita was there. I would be much further along than I am now."

"It's never too late, Wes. Just be glad that you started now. Look at all of the possibilities that are coming your way. Enjoy the ride, my friend."

"Hello, Leroy," Grace interjected. "What brings you here?"

Leroy turned to face Grace Jenkins, who was clearly annoyed to see him. No matter what he did, she would forever dislike him. In fact, he believed that she would hate him until the day she died.

"Nice seeing you too, Grace."

"Wes, can you go to the store and pick me up some graham crackers? I need to finish making my cheesecake, and I ran out."

"Sure, Grams. You need anything else?"

"No, that's it. Do you need some money?"

"Nope, I'm good. I'll be right back." Wes kissed his grandmother on the cheek and headed out the door, leaving Grace and Leroy in the living room, simply staring at each other in silence. Finally, Grace broke the ice.

"Now, do you wanna tell me why you're here?" Grace demanded an answer from Leroy, who was looking for something all around the room.

"Miles Davis. He's one of my favorite jazz musicians. Did you know that?"

"Why would I know that? What the hell are you talking about?"

Leroy pulled out a CD placed in the music rack and bent down to put it in her player. "Why don't we listen to it?"

Grace crossed her arms and was about to go off on him, but he placed his finger to his mouth as a way to quiet her down. She decided to go along with whatever game he was playing. "Well, sure. Go ahead. Play some Miles and make yourself comfortable. I'll bring us some tea and cookies. And then we can have a nice chat."

Grace went back to the spotless kitchen and pulled out two teacups, tea bags from the cabinet, and ginger cookies, placing them on a tray. After heating water from the tea kettle, she poured the hot water into the teacups and walked back into the room, where she observed Leroy touching different spots on the furniture, including the coffee table and couch.

"Here you go, Leroy."

"Let me help you with that tray."

"No, I can handle it. Please, sit."

Leroy sat down on the side chair next to Grace, who sat on the couch.

"Now, why don't we discuss your visit. Why are you here, Leroy?"

Leroy picked up the cup of tea and blew on it to cool it down. "I know it's been awhile since we've talked last, and I thought it was time for a visit."

Trying to contain herself, she picked up a ginger snap and popped it into her mouth, followed by a sip of tea. "And why is that, Leroy? Is there news that you want to share with me?"

"Actually, there is. I've been in communication with your granddaughter, and she misses you. How would you feel if I was able to set up a visit?"

"Well, ain't that something. You know that I would give my life for Benita. All you have to do is tell me when and where, and I'll be ready."

"Well, there's a tournament coming up, and I would love if Wes would compete. I'm sure that he would do great there and meet so many different people. You know what I'm saying?"

"I hear you loud and clear, Leroy. Loud and clear."

Leroy sat for a little while longer and saw that Grace was relieved that she would finally see her granddaughter again. The former agent was also happy that he had given Benita's grandmother the opportunity to figure out a way to make this meeting happen. What a surprise it was for him when Grace thanked him for being there for her granddaughter even though she disliked him for deserting Benita's mother years ago.

After the sensei left, Grace walked to her bedroom and pulled out a postcard that Benita had sent her a few months ago. She read it several times, savoring each word on how Benita saved the world from the bad guys. She wasn't sure how her grandbaby ended up in this secret organization, but she prayed that she was in a safe place. She had often wondered where Benita was and what she was doing, and now she would find out all of that.

Leroy had warned her that she and Wes would have to keep their future meetings with Benita a secret to keep them safe. He explained that the organization was not to be trusted and that if they found out that Benita had been communicating with them, they would send her away to an undisclosed location, and not even he would be able to contact her.

Unlike now, he had worked it out that they could see each other. And the good thing was that she was living in New Jersey, and it was easy for him to see her. Before he left, he told Grace that he would be in touch once everything was set up for the meeting.

Wes had finally come back from the store and found Grace crying in her bedroom.

"Grams, are you okay? Where's Sensei? Did something happen?"

"I'm fine. Everything is going to be all right."

Wes was not sure what she meant, but he didn't press her to explain. He saw that she was looking at Benita's postcard and knew that she was crying over Benita. He so desperately wanted to tell her that he was in touch with Benita, but his sister had made him promise to keep it a secret.

"Baby, why don't we go for a walk? I wanna share some things with you." Grace stood up and headed to the door.

"All right, Grams. Where do you wanna go?"

"Oh, it doesn't matter. I just want to get some air."

The grandmother and grandson duo walked around the neighborhood, and Grace shared the news about finally getting to see Benita. She warned him that they would have to keep their plans quiet to protect Benita and them from any blowback. Wes put his arm around Grace's shoulders and bopped his head up and down. There was a new pep in their steps as they strolled through the neighborhood.

"So, what's next, Grams?"

"We need to wait for him to get back to us. I never thought I would say this, but your sensei is coming through for us. And for that, I am forever grateful. Now, how about we grab something to eat?"

Chapter 31

Benita was exhausted after Sean's interrogation. She and Evan made their way back to the main house while Sean was escorted to one of the bungalows on the other side of the estate. She definitely didn't want the two brothers around each other because she wasn't sure how Doug would react once he saw Sean. She couldn't think about anything other than grabbing something to eat. She would deal with Sean in the morning after everyone got a good night's sleep.

The two agents said their goodbyes and headed to their respective bedrooms. Benita was starving, and when she arrived in her room, she found a small, wheeled table filled with several cloches located near the window. She picked up a note placed near the plate cover, condiments, bottled water, and canned Diet Dr. Pepper, summarizing the menu, including steak, potatoes, and a salad.

As she nibbled on a roll and looked at her meal, she poured herself a glass of soda. Although she was ready to enjoy her dinner, she wanted to take a shower first and wash away all of the day's events. As the hot water ran down her body, Benita's mind kept going back to the conversation that she had with Miguel earlier. She was questioning her feelings for him. The more aggressive he was becoming toward her, the more she wanted to pull back from him. She knew that his feelings were deep for her, but she wasn't sure if she could reciprocate. Things had taken a turn for the worse, and she was tired of his power tripping. Now, she had to figure out a way to pull away from him without alerting him to her next moves to spend time with her family.

She slipped into a pink loungewear set that hung in her closet and finally sat down to enjoy her meal. The food was beyond delicious and hit the spot to ease her grumbling stomach. Sipping on her water with lemon, she leaned back in her chair, thinking about Doug. She hadn't spoken to him at all that day and wanted to see him. So, she decided to visit him, and just as she was about to leave, her other phone vibrated from her bag.

She smiled as she slipped on her pink, fluffy flip-flops. Pulling out the second phone, she walked downstairs and headed outside toward the row of bungalows. She made sure that no one was around as she returned the call. "Hello? Sensei?"

"Hello, my beautiful daughter. Weren't you supposed to call me back? It's been a minute, and I was getting concerned."

"I'm fine. It's just this case—"

"It's a case now?"

"Yeah, it's a whole case. It seems that my intuition was right. There seems to be a link between Doug's grandmother's kidnapping and a group of criminals who run an illegal fight club called the Black Hole. Have you ever heard of it?"

"No, honey. There are a thousand of them popping up every day."

"Yeah, well, I had the pleasure of interrogating Doug's brother Sean, who plays a critical role in not only finding his grandmother but also helping to shut this group down."

"Well, good for you. And how are things with Agent Perkins?"

"He decided to assign me to another agent. Willard Cole."

"Oh, I see. How's that working out for you?"

"He's very interesting. But I'm learning his style and how he reads people."

"Just make sure he doesn't spend too much time reading you because heaven forbid he finds out what you're doing behind the Agency's back."

"I will, Dad. I'm being very careful."

The two continued talking about the next steps when it came to seeing her family. The plan was now in motion, and she would need to be ready to make herself available when the time was right. She hung on to his every word because she wanted to follow his orders precisely to protect her family. After getting off the phone, she breathed a sigh of relief because she felt confident that her father's plan would work. She hugged her body tight as a way to comfort her tortured soul. *Thank you, Dad*.

Just when she was about to walk toward Doug's bungalow, she sensed that she was being watched. She looked around and didn't see anyone, but she thought she saw someone peering out when she looked up at a light in the window. She brushed off the feeling and continued down the path leading to Doug. She knocked on the door, and after a moment, Doug opened the door while putting on a T-shirt.

"Oh, hey, Agent Jenkins."

Benita smiled and playfully rolled her eyes at him. "Jeez, can you just call me Benita? You don't have to act so formal with me. I thought we were past that. Can I come in for a few minutes?"

"Yeah, sure. I was just watching a little television." He stepped out of the way, allowing her to walk into his place. "So, any updates about my grandmother?"

Benita sat down on one of the matching chairs close to the window and watched as Doug sat down on the corner of the freshly made bed. "Not exactly, but we're pretty sure we know who has her. There is something that I have to tell you, and I wanted you to hear it from me."

"What is it? Is my grandmother okay?"

"Yeah, yeah. She's fine. This has to do more with your brother, Sean. He's here."

Doug's fists tightened. "*Here?* Why is he here? What's going on? Did he tell you where Nana is? What are you *not* telling me?"

"Wait. Doug. Calm down. Please. Listen. Your brother has been dealing with a bad crop of criminals, but he is cooperating with us to find them and take them down while at the same time, finding your grandmother."

"Benita, you can't trust him. Not one bit. He is slick and will bail on you at the first chance he gets."

"Well, I'm here to tell you that he is our best chance at finding your grandmother. I believe him when he says that he didn't plan for any of this to happen."

Doug remained quiet while he started bouncing his right leg. He wasn't sure what to say next because he was filled with both rage and fear.

"Listen to me. I promised you from the very beginning that I would find your grandmother, and that's exactly what I'm going to do. Do you understand?"

"Yeah, I understand."

"I was thinking that we could go running in the morning. There's this great trail behind the compound, and we can work off some of this energy that both of us have. Would you like that?"

He thought about her suggestion and begrudgingly relented to her request. "Yeah, why not? It's not like there's so much to do in this joint. I could definitely get some much-needed training if I'm going to fight for my life."

"That's what I'm talking about."

"So, what else did my brother talk about?"

"He talked about you and your grandmother and how he has really made a mess out of his life."

"Well, that's true."

"But more importantly, he does love his family. He knows how much he's hurt the two of you."

"So, what's next?"

"That's what we'll be discussing tomorrow. But for now, let's all get a good night's sleep."

Benita was about to leave, and just when she passed by Doug, he quickly stood up and gently held on to her wrist. When she looked at him with curiosity, he let her go. "I'm sorry. I just wanted to tell you that I'm thankful for all of your help. I know that I was a real jerk when we first met, but it's hard for me to trust people. You know?"

Benita was moved by how sincere Doug was being, and she touched his face. "Doug, you can trust me. When I say that I'm going to do something, I'm going to do it. And right now, you are my top priority."

He placed his hand over Benita's and nodded. "Who the hell are you, Benita Jenkins?"

Smiling back at the handsome boxer, she sighed. "I'm just a woman who will do anything to make things right. Doug, I promise I won't let you down."

"And you know what? I believe that."

They both smiled as they stood there looking deeply into each other's eyes. Just when it looked like they were going to kiss, Benita broke the stare. "Well, I think I should leave now. Will I see you in the morning? Seven a.m.?"

"Yeah, that's cool. See you in the morning."

Benita left the room, leaving both of them surprised by the recent developments. Hopefully, a good night's sleep for both of them was necessary to clear their heads because the last thing they needed to happen was for a budding romance amid so much chaos surrounding them.

Chapter 32

Miguel and Willard walked to the private dining room, where they planned on discussing the day's events. Even though Miguel wanted to speak to Benita privately, he thought it best to keep his distance since their conversation from earlier ended badly. He would apologize to her for his untimely behavior. He watched as his friend Willard dug into his chicken alfredo pasta and was happy that they were working together again. "Agent Jenkins did a great job interrogating that Sean character," Willard shared.

"Yeah, it was impressive. But I'm not surprised. That's one of the best qualities about her. When she's focused, she really delivers. You should have seen her in action on the last case."

"I'm sure she was something."

"Yeah, she is something," Miguel acknowledged.

"So, Perkins, you wanna talk about it?"

Miguel gave him a curious look. "Talk about what? What do you mean?"

"Look, you and I have been friends for a long time now, and I know when there is something on your mind. Spill it."

Miguel rubbed his finger over the top of his glass several times before he answered. "We've been doing this job for a long time now, and I guess I was just thinking about how different my life would have been if I had chosen another profession."

"Boring. That's what it would have been. Damn boring," Willard commented as he took another bite of his food.

Miguel chuckled as he watched his friend chow down on his dinner. "Have you ever thought about having a family?"

Willard put down his fork and stared back at Miguel with a perplexed look on his face. "Oh, okay. I now see where this is going. You got the hots for Agent Jenkins."

"No," Miguel quickly lied to his friend. He couldn't share his feelings with anyone, including Willard, because he knew that there would be terrible consequences if anyone found out. "Benita? No. I don't have feelings—"

"Well, you could have fooled me. And I'm no fool. I see how you look at her, and it is not just because she's a damn good agent. Look, Miguel, I'm your friend, and I saw how the last relationship you had ended badly. I just don't want you going down that road again."

"Nothing's going on with us."

"Even if it isn't, you need to think long and hard about getting involved with someone who reports to you. You and I both know what would happen if you crossed that line. You can't allow your feelings to get in the way of the job because every day we step out there, we put our lives on the line. And when you allow feelings to get in the way—"

"I hear you, Willard. Loud and clear. Now, can we just change the subject? We need to figure out our next steps in order to use the information that Sean has given us to bring down this crew."

"How about we just enjoy our meal, and I can finish up my Cognac?"

"You and your Cognac."

"It's one of the finer things in life that I will never give up," Willard commented.

Just like Willard would never give up his favorite drink, Miguel wasn't ready to end things with Benita. He was in love with her, and he would continue to hide his relationship from everyone at the Agency, including his best friend. For now, he needed to remain focused on the case while he worked to get back into Benita's good graces.

After dinner, the two agents parted ways, and Miguel went to his bedroom to finish up reviewing other cases that were currently open. His mind wandered back to the last conversation that he had with Benita. He couldn't shake the feeling that things were different between them now. He thought about calling her but decided to keep his distance with so many agents swarming around them. He shouldn't have blown up with her, and more importantly, he probably shouldn't have assigned her to work with Willard. But there was nothing he could do about his actions now except to allow things to play out. A few hours had passed, and she hadn't reached out to him either. He hated that she acted so distant with him. *I'll make it up to you, B.*

He had gone too far with his controlling behavior. Having worked at the DTCU for more than ten years, he had learned early on to perfect the art of manipulation, which was imperative if he was to be successful in closing cases. As he worked undercover with some notoriously dangerous men, he had quickly learned how to pivot his behaviors to fit into their worlds.

Thinking about how he swayed the events leading up to Benita becoming an agent at the agency, he often felt a pang of guilt. However, he knew that what he did was for the greater good, and to his mind, Benita would serve a bigger purpose working for him than still being a hairstylist. He smiled when he thought about the first time he saw her defending herself in the mean streets of Brooklyn, and he was instantly attracted to the gorgeous, brown-skinned woman. Obsessed with knowing everything about her, he later convinced his boss, Director Jeremiah Bolden, that she was the right one to close the Carl Johnson case. He needed her on his team, and he needed to possess her mind, body, and soul. All he could think about was being with Benita, and as time continued, his feelings only grew stronger for her.

Whenever Benita spent time with other people, he became jealous. He wanted to be the one she turned to when she felt sad or happy or even mad. Ever since he had gotten back from Africa, things had been rocky between them. He didn't want to push her away, and he didn't want to spend another minute without her.

Miguel knew he was hypocritical when it came to Benita. He couldn't help wanting to control her every move, and that wasn't fair. But he also wanted to make sure that she was okay as she navigated through the more dangerous cases that came her way. He was pissed that she had found her own case, but his mind eased when he saw how she galvanized her team. It was essential not to get personally caught up with any of these situations because it would be tough to separate fantasy from the real world.

They were undoubtedly playing a dangerous game of keeping their love affair a secret while interacting with others in a professional setting. And Miguel didn't care that he was putting his career on the line for Benita because, in the end, she was worth losing everything for. He picked up his phone and was about to text Benita, but he changed his mind. He decided to give her some space because the last thing he wanted was to push her away even more. He had to learn to be patient and let her deal with her own emotions. This was something that he couldn't control. He needed to sit back and let her come to him.

Just when he was about to put his papers away and settle in for the night, Miguel looked out his window and was surprised to see Benita walking toward Doug's bungalow. He felt himself getting heated at the thought of her paying attention to someone else. He was furious that she had started to take him for granted when he had been there for her from the very beginning. He stared outside as she knocked on the door and waited until Doug let her in. Thinking about what he just observed, he decided to take a shower to clear his head. He would make it a point to ask her why she was visiting Doug so late at night. But for now, he had no other choice but to deal with his insecurities before they affected his work.

Chapter 33

Benita was dressed in her workout gear, stretching while waiting for Doug to meet her at the trail located behind the row of bungalows. She smiled when she thought about her conversation last night and was happy he'd finally lowered his guard and began to trust her. In fact, she felt invigorated after spending time with him, and now, she was psyched about seeing her own family again. It was strange for her to understand finally that helping Doug was also helping herself. She didn't realize just how she had gotten to such a low point in her life since being cut off from her grandmother and her brother.

Even after spending six months in jail, she knew that she had contact with her family. And after speaking to Doug, she felt that all hope was gone for her. She wondered if this was how people had felt before giving up on everything. Thank goodness that she had her father to bring her back to reality. She now had two things to look forward to . . . one was to find Doug's grandmother, and the other was to see her family again.

She looked up to see Doug jogging toward her. Her eyes lit up when she saw the tall, handsome boxer smiling back at her. She thought about the very first time she had met him and how he had given her shade. But now, things had changed. He was filled with hope and an unwavering strength that was necessary to see this tragic time through.

Doug flashed his beautiful smile, and this was the first time that Benita had actually seen just how gorgeous he was. "Agent Jenkins. Funny seeing you here."

"I know, right? I mean, who runs a long-ass trail in the middle of nowhere?"

"I can't believe you talked me into running with you this early in the morning," he teased.

"Wow, Doug. I thought you were a tough guy. I mean, I have seen you chow down, my friend. You gotta keep that figure tight and right."

"Whatever. You act like I'm out of shape or something."

"Or something." Benita was happy to see Doug preparing for the upcoming fight. Her father told her that part of being a great agent was to learn to look at every accomplishment as a win. Even though this was a small thing, it was still a win. She needed to see Doug fight for his grandmother's life. And it was up to her to make sure that he stayed on course. That would be the only way that they both would be able to move forward.

"Hey, you two. Mind if I join?"

Benita was shocked when she saw lover boy standing behind her. "Miguel, what are you doing here?"

"Well, I saw that you were stretching and about to go for a run. I thought that I would join you. You're not the only one who needs a workout. Nice seeing you getting prepared for the fight, Doug."

"Yeah. Thanks to Benita, she really is helping me see things more clearly."

Miguel cocked his head to the side as he looked over at Benita. "Yeah. She certainly has a way to do that. What is most impressive is her ability to push people to their full potential. Very admirable of her."

"Yeah. She hounded me like none other until I listened to what she had to say."

"All right. All right. I think you both have made your point. Agent Perkins, can I have a word with you? Doug, give us a second, okay?"

Doug smiled and nodded in agreement. "Sure, I'll be here."

Benita and Miguel stepped out of earshot of Doug while he continued stretching. She turned her back to Doug and tried to contain her anger toward Miguel. "What are you doing?"

"I saw you were going for a run, and I thought I would join you. You know . . . surprise you. It's been a minute since we've had quality time."

"You are unbelievable, Miguel. I mean, we're on a case, and you care about squeezing in some *quality time?* I can't do this right now. I'm really trying to stay focused on closing this case."

"I'm sorry. Look, things have been tense between us, and I just wanted to talk to you without the distractions."

"Miguel, don't take this the wrong way, but one minute you're reprimanding me for doing everything wrong, and then when I finally start to make headway, you now want me to shift my focus to you. Well, unfortunately, I can't do both."

Miguel listened to his lover and knew that she was right. But in his mind, she was starting to pull away from him, and he wasn't ready to let go. All he ever wanted was for her to see him as her protector, but now she saw him as something other than that. He was a man who was scared of losing her, and he didn't know how he would handle that if he didn't have her in his life. He loved her and simply wanted to be with her. "I'm sorry that you feel that way. I just wanted to see you."

"I know, and we'll have plenty of opportunities to make up for lost time. But for now, I can't be looking over my shoulder to see you breathing down my neck. I really need the space to continue to build a relationship with Doug so that when the time is right, he is strong enough to do his part to save his grandmother. Are you okay with that?"

Miguel thought about what she said to him, and he knew that she was right in her approach. He agreed to give her room to work things out with the case and Doug. He wasn't happy about his decision but knew that it was the right thing to do. "Okay, Benita. You win. I don't want to stand in the way of you planning your next steps with Doug."

Benita smiled at him and then looked down at her watch. "Thank you. What do you always say? When we're on a case, we need to focus on the task at hand? Okay, I'll see you in an hour. It looks like Agent Cole has set up a meeting to go over the next steps."

Benita turned around and walked back over to Doug. They started jogging down the trail while leaving Miguel to figure out how to get this case closed. That would be the only way for him to spend quality time with Benita. He walked back to his room and prayed that she wouldn't cross the line with the likes of Doug Gibson.

Meanwhile, Benita was trying to keep a straight face after the confrontation that she just had with Miguel. It was disturbing that he would take it upon himself to just invite himself on her run without letting her know first. She didn't like that he watched her every move, and now, that frightened her. *You don't trust me.* This was becoming a bigger issue than she first thought. *You* really *don't trust me.*

When Miguel first started tracking her when she began at DTCU, she thought that he simply cared about her, but the more she thought about it, the more her mind began racing. *He's stalking me.* She would need to get this situation in check before she saw her family in person. Who knew what else Miguel had up his sleeve, or who else he had watching her? She didn't want to mess around and have him pop up any time he felt like it. *You will not blow up my spot, Miguel. I will kill you first.*

So now, she thought about how important it was for her to play the game of chess. She was the queen that needed to anticipate this man's every move. She used to give Miguel a pass when he would just pop up at her apartment because she loved the attention. The chemistry was so strong that she could hardly contain herself when she was around him. The lovemaking was incredible, and he had no problem taking her to the brink of ecstasy several times before setting off fireworks in her body that they enjoyed together.

Living a double life, bouncing between the official job at the DTCU and their secret love affair, was electrifying. But today, Miguel had gone too far when he showed up without her knowing. He had totally crossed the line. Trust had been broken.

She began to remember when she first started at DTCU, and there were cameras set up everywhere in her apartment. But as time passed, Benita convinced Miguel to remove them. She told him that he could trust her, but trust had to be both ways. He removed them, and he would only track her car when necessary. That brought her some comfort, but she still knew that she had to be careful when speaking to her brother and ended up purchasing several burner phones so that she and her brother could text freely.

And just when she thought she had some kind of freedom, Miguel had dispelled any fantasy of her having a normal life. Was there still a tracker on her car? Probably. Were there cameras still in her apartment? Most definitely. So, she now concluded that Miguel was the perfect secret agent. He could look directly in your face and lie with ease. This was now highly nerve-wracking to her, and any trust that she may have had for him was gone. *I don't trust you, Miguel. Not even a little bit.* She was also sure by his actions that he didn't trust her either. That made her sad because she did care about him, but now that the veil had been lifted, she wasn't so sure just how she felt.

Your intentions aren't genuine, Miguel. Now she needed to start building a cover story that protected every step she made. She needed to keep any level of suspicion down to a minimum. She could use this time to put Miguel on the back-burner until she figured out a solution to this complex situation. She now had a reason to keep her distance from him, if only for a little while.

This morning, she just wanted to enjoy her run with Doug. She watched him as he remained focused on his running and didn't question anything except for what happened to Agent Perkins. She told him that Miguel had to make a few calls and apologized for not being able to run. He would catch up with them later. Doug was real for her. In fact, he was the first real thing that she had encountered in a long time, and she gave herself permission to enjoy her run with him.

After their workout, Doug focused on his boxing moves while Benita practiced her jujitsu combinations.

"Hey, where did you learn some of those moves?"

"I'm a third-degree black belt. So, I've been training for a long time."

"Wow. Impressive."

"You're impressive too, Doug. When did you learn how to fight?"

Doug plopped down on the ground and started stretching out his sore limbs. "I started when I was in high school. I was on the wrestling team, but I didn't like that type of contest. I started watching boxing matches when I was a kid and fell in love with the sport. And when I met my coach, I knew that I wanted to pursue a career. Hey, I hate to ask you, but would you be down to spar with me?"

Benita cocked her head to the side and placed her hand on her slim waist. "Yes, sir. I am most definitely down. I just hope I don't hurt you too much."

"Oh, okay. It's like that?"

"Yes. It's like that."

"Hey, gentle, please. Gentle."

Benita smiled at Doug as she stretched out her legs. "You ready to do this, big guy?"

As Doug turned to her, he smiled his pearly white teeth. "I'm always ready. The question is . . . Are *you* ready, Agent Benita?"

Benita laughed as she tapped her closed fists together. "All right, mister. Let's go."

They positioned themselves with a new sense of purpose. But more importantly, they were ready for a friendly rumble as they used the practice to work out any frustrations that may have clouded their judgment.

Chapter 34

Sean was annoyed when he was awakened by birds chirping outside his room. He had a hard time falling asleep the night before after Benita questioned him about the disappearance of his grandmother and the Black Hole. He tried avoiding answering her questions, but she had convinced him that he was the only person who could get his Nana back. Sean had finally let his guard down and told her everything he knew about the men behind the illegal boxing ring. He never liked being labeled a snitch, but he wanted to do the right thing, even if that made him feel uncomfortable doing it.

And now, as he lay in bed thinking about everything he had done leading up to this situation, guilt consumed him. He wiped away one single tear when he thought about his grandmother. He could never live with himself if anything happened to her. He finally climbed out of bed and walked over to the window, where he saw nothing but farmland. When he turned to look in the opposite direction, he saw some horses eating hay in the field. There was a beautiful house standing in the distance.

He wondered if his brother was staying near him. When he asked Benita, she told him that Doug was safe, and if he cooperated with her, she would bring him to his brother. He thought about what he would say to settle things with his sibling, even though he knew Doug would not forgive him. Sean was still going to try because family was important, and if he had a chance to prove to them he'd changed, he would. But maybe since he was there and working with the agents, that would be enough for Doug to see he was serious.

He picked up his phone and checked to see if he had any messages, but there were none. Sitting back on the corner of the bed, he started rocking back and forth, thinking about all of the damage he had caused his family. Never had he felt so alone as he did right now. This was the second time that he felt totally abandoned. The first time was when his mother left him and Doug at his grandmother's house.

His phone started ringing. He looked and saw it was Reggie. At first, he contemplated not answering it, but then he gave in. "Hello?"

"Hey, man. What's up? Been looking all over for you."

"Whatchu want, Reggie?"

"Look, I know that things didn't work so well between us, but we boyz. And boyz sometimes have disagreements. I just want you to know that I apologize for my part in how things went down with your grandma."

"Well, yeah, things are fucked up right now."

"You find her yet?" Sean asked Reggie, knowing he wouldn't have an answer.

"Nah. All I know is that A-Roc got her somewhere. I heard that he'll release her after your brother fights. You heard from Jermaine? I think he's going to be reaching out to schedule the fights. Should be happening sometime this weekend."

"I'll reach out to him. Look, I gotta go. Thanks for calling."

"Of course, no matter what, man, we fam."

Sean hung up the phone and thought about touching base with Jermaine. He had also promised Benita that he wouldn't do anything that might jeopardize his grandmother's safety. He went to take his shower. He thought about how he could use this information to find his grandmother. After getting dressed, he called Benita and left her a message on her voicemail letting her know that he would do whatever it took to get his grandmother back. He stood by the window, watching the horses being carefree in the pasture. He wondered . . . Would he ever be able to live his life as carefree as these animals? It was time for him to make a change in his life, and maybe this was the time.

Benita leaned on the corner of the table with her arms crossed as she looked at the virtual board covered with confidential data that Huey had pulled on the Black Hole illegal boxing ring. Photos were there of A-Roc and key members of the Ortez crew, as well as Jermaine Thomas, with an unknown suspect. She took a closer look at the photos and thought that she recognized the nameless man, but she couldn't place him.

"Wow. What a cast of characters. I see you've been doing your homework, Huey. Did you even get any sleep last night?"

"Very little. No rest for the weary. When I'm on a roll, though, I just can't stop. Agent Cole gave me access to his confidential files, and I just combed through them, gathering as much intel as possible."

"Huh. Well, you are undeniably thorough."

"What did you come up with, Huey?" Both Benita and Huey looked up when they heard Agent Cole's voice coming from the entryway.

"Morning, Agent Cole."

"Morning to you, Agent Jenkins. So, I'm assuming that the files were helpful?"

"Yes, sir. I was able to pull background checks as well as financials from most of the men."

Miguel, Luciana, and Evan eventually joined the meeting. Benita and Miguel looked at each other, but Benita quickly glanced away. Luciana noticed the exchange as she commented on Benita's missing breakfast. Standing next to Benita, she started reviewing the board. "We were wondering where you were, Benita. Evan thought you left him and went rogue."

Benita smiled at Luciana and then looked at Evan. "Now, when have I ever just left you high and dry, Evan?"

"Don't listen to Luciana. She's the nervous one. I told her that yesterday was a long day for both of us, and you were probably just getting a little extra sleep."

Benita looked over her shoulder and watched as Miguel poured himself a cup of coffee. She refused to acknowledge him more than she absolutely needed to. In fact, she was wondering why he was even involved right now since this was Agent Cole's case.

"Damn, Perkins. You sure do love our coffee," Agent Cole said. "Okay. What did you all find that might be helpful?"

"Well, after going through all of the files that you had your tech person send over, I was able to narrow down the key players who are involved in the Black Hole. See the photo on the left? That's Abril Roco, aka A-Roc, along with his lieutenants, Carmelo Cortez and Diego Madina. They are currently involved in drug trafficking along with dogfighting. Several crack houses are strategically set up in a thirty-mile radius but mostly centered around the Perth Amboy area. Then there is Jermaine Thomas, a former boxer who is heavily invested in real estate. He seems to be the one running the show. He started the Underground Fighting League, where he recruits amateur fighters to become members. This league is completely unsanctioned. The refs aren't certified. None of the fighters are insured, and the rules aren't set in stone. This guy is smart. Really smart. He's found loopholes to keep him and his little league under the radar. All of his fights are in secret locations, secret passwords, and most of the goers don't talk about the fight club. That's why the DTCU has had a hard time shutting these fights down, that is, until now. I finally found a link between him and the Ortez Gang."

"Good job, Huey. I'm looking forward to seeing these men finally out of the illegal boxing game," Agent Cole said.

"Sean mentioned Jermaine during the interview last night. He clearly is the person that we need to get to know."

"That's good to hear, Benita. It's always best to hit as many angles as possible. We need to find the guy who made the call to Doug. He's lower level, and I'm sure we can flip him," Luciana mused.

"Willard, were any of your agents able to get in good with the gang?"

"No, Miguel. Unfortunately, we've had a few try, but they weren't able to get close to A-Roc. It takes a long time before A-Roc will allow any of the movers and shakers up in the ranks. And we just didn't have the time or manpower to keep someone working undercover. The case began to take a backseat to more important ones."

"But it's perfect timing now, sir," Evan pointed out.

Benita looked closer at Abril and Jermaine's photos. "How do you think these two met? They seem so different. One is a leader of a gang, and the other one seems more clean-cut."

"Those are the best ones, Benita. You never see them coming," Luciana said.

Huey reviewed more information on his laptop. "According to the dark web, chatter about the illegal fights started about eighteen months ago. But it looks like A-Roc and Jermaine knew each other while they both spent time in juvie together. After leaving, they took different paths. A-Roc has been in and out of jail, while Jermaine went on to attend William Patterson University and graduated head of his class. He did a small stint on Wall Street and became a professional boxer. He undoubtedly is the mastermind behind this."

"I guess Jermaine believes in multiple streams of income," Evan commented.

"Very interesting. Very interesting, indeed. Now, we have a clearer understanding of who we are working with. Agent Jenkins, what do you think we should do next?"

"Well, Agent Cole, I think that since Jermaine is the mastermind behind the Black Hole, we should focus on getting to him. We can create a cover for me. I'm Doug's manager, and Sean can set up a meeting for us to discuss logistics and maybe even ask about some sort of payment. I think this would be a great way for me to get inside of their organization and find out when the big fight will happen. Maybe I can convince him to bring the grandmother to the fight so we can do an exchange."

Miguel looked at Benita and shook his head. "No. I don't think that's a good idea."

"Excuse me?" Benita narrowed her eyes. "What do you mean it's not a good idea? It's a great idea. Sean and I can walk into the place, meet with Jermaine, and now, we have an in—especially since we don't have eyes on these people. I can drop a few cameras and voilà. We got surveillance."

Agent Cole nodded in agreement with her. "Perkins, we have one shot at making this happen. If Doug has to fight, then Benita will serve as the perfect proxy to get inside the circle."

"Yeah, but we need to make sure she's not putting herself in a situation where she doesn't have the proper backup."

"Miguel, it's not like this is the first time that I've gone undercover, remember? And guess what? I had to take on another identity. Look, how about this? Evan and Luciana will be my backup. They can be situated outside the building when I speak to Jermaine. And Huey will be able to follow me when I wear those surveillance glasses."

Luciana watched as Miguel tried to wrap his head around sending his agent into a situation that had not been fully vetted. She finally spoke up to her boss to let him know that no one would get hurt during this meet. "Miguel, listen, with all of the surveillance equipment and us being there? We'll make sure that nothing happens to Benita or Sean. We need to do this because, otherwise, we may never get an opportunity to bring this group down."

Miguel finally relented and agreed with the other team, even though he was concerned about Benita's safety. He wished that he could go in with her, but he didn't want to show how much he cared about her. "Okay, Luciana. You're right. But I want to make sure that we have an exit strategy, in case things go left."

"Good. So, now that we're on the same page, let's talk logistics," Agent Cole stated to the group.

"Yes, sir. I plan to speak to Sean and let him know that we need him to set up a meeting with Jermaine today to do a proper introduction. Evan can prep him, letting him know that he will call Jermaine and that he wants to bring me, Doug's manager, to his office for an introduction. And while he's doing that, I will change into my *manager* look."

Evan looked at Benita strangely. "Your 'manager look'?"

"Yes, Evan. You don't think I would go anywhere looking like this, do you? I've got to make sure that I play the part."

Agent Cole continued looking at the board filled with photos. "Well, whatever you do, I want to make sure that Gibson stays on script. I don't want to hear that he fucks up and creates a fiasco that pushes this asshole Jermaine away. He needs to introduce you, and you do the rest, Benita. I need you to find out when the next fight is and convince him it would be in his best interest to make sure the grandmother is there. You want to do the exchange. Understood?"

"Yes, sir. Loud and clear."

"Okay. Now that we have that settled, I'll leave you agents to flush out the plan. Perkins, can I have a word with you?"

The two men walked out of the conference room and headed outside. Willard was fuming at his friend and didn't hold back on his feelings.

"Perkins, what the hell was that about? I mean, *you're* the one who told me that the team could work with me on this case, but then you're doing everything in your power to cock block them—*especially* Agent Jenkins. Now, do you want to tell me why you continue to question her judgment? I mean, she *is* doing her job, and for some reason, you are not happy with her decisions."

Miguel bit his lip before answering him, and he really wasn't sure what he was going to say that would provide a reasonable answer. "Look, I'm sorry. I'm not trying to step all over your case, but I just feel like things are moving too fast, and there hasn't been enough time for a real strategy to be put in place."

"Well, unfortunately, if it were any other circumstance, I would agree with you. But as we both know, time is of the essence, and we need to get in as fast as we can. We have the perfect weapon to infiltrate this group. And that's Agent Jenkins. At this point, we have no idea where the grandmother is, and I would prefer for us to find her alive instead of in a body bag. You told me that Benita was one of your best agents, and I'm asking you to fall back and let her do her job."

Benita, Evan, Luciana, and Huey were left in the conference room discussing the friction between

Agents Cole and Perkins. Benita decided to remain quiet because she knew why Miguel was acting the way he was. He was jealous that she was working with his colleague.

"What the hell, man? It's as if Miguel's not in control," Evan commented.

Luciana defended her boss and let the team know why Miguel acted the way he did. "Guys, I've known Miguel for a long time. Much longer than any of you. Yes, he's a control freak. Yes, he is a perfectionist. But he means well. He just wants to make sure that all of us have our ducks in a row so that we protect ourselves."

"No disrespect, Luciana, but Miguel is not running this case. Agent Cole is. And *he's* the one who made Benita the lead agent on this case. I don't understand why Miguel thinks that he has to run point. That's all I'm saying," Evan replied.

Benita cocked her head side to side, stretching out her neck to help release the built-up tension that she was currently feeling. She knew all of Miguel's antics were about controlling her every move. Anger was boiling up inside of her, and she fought hard to keep from blowing a gasket in front of her colleagues. She changed the subject and worked to keep the team focused on the case. "Look. We can't control how Miguel behaves. We have a case to close, and I want us to create our plan and execute it well. Because the quicker we get our shit together, the quicker we can finish all of this, no matter what. We got this handled."

"So, do you think that you can trust Sean to be able to pull this off?"

"He has no other choice, Luciana. After last night, I think he finally understands the importance of working together to get his grandmother back in one piece. We got a single shot at this, and I refuse to let this dude fuck things up, okay? So, next steps. Evan, can you and Luciana speak to Sean? I need to speak with Doug."

"No, Benita. I don't think that's a good idea." Benita turned around to see Agent Cole standing at the door. "I think you and Evan go pay Sean a visit while *I* speak to Doug. We're going to play hoops."

"Hoops, sir?" Benita glanced at the others in surprise.

"Yes, Agent Jenkins. Hoops. I'm a man with many talents. Now, please proceed. Handle your business. I'm around if you need me."

And just like that, Agent Cole was gone. Benita wanted to bring the brothers together so that Doug could see that Sean was serious in helping to bring his grandmother home. But she learned to stay in her lane and not push things too much. Agent Cole had finally started releasing the reins a bit, and she would take advantage of his efforts to make way for her family. Now, she just had to figure out how to get Miguel off her back since he was watching her every move. She went back to laying out the plan with the team while thinking about her next move to get her one step closer to solving this case and seeing her own grandmother and brother.

Chapter 35

When Benita and Sean made it to 505 Blades Street, it was completely dark, and no other people were in sight. They had walked past a few abandoned row houses and dilapidated buildings before arriving at the entrance of a boarded-up structure. Sean kept staring at Benita's outfit that had transformed her from natural beauty to a superhot vixen. She'd put on her signature short, asymmetric, burgundy-colored bob and a letter print knotted, low-cut black-and-white jumpsuit with black peep-toe booties. The oversized, black-framed glasses she wore housed a tiny, microscopic camera.

Benita asked, "Wow. Is this really the place that Jermaine works out of?"

"Yeah. This is it. What'd you expect, Princess? A fucking mansion? Plus, no one told you to get all dolled up to meet the guy."

Benita bit her lip so that she wouldn't go off on Sean. No matter how many times she explained that he needed to watch his mouth, he still didn't miss an opportunity to speak to her disrespectfully. She wondered if he ever thought about how horrible a person he was or how he was the center of all of this mess. She thought about Doug and how he was willing to sacrifice his career and life for his no-good brother. If it were up to her, Sean would be in jail and far away from his family. Instead, she focused on the objective at hand.

She then turned her focus back to the job, which was to meet Jermaine to learn more about the inner workings of the illegal boxing club. Unfortunately, she had to depend on Sean to make that introduction, and he was becoming more of a liability than an asset. However, she had no other choice but to deal with his antics to gather information about the upcoming fight and what he might know about Doug and Sean's grandmother.

Sean knocked hard on the rusted metal door, and when there was no answer, he banged again. That's when a huge, six-foot Black man with dreads came to the door. Dressed in all black, he spotted Benita and Sean standing there. "Yeah?"

Sean smirked. "I'm Sean Gibson. We're here to speak to Jermaine about my brother, Doug, who's one of the fighters."

The oversized man looked at Benita. "Okay, but who the hell is she? His groupie or something?"

Benita placed her hands on her hips. "I'm nobody's groupie, son. I'm his *manager*."

The big guy crossed his gigantic arms and laughed. "His fucking *what?* Get the fuck out of here. Bitches can't be no manager."

"Really? And just how do you know? I mean, you're at the door. Some kind of two-bit bouncer. Bet you ain't even got a high school diploma, and *you're* telling *me* I can't be no manager?"

"Hey, you don't talk to me that way."

"I'll talk to you any kind of way I want. You want respect? Then you give it."

Sean tried to defuse the escalating situation and pulled Benita back. "Hey, B—you need to chill out. Man, she don't mean no harm. She's just super hyped about her fighter. It's all good. She's cool."

"Yeah, okay. But she needs to watch her mouth."

Benita was about to respond, but Sean pulled her close to him. "Benita, we're not here to cause any problems. We're just here to speak to Jermaine. Got it?"

Benita calmed down and smiled at Sean. "Yeah, you're right. I'm not trying to cause any problems." She turned back to the big, burly guy and flashed one of her million-dollar smiles. "Sorry. Do you think we can speak to your boss?"

"Yeah, whatever. Wait here." The bouncer closed the door, leaving them outside.

"You know what? These fools will really try you. You guys seeing this place?" Benita commented as she tapped on the earpiece linked back to Evan and Luciana, who were currently waiting for them in a van about half a block away.

"Yeah, what a great view," Luciana drawled.

"Well, you just make sure you look at everything once we get inside," Benita said.

"Copy that, B," Evan promised.

Sean looked at her, and for the first time, he realized just how beautiful she was. He had seen and experienced her tough side, but he was shocked to see a totally different side now.

"What? Why are you looking at me like that?"

"Nothing. Just seeing how you can go from zero to a hundred like at a drop of a dime."

"Well, it's like that sometimes. You gotta be ready to move and pivot for what life throws at you."

"If you say so, Benita. I, for one, don't think that one has to change that much."

"Well, no one asked for your opinion, did they, Sean?"

The bouncer came back and ushered the two of them into the building, then slammed the door once they got inside.

Benita whispered in Sean's ear, "Remember, you need to keep things cool. Our job is to find out where the hell your grandmother is and when the next fight is happening. Understood?"

Sean grinned at her. "You got it, sweetheart. I'm just here to make the intro. I'll let you do all the rest."

As Benita and Sean slowly walked down the corridor, the bouncer pushed them forward. "Keep moving, will ya?"

Benita stared back at the bully. "What's your problem? You seriously need to check yourself. Where the hell are we going, anyway?"

"You see those red double doors? *That's* where you're going."

Benita was surprised by the size of this building. The long hallway had fifty-foot ceilings, and it was a hell of a walk to the huge red double doors. She spotted an electronic button located to the left of the doors and pressed it, causing the doors to automatically open into a gigantic room decked out with flashing lights, a caged boxing ring, and hundreds of spectators. There was even a DJ booth blasting music from the second floor.

Benita was amazed at the setup. "What the hell is going on here? This is crazy."

"Welcome to the Black Hole, Benita. It doesn't get any crazier than this. Speaking of crazy, get ready to meet Jermaine," Sean boasted.

Benita observed a clean-cut, handsome Black man walking toward them. He wore everything black, from his oversized Ray-Ban Wayfarer sunglasses to his black New York Yankees baseball cap to his black cardigan and plain black T-shirt. He was even wearing black baggy Givenchy jeans. But what made Benita smile back at him was when he flashed the most beautiful white pearly teeth that she had ever seen. Two large men walked behind him.

"Sean, my man, how's it going? Glad to see you again. Hope things are going well with you. You must be the beautiful lady that Sean told me I had to meet. I'm Jermaine, one of the partners at this here establishment."

"Yeah, this is Benita Jackson. She reps my brother, Doug. She insisted on meeting the owner behind the club before agreeing to have him fight for you."

Jermaine chuckled at Sean. "Look at you, Sean, trying to broker a deal. I like it. I really like it. I can see big plans in your future." He turned around and smiled at Benita. "And you are one fine, gorgeous lady."

"Thank you," she replied.

Jermaine grabbed Benita's hand and pulled her close to him as he continued to smile at the agent. "So, you in the managing game? Well, you better work it, baby. Because I hear your boy is a local legend. In fact, I know for sure that peeps in the streets know who Douglas Gordon Gibson is and that he has the skills to become a real champion. I'm just happy that he decided to fight for me."

Benita placed her hand on Jermaine's chest and stepped back from him. She didn't like the fact that he was getting too close to her. "That's why I'm here to discuss some terms," she calmly answered.

Jermaine snickered. "Oh, I love your style, my love. Love your style. Of course, we can discuss some terms. But it's going to be hard the more that I look at you. You're the type of woman where men can just get carried away."

"Jermaine, can I speak to you for a minute? Privately?"

Jermaine agreed to Sean's request, and the two men stepped out of earshot from Benita. Of course, this didn't make her happy, and she tapped on a tiny microphone hidden on her crossbody bag.

"Jermaine, I need to know where my grandmother is," Sean yapped.

Jermaine's smile turned into a scowl. "Your grandmother is where she's supposed to be. Now, once you get your brother to fight on your behalf, then you'll see your grandmother. You feel me?"

Sean now had a look of desperation on his face. "Jermaine, can I see her? Maybe talk to her?"

"Sean, you need to chill out and fall back for a minute. You heard what I said, right? All will work out the way it's supposed to if you do your part. I'm not going to tell you again."

Sean balled up his fists by his side and was about to hit Jermaine, but Benita walked over to the two men. "So, Jermaine, how about we set up some ground rules. You ready to talk business?"

Without missing a beat, Jermaine turned to face her. "Damn, you are fine as hell. I bet you can make the toughest man weep. Of course. Let's do it, Queen."

"Okay. I'm ready when you are," she seductively answered.

Sean pressed his lips together and remained quiet.

"Why don't you follow me to my office, and we can get some things straight. 'Cause fight night is upon us, and I want to make sure that we give you all the information you need."

"Sounds good to me. Lead the way," Benita said.

"Sean, you got the right one here. Listen, why don't you hang out here for a bit because your girl here and I got business to conduct. You did your part; now let me do mine."

"Nah, I think that I should be there if you're talking about my brother," Sean pleaded to the well-cut gangster.

"No, Sean. It's okay. I'll fill you in on how the meeting goes. Don't worry. I got things covered."

"Yes, baby girl. You *definitely* got things covered. You ready? 'Cause I'm sure as hell ready to see what kind of negotiating skills you got going on." Jermaine rubbed his chin as he gave Benita a heated gaze.

Benita turned to Sean and squeezed his hand. "I got this, boo. You make yourself comfortable. It shouldn't take long to solidify the deal."

Sean nodded his head in agreement. "Hit me up if you need my help."

"Ah, ain't that sweet. Damn, Sean, I think you got a crush on this lady. No worries, though. I won't steal her from you. Okay, let's go talk business. Now, follow me, please."

Concerned, Sean watched Benita walk off with Jermaine.

Chapter 36

Benita finally realized that a part of her job as an agent was to be a chameleon and give people what they wanted. After meeting with Jermaine, all she wanted to do was to wash away all of his sleaziness. Between dealing with him and Sean, she'd had enough of these slicksters. Jermaine had escorted her into his office, where he spent at least thirty minutes talking about himself. She finally had him focus on the fight, and that's when everything changed. He was no longer the flirty Casanova. He quickly turned into a crafty businessman. "So, Benita, you want to discuss what's in it for you and your boy, Doug? Well, I'm here to tell you that you just need for him to show up to the fight."

"Oh, he'll do just that, but I need to know what's in it for him?"

"Now, you know exactly what's in it for him. He fights; his grandmother lives."

"Speaking of his grandmother, will she be at the fight? I mean, we can do an even exchange."

"Not so fast, sis. I generally don't mix business with pleasure."

Benita was surprised by his comment. "What are you saying right now? What pleasure?"

Jermaine leaned in close to her and whispered in her ear. "You see, I would hate to see Doug's grandmother see her grandson get beat to a pulp because, unfortunately, these fights are quite grueling."

"Ah, and that's your pleasure?"

"See, not only are you a beauty, but you are also a smart one too."

"Well, I was hoping that we could discuss a wager. Double or nothing. My guy beats the shit out of your guy. And you let his grandmother bounce before the second fight."

"Oh no, ma'am. You mean *guys*. He will need to commit to *four* fights. That's the minimum."

Benita leaned over the desk and smiled back at Jermaine. "Fine, then, for every fight he wins, you'll owe me twenty-five grand."

Jermaine flashed his beautiful smile and crossed his arms. "Ah, so, you want in on a real game, huh?"

"Jermaine, I want in."

"You want in? Care to elaborate?"

"Yeah. If Doug does what I think he's going to do, then I want to become a member of your exclusive club. See? I have more than one fighter to bring to the table."

"Oh, I understand. Well, that just might be arranged. I need to speak to my partners first, but I'm sure that won't be a problem."

"Good. And I still want the grandmother at the fight. Even if you keep her somewhere close. We want her back. Safe and sound."

Jermaine rubbed his chin and went into deep thought. "Sure, why the hell not? I mean, it's not like we'll need her after this fight. I tell you what. Let me check my schedule to see when the next fight is happening."

"Let's hope that it's sooner than later because my fighter is getting antsy."

As Jermaine pulled out his laptop and began reviewing his schedule, Benita stood up and started looking around the beautifully decorated room filled with walls and walls of books. She adjusted her glasses to make sure that Evan and Luciana got a full view of the room. "You know what I don't understand?"

"What's that, sweetheart?"

"You have this incredible office space, but the outside is surrounded by nothing but vacant lots and dilapidated buildings. What gives?"

Jermaine sat back in his chair and smiled at the gorgeous woman. "Because I prefer to keep the bad elements away from my businesses. No one needs to know what I have. So, I let them keep thinking that there is nothing here but an empty, run-down building. I don't have to stay awake at night worrying about someone taking my shit."

"I'm assuming that you have boxing clubs all over New Jersey?"

Jermaine walked over to Benita, who had picked up the book *Think and Grow Rich*. He stood so close that she could smell his cologne. She took a whiff of it and found herself becoming a bit aroused. She took a step back and faced him while she was holding the book. "Is this the original?"

Jermaine gently took the book out of her hands and flipped through it. "Yup. I picked it up at a garage sale for two bucks. *Think and Grow Rich,* written by Napoleon Hill in 1937. When I first read this book, I didn't realize how much it would change my life. It helped me become the man I am today. He was a genius when it came to personal development and self-improvement of one's self."

Benita took the book back from him and smiled. "Quite inspiring. I like it."

She turned away from him and placed the book back into its rightful place, but she then slipped a small microphone under the shelf just as Jermaine turned to walk back to his seat.

"So, you see? I learned to think bigger and better. I have multiple fight clubs happening statewide. And on any given day, I got people lined up to see some of the greatest fighters in all of the tristate area."

"Huh. But why do you need to force fighters to be a part of your fight club then?"

"Oh, I see where you're going with this. You see your boy out there? Well, he owes me a lot of money, and it seems the only way for him to repay his debt is to have his brother fight on his behalf. And I'm not the one who will say no to a good-ass fighter. So Doug is precisely who we need as a part of the roster."

Benita bit her lip and nodded in agreement. "You can't blame me for asking."

"Never. Never blame you. Now, let's talk about you wanting to join my membership."

Benita sat down in front of Jermaine and listened to him discuss how she could join his club. She felt she made serious headway with the sociopath and thought about the next steps to get Doug on the books to fight. She wanted to talk to her father, who could help her figure out how she could remain focused on the case while working with him to see her family. She realized that she needed to see them now more than ever. Unfortunately, she would need to debrief Agent Cole and her team while still dealing with Miguel.

Benita was exhausted after dealing with Jermaine and how she had to play nice to gain access to the next fight night. When she left his office, Benita and Sean exited the building and walked toward the van where Evan and Luciana were parked.

"So, how did it go? Did he tell you when the fight was going to happen?"

Benita was annoyed at the very sight of this two-bit criminal, but she kept her cool. "Yeah. It's happening in two days."

"Two days? Wow. Okay. That's good, no?"

Benita and Sean finally made it to the vehicle. Evan jumped out, leaving Luciana looking at the feed from the camera that Benita had placed under the bookshelf facing Jermaine's desk.

"Man, I thought that meeting would never end," Evan said to Benita.

"You? All I wanted to do was to get the information and get out of there, but he loves to talk."

"I see he's serious about his business and his ladies," Luciana yelled from inside the van.

"A real live ladies' man. I'm so glad that I'm out of there."

"So, whatchu need for me to do? I mean, if you want, I can call A-Roc. Then we can head over there," Sean chimed into the conversation.

"No, Sean. You got us to the person we needed to get to. You did good," Benita replied.

Just as she finished her comment, the agent's phone buzzed. She received a text from her father. Hey, B. On my way to Grady's. Can you meet me? She quickly replied. Yeah. Give me twenty minutes.

"Hey, guys. I need to meet my father. Do you mind taking Sean back to the Black Creek Hills? I won't be too long. Just need to get a little advice. You know what I'm saying?"

"Of course, Benita. Come on, Gibson. Let's roll." Evan and Sean jumped into the van and headed back to the farm while Benita went over to Grady's gym to meet Leroy. She hated how she had to control her temper, but her father had told her that the key to being a great agent was always to keep her emotions in check. All she wanted to do was to end this case so that she could see her family.

Benita drove to the parking lot near Grady's Gym while waiting for her father to arrive. She was still very emotional after leaving her meeting with Jermaine because she had to hide just how much disdain she felt for him and his underground fight club. But she kept her focus and hid her true feelings. She was learning to play the game when it came to dealing with her mark. She smiled, nodded her head in agreement, played humble, and remained mysterious. Of course, that had been hard for her since she had always been transparent when it came to her being so vocal. She never used to hide her true feelings, but now, she saw the sense of urgency to do so if she wanted to see her family.

What concerned her most was Miguel. He knew just what she was thinking when she was thinking it, which had always bothered her. And now, tension was building up between them, and she began pulling away. However, he made sure that he was not going to let her off the hook so quickly. She was working hard not to crack under pressure, but it was becoming more difficult by the minute every time he started pushing her buttons.

She refused to let her lover-boss get to her. She really didn't want to be bothered by him. No way was she going to let him see her feeling so vulnerable. After their big blowup when he first assigned her to Agent Cole, Benita sensed that their relationship had changed. It was like she saw another side of him that she didn't like. He was vindictive because he perceived her actions to be nothing but careless. But now, it was clear that if Miguel didn't get his way, he would show her who the *real* boss was.

Placing her head on the steering wheel, she thought about what she needed to do to keep Miguel from becoming suspicious. It was essential to create some space between them, and thank goodness she could use the current case. What concerned her was that he wanted to control her every move, which didn't sit too well with her. Once this case was over, she would see if she could permanently work on Agent Cole's team. That would at least provide her with another way to separate from Miguel.

What was sad for her was how she couldn't be honest with Evan and Luciana. Her father warned her that she couldn't trust anyone she worked with. No matter how difficult it would be to remain quiet, she needed to do this because, in the end, any one of them would throw her under the bus if push came to shove. Her fears were creeping up inside of her, and now, she was becoming overwhelmed. Perhaps she would give Agent DeVreau a visit to help ease her mind. In the end, she needed to figure out a way to deal with her feelings instead of keeping them all bottled up inside.

Someone suddenly knocked on her window, and when she turned around, there stood a handsome, middle-aged man smiling down at her. "Hey, pretty girl. You waiting long?"

"Dad, where have you been? It's not like you to be late."

"Sorry. Traffic from Brooklyn was a beast. Come on out of the car, young lady, and let's take a walk."

She gathered her belongings and did as she was told. She gave him a half smile as she locked the door, and they started walking. Exhausted, Benita remained quiet for a part of their walk until Leroy broke the silence. "So, how did the meeting go?"

"I think it went as well as could be expected. Thanks for the advice. I remained cool, calm, and collected. I got the information that I needed from the suspect. And I didn't flinch even once."

"Good job, Benita. I'm sure you did the right thing."

"I don't know if I can continue to do this . . . always having to act like someone I'm not. I mean, when I really think about it, I have to think quickly on my feet and be ready to pivot at any given time. I thought I could do it, but I just can't pretend that I'm okay with not being around my family. They were my rock and pushed me to be the best I can be. And now, since I don't have them in my corner, I have to rely on myself to get the job done. All I want to do is disappear so that no one would ever find us."

Leroy felt bad for his daughter, who was struggling in her new reality. He was shocked when he found out that the DTCU was watching her but felt more at ease when he thought she was taking on a cause that fit into her ultimate dream of working in law enforcement. Never in a million years would she have ever agreed to walk away from her brother and Grams.

Unfortunately, she had made the decision that she now regretted. Leroy had long let go of the guilt he felt with every time he worked undercover and was responsible for sending mostly brown and Black men to jail. There were times when his decisions had left him empty, but he rationalized that what he was doing was for the greater good. But after being in the organization for so long, he knew better. He was a step above the bad guys and learned to walk in their shoes to get what he needed to be accomplished.

He didn't want that for his daughter. He may not control how deep she will be in the DTCU, but he could at least provide the support she desperately needed. He knew that she could definitely make a difference, but at what cost?

"Benita, honey, I know what it feels like to be confused by this job. And I know how hard it is for you to take a step back and allow others to control your every move. But I also know that you will need to dig deep down in your soul to get past these feelings. You're my daughter, and I've seen you defy every odd. You grew up to become one of the most resilient women I know. You competed in some of the toughest tournaments and won against other champions. You took down one of the worst criminals in Brooklyn. You can't tell me that you're not skilled up and ready for battle. You are an anomaly, and I know that, in the end, you will see that what you do at this organization will have a huge impact on others around you."

The loving father placed his arm around Benita's shoulders as they walked down the street. He had always had a special place in his heart for Benita, but now his love for her was so overwhelming that it hurt. He didn't want to see her give up because he knew it was a dangerous game she was playing.

It was his job to convince her to learn how to play the game while finding a way to live with her decisions.

"Dad, do you think that I will ever have a normal life?"

He cocked his bald head to the side and inquisitively looked down at her. "Define 'normal.'"

"You know what I mean. These ups and downs can drive anyone crazy. I had a dose of reality when I saw how Doug handled the disappearance of his grandmother. What would happen if I don't find her? I don't know what I'll do."

"But here's the thing, Benita. You can spend time thinking about all of the *what-ifs*, or you can think about how you need to close this case and save the woman's life. You are a true warrior, Princess. Let's not lose focus on that."

"I never thought about it that way," Benita confessed.

"Benita, you didn't make the biggest mistake of your life joining the DTCU. But now, you have to pivot and start keeping a low profile and staying under the radar. But once you plan a life outside the system, you can have anything you want. The world needs Benita Renee Jenkins."

Benita thought long and hard about her father's words of encouragement, and at that moment, she realized that she did have a lot to offer the world and wasn't going to lose hope. "Thank you,

Sensei Leroy. I guess I just needed some kind of confirmation."

"Well, you know you got me to lean on. Listen, let's talk about how we're going to get you and your family together again."

Benita smiled at him with much admiration in her eyes. "We really doing this? I mean, we're really going to make this happen?"

"Yes, my love. It's already in the works. I spoke to your grandmother, and she understands that it will require complete secrecy on her part. She's anxious to see her granddaughter again."

"Oh, I can't wait to see that sweet face of hers. When is it going to happen?"

Leroy cocked his head to the side. "The most important thing for you to do right now is to act like nothing is wrong. You need to control your emotions and not let anyone know your plans. Make no mistake, these people at the DTCU are like sharks and can smell blood. You may think that they have your back, but sure as the day is long, they will throw you under the bus."

Benita remained silent as she listened to her father's advice.

"Do you hear what I'm saying, Benita?"

"Yes, sir. I hear you loud and clear."

"Good. Because if you're going to get what you want, you need to listen 100 percent of the time. No getting caught up in the moment and letting anything slip. It's time for you to do your job and keep your distance. Remember, these people are always watching—every last one of them. Now that we've gotten that out of the way, let's go through our next steps."

Leroy and Benita continued talking as they made it down to Main Street, where a few shops were still open. As he mentioned that Wes would be competing in his first jujitsu match held in Connecticut in four days, suddenly, Benita felt a sense of panic when she heard the date. This was the day after Doug's fight. The joy she felt quickly turned to anxiety.

"Dad, Doug's fight is the night before Wes's match. We have a lot riding on this fight to find Doug's grandmother and shut down the boxing rings, but what if things don't go as planned? How am I going to meet you in Connecticut? I mean, it's almost impossible for me to commit to this day."

"Benita, relax. One thing at a time, my dear. First, you need to focus on closing the case so that you'll be able to use the next day as a much-needed break. All agents are told to use postcase periods as downtime. Second, I know you'll do everything in your power to close this case. You got a lot riding on this. I have every faith in you that you will be able to make this happen. If not this time—"

"No, Dad. I am *definitely* going to make sure that I see my family. No *ifs* about it. Even if it's only for a few minutes, I need to be with them."

She started crying, and Leroy pulled his daughter close to him. "Don't worry, Benita. I promise you will see them soon. Just hold things together for a little bit longer. I just need for you to be ready to roll when it's time."

Benita took a deep breath after her father helped calm her down. Now was *not* the time for her to have a total breakdown. She would also think about how she could devise a plan to step away from the group. As they continued discussing their next steps, a black SUV watched them from across the street. Looking through binoculars, Miguel watched the father-daughter duo. He had promised himself to give Benita some space, but he needed to know what she was up to. His mind eased once he saw her with her father. He took a deep breath and pulled out, leaving Leroy and Benita unaware of him watching them.

Chapter 37

Sean paced back and forth outside of the bungalow he was staying at for the past few days. Benita had texted him earlier, letting him know they would be leaving shortly to go to the fight. He was happy that things were finally happening because he was tired of being cooped up at the farmhouse without seeing anyone but a few agents assigned to guard him. He was past being antsy. When he asked Benita if Doug was going to join them, she told him yes. He wasn't sure how things would go down since the last time they saw each other, a huge fight broke out.

He couldn't help but be hurt by the fact that his younger sibling had stopped texting him back. However, at least he knew that his brother was still on track to fight later that evening. He thought about a million and one ways that he would make things up to Doug, and once he was given a chance, he would make him understand he was sorry for putting Doug and their grandmother in this terrible situation. Looking down at his phone, he saw no messages or calls. *Damn it. Where are you guys?*

Finally, two black SUVs drove up in front of the circled entrance, and Benita, dressed in a royal blue leather jumpsuit that hugged every curve of her muscular figure and wearing a burgundy bob, got out of the second vehicle. She opened the back door on the passenger side and looked over at Sean.

"It's about time. I've been waiting for thirty minutes," Sean whined.

"Well, good to see you too, Sean. Okay, let's go," she said sarcastically.

Just as Sean was making his way over to Benita, Doug jumped out of the other car and ran directly at Sean. He punched him in the face, and Sean fell to the ground. He grabbed his face as anger took over him. Sean quickly got to his feet and lunged at Doug, knocking him down. The two of them began to roll on the ground, but Benita and one of the agents pulled them apart. "Doug, stop it! What's wrong with you two?"

Doug jerked his arm away from Benita and looked at his no-good sibling. "That's for putting our family in danger, you son of a bitch."

"Good to see you too, bro. You got a helluva punch. I'm sure you won't have any problem taking out those dudes tonight."

Benita stood between the two brothers. "Okay, I'm going to say this once. It's going to be a long night, and I don't want to worry about the two of you breaking each other's skulls before we even get to the fight club. I'm telling you right now, both of you need to get your heads straight. Whatever bad feelings you may have for each other needs to be squashed—like *now*."

Sean watched as Doug turned his back on him. "I don't have problems with my brother. I'm actually happy to see him."

Doug turned around to face his brother and gave him a blank stare. "Of course you are. I mean, it's not like you gotta go into the ring and fight for your life."

"Well, I've got a lot to lose too. Trust me."

Doug threw his hands in the air in disgust. "Wow. Trust you? I mean, there is *no* trust. You're a fucking loser. We may never see Nana again."

Benita watched as the two brothers continued to hurl insults at each other. Finally, she had had enough. "Listen, shut up—both of you. Now. I'm sick of this bullshit. I think we all know what has transpired over the past couple of weeks, and it's time for us to all focus so that we can end this shit tonight. Doug, get back in the SUV, and, Sean, you ride with the nice agent here. Let's go."

Benita pulled Doug back to the second car while Sean entered the first. He shook his head, hating the fact that this woman had so much control over them. After getting situated, the SUVs headed to the undisclosed location twenty minutes outside of Perth Amboy.

Benita looked over at Doug as he stared out the window. "You okay?"

"Oh, I'm just peachy."

Benita adjusted her eyewear and bit her lip, thinking about what she could say to ease his anger. "You know, you're going to be fine, right?"

Doug glanced over at Benita and shook his head. "I don't know about that. I don't think I'm going to be fine until I see my grandmother again."

Placing her hand on Doug's arm, she took a deep breath. "You'll see her. I promise. Now, why don't you rest up? We've got some time before we arrive."

Doug made himself comfortable, closed his eyes, and without missing a beat, he fell fast asleep.

Benita pulled out her phone and called Evan. "Hey, you guys on your way?"

"Yeah. How far out are you?"

Benita looked over at Doug as she continued her conversation. "We're a few minutes behind. Had a situation between the brothers."

"Well, I told you to send Sean with me. I knew there might be trouble."

"Things are fine. I thought it was important that they hashed out their temper tantrums and got their minds ready for the fight tonight. Is Luciana with you?"

"Yeah, I'm here. I can't wait to play our roles. It's going to be fun," she chuckled.

"Yeah, real fun. Two more of your fighters. Seriously, Benita? This is the *best* you could come up with?"

Benita smiled and smoothly commented, "Listen, I think it's cool to have two of the prettiest fighters out there. Love how you are Pretty Ricky and Bombshell Brenda. You know Jermaine is all about looks. I need you to play the roles you have been given."

"You don't have to worry about anything, Benita. We got this. See you in a few," Luciana said.

Benita hung up with her colleagues and sent a few back-and-forth text messages to Agent Cole, who worked with Miguel on making sure the tactical team was getting in place. Unfortunately, they had to be on standby when Jermaine finally sent the address to the undisclosed location. She hadn't gotten confirmation about Elsie Gibson, but she was confident that he would make sure she was there. As soon as they got word from Huey, they would make their move. But in the meantime, she relaxed her eyes and quietly meditated to calm her anxieties.

***

Jermaine tapped his fingers against his desk as he waited for A-Roc to answer his phone.

"Hello?"

"It's Jermaine. Where you been?"

"You know, I always got business to attend to. What's up? We set for tonight?"

"Yeah. Listen, I need for you to bring the Gibson lady to the fight."

"Hell no," A-Roc snarled.

"Look, I figure when he sees her and knows she's alive and kicking, it will incentivize him to do his best. Plus, I need for him to be mentally prepared to fight. Because, baby boy, I got a big surprise for him," Jermaine chuckled.

"I hear whatchu saying, but I can't let anybody know that we're involved in a kidnapping."

"Nigga, it's all good. Just keep her at a distance. You can even have two of your boys keep her in a van outside the club. Snap a few photos to show Doug we mean business. And then—"

"And then we'll make sure that I'll make sure that I tie up loose ends after the fight," A-Roc interrupted.

"And then, we'll handle accordingly. Man, you gotta think big picture. This guy can make us a lot of money. We don't kill the lady if we don't have to. All we need to do is to let him and his brother know that we can get to them at any time. That's all we need to do. You feel me?"

After a brief silence, A-Roc breathed heavily in the phone. "Fine. We'll do it your way, but I'm telling you, I'm not going to jail for any of these bitches. Understand me?"

Jermaine chuckled at A-Roc's comment because he knew that his partner didn't mince words. His gangbanging partner always resorted to violence, while he, on the other hand, focused on making things happen the least violent way. That's why he was highly successful in all of his business ventures, even if most of them were illegal.

"Excellent. This is gonna be one helluva of a night, my friend. If everything I've heard about Doug Gibson is true, then he is a sure bet. At least on the first three. But the last one? Well, that's when my secret weapon will come in and whoop his little monkey ass. No way he gonna win against that guy."

"Just who you got planned for the last fight?"

"Come on, A-Roc. You know it's gonna be my ace in the hole. Iron Mike, baby. I'm going all the way in."

"Oh snap. That dude is no joke. I like your plan, Jermaine."

"It's all about the paper. Oh, and by the way, make sure you got Grandma cleaned up. I want her to look her best for her grandson. Doug needs to know that she has been taken care of. The last thing we need for him to see is her looking like some tortured soul."

"Man, we've been taking care of her. No bumps or bruises. At least not yet. But I hear you. Okay, I'll hit you up when I get to the club."

Jermaine hung up the phone and sent a text to Benita letting her know that Doug's grandmother would indeed be at the fight. He made it clear to her that he kept his end of the bargain, and now it was up to Doug to do the same. Then he pulled out a cigar from his desk and lit it. Leaning back in his chair, he smiled when he thought about tonight's fights. He always had a packed house and bankable fighters, but tonight felt different. After taking a long puff of his cigar, he closed his eyes, a ritual that he had done a million times. He took one more puff and headed to his home, where he would rest up for another exciting night at the Black Hole.

An hour and a half later, Benita and her team pulled inside an empty warehouse where the DTCU tactical team surrounded her. Evan and Luciana were already there waiting for them, and they were talking to Huey, who had set up shop in the right corner of the building. Agent Cole and Miguel were also there speaking to several of the agents dressed in all black.

After exiting the vehicles, Benita escorted Doug and Sean over to her bosses.

"I see you finally made it here in one piece," Agent Cole commented. "Doug, how you holding up?"

"I'm good, sir. Ready for this night to be over."

"And it will. Sean? You good?"

Sean, surprised by the agent's concern, especially after their first meeting, shoved his hands in his pockets and nodded. "Yes. Yes, sir. I'm good."

"Great. Now that everyone is fine, why don't you fellas go over there with Huey and the rest of the team while I speak to Agent Jenkins for a minute?"

Doug and Sean made their way over to the other agents while looking back at Benita.

"Agent Jenkins, now, I don't have to tell you what will happen if this fails, do I?"

"No, sir. You don't. I've spoken to the team, and they are ready. I'm ready."

"I can see you are. Nice outfit, by the way. I'm sure you will fit right in. Make sure you stay in contact because we need to know where you are at all times. Isn't that right, Perkins?"

Miguel, who had remained very quiet, finally broke his silence. "Absolutely, Cole. We want to make sure that everything goes smoothly. Benita, Huey has a few gadgets that he wants to share with you. He's updated the glasses with a highly sophisticated camera along with a microphone chip that you can attach to your outfit."

"Okay. Will do. And the tactical team? Are they ready to move when necessary?"

"Absolutely. Now that we have the location, we'll make sure the place is surrounded," Agent Cole answered.

Benita excused herself and headed over to her team while Agent Cole and Miguel continued devising their plans to lock down the site. Without looking at his friend, Agent Cole commented to Miguel. "Well, I can say one thing, Perkins. If you were ever interested in this woman, I could see why."

"Willard, why don't we focus on our job and leave my social life out of it?"

Agent Cole laughed as they moved over to the tactical team.

Moments later, Benita adjusted her new eyeglasses, which contained a tiny camera linked to Huey's computer. She also tested out a hidden microphone strategically placed on the back of her collar. Then, finally, she tapped on her earpiece to get a response from Huey.

"Testing. Testing. Huey, can you hear me?"

"Loud and clear, Benita," he responded. "Okay, now, turn toward the entrance so that I can see the entire room."

Benita turned around while Huey adjusted the feed on his computer. "Okay. How's that?"

"This is good. And the good thing about this camera? There is a Varifocal technology in the glass so that we can see at night and other people. You're good to go here."

Benita adjusted her earpiece, making sure that it was in place. "All right. I think I'm ready. Are we set with the password?"

Huey scanned through his computer and found the password. "Yup. I've created a program that allows all of our agents going in with the crowd to be sent the password. Just show it, and you'll be fine. Oh, and one last thing." Huey pulled out a box with three weapons made out of plastic and stainless steel. "Okay, so these guns have been specially manufactured *not* to be picked up by metal detectors."

Luciana picked up the gun, which was smaller than a standard handgun. "Cute, but, Huey, what are we supposed to do with them? They're not even large enough to get off one shot, let alone multiple rounds."

Huey smiled back at her. "Well, actually, these are the latest weapons that the DTCU has been developing for the past few years. They don't release bullets. These are powered lasers. One shot, and your suspect is immobilized for a few minutes. Similar to a taser but stronger."

Evan also picked up the gun and examined it. "Well, I'll be damned. There is some serious firepower in this little puppy."

Looking at her gun, Benita pointed in the direction where there were no people in her line of vision. "Just what I always wanted. A baby gun of my own. Huey, you never cease to amaze me."

"I aim to please. But there is only one caveat. Hopefully, the metal detectors are not running on a higher frequency to induce a current in the stainless steel. If this happens, then, well, you may have a problem."

"But, Huey, isn't there a way to block the metal detector if that happens?"

Huey sat back down at his computer at Benita's question and started looking through the schematics. "When you get close to the metal detector, make sure you point your camera in the direction of the bar code. I can quickly analyze the machine to figure out the make and model. If it's a later model, I can tap into the company's system and place a bug on the machine. Either way, you should be able to make it through without getting stopped."

"You see, *that's* what I'm talking about. We have our own MacGyver up in here." Benita rubbed Huey's shoulder. "Now, we just have to wait until it's showtime."

As the brothers stood in silence, Benita noticed Sean trying to start a conversation with Doug, who ignored him. In fact, Doug was becoming more anxious, and that concerned her because she didn't want him to fall apart before his first fight. She walked over to them. "Sean. Doug, how are you two holding up?"

Sean didn't look at Benita and just mumbled that he was okay. "I'll be glad when this shit is over, you know?"

Doug rolled his eyes at his brother and looked at Benita. "I'm fine."

Benita placed her hand on one of Doug's shoulders. "Good, because we need you more than ever to help us end this shit. Once and for all."

Chapter 38

The oversized bouncer pulled out a walkie-talkie and spoke into it. "Yeah, Benita Jackson is here to see Jermaine. And she got an entourage with her."

After a few minutes, a faint, deep voice replied, "Yes. Send her back. Have them walk through the metal detector."

The bouncer turned off his walkie and looked back at Benita, Doug, Sean, Evan, and Luciana. "Follow me."

Just as they began walking down the hallway, Benita tapped on her earpiece and quietly spoke into her microphone. "Okay, you see the detector?"

"Yeah, I see it. Zoom in on the label."

Benita acted like she was fixing her hair as she moved her right hand to the side of the frame. "How's that?"

"Perfect. Now, give me a second to check," Huey said as he typed on his keyboard.

The bouncer turned around when he heard Benita's voice. "Did you say something?"

"Yeah. I said that I'm glad that you have metal detectors. Can't be too safe," she replied.

"We don't need anybody coming up in here and shooting up the spot."

"That's great to hear."

Huey finally reported that the model was one of the later ones. "Okay, I've just overridden the company computer system and deactivated the frequency, so you guys should be all set."

"Let's hope you're right," she mumbled.

They walked through the metal detectors without setting off the alarm. Once they got to the other side, another bouncer checked Luciana's and Benita's bags. Fortunately, they had placed their guns in hidden compartments, and they went unnoticed. After making sure the group was good to go, the bouncer started walking down the hallway. "Okay, follow me. I'll take you to Jermaine."

At the end of the corridor, the bouncer stopped in front of a set of double doors, pressing a red button. Once the doors opened, the group was surprised by the size of the gigantic room.

"Wow. I heard that these illegal fighting rings were off the chain, but this one is better than a traditional fight scene. Everybody living their best life," Huey commented.

Benita looked around, eyeing the entire scene. She had never attended any fights in Atlantic City or Las Vegas, but she had heard that people really got dolled up to attend these events. So she was surprised to see how many of the patrons dressed to impress and were wearing expensive outfits from head to toe. "Unbelievable. These people are seriously treating this like a real event."

"Well, they *are* attending a real live event. Except that many of the fighters may get seriously hurt or die. Make sure you keep your glasses on so that I can capture everyone there," Huey said.

"Yup. Will do, Huey. Signing off."

Benita tapped on her earpiece, turned, and watched Doug, who was staring at the boxers currently in the ring. Horrified by the sight of the bloody fighters, he couldn't help but stare angrily at his brother. "Hope you're happy, Sean. That will be me in a little bit. A bloody mess—just so that you can pay off your debt. I've been training to be a legitimate fighter since high school, and now, I'm about to throw it all away before I even start my career." Sean avoided his brother's gaze, and this pissed Doug off even more. "You ain't got nothing to say?"

"Hey, save your energy for the ring. Pull it together. We have a visitor coming." Benita observed Jermaine walking toward them with two of his bodyguards. Dressed in a black Versace suit with a black and red Sergio Tacchini polo shirt and black Vans, neither Benita nor Luciana could deny how gorgeous he was and how tastefully dressed he was. What was even harder was not to get sucked up in the essence of this man when he flashed his beautiful, white, pearly teeth. Too bad he was engaging in illegal activities because he was the kind of guy most women dreamed of under any other circumstances.

"Damn, Benita. You didn't tell me how fine he was. I mean, papi got it going on," Luciana whispered in her ear.

"Hey, I heard that."

"And I said what I said," Luciana winked at Evan.

Jermaine greeted the group and pulled Benita closer to him. He kissed her on the cheek. "Benita, my love. Glad you made it."

"Thanks for the invitation. As promised, I brought my prizefighter, Doug. Doug, meet Jermaine Thomas. He runs this fight club."

Sean suddenly stepped in front of Doug and stared back at Jermaine. "You don't need to talk to my brother, Jermaine. Where's my grandmother? Is A-Roc bringing her?"

Jermaine chuckled at him. "Look at you, Sean, trying to be a big man. I like it. I really like it. I can see big plans in your future." He turned around and smiled at Luciana. "Now, who is this gorgeous lady?"

"I'm Roxanne—"

"And I'm Kareem," Evan commented.

Benita gave Evan a surprised look and smiled back at Jermaine. "Anyway, these are the other fighters that I mentioned to you earlier. I told you I could deliver the project if you can deliver the paper."

Jermaine grabbed Luciana's hand and pulled her close to him as he continued to smile at Benita. "Benita, you ain't playing around, baby. I mean, here we got a local legend with Doug. Listen, the streets know all about Douglas Gordon Gibson and that he has the skills to become a real champion. I'm just happy that he decided to fight for me. And then, you brought me two other gifts. I feel like I'm in heaven."

Just as Jermaine looked like he was trying to hug Luciana, Evan stepped between them, guarding her with his body.

"You need to fall back, man. Show some respect," Evan ordered.

Jermaine snickered. "Sorry, big man. Didn't mean to offend. You got a serious looker here, and I guess I got carried away. I meant no harm."

"No worries. I can take care of myself. I'm just happy to meet the man who can help raise the stakes," Luciana purred.

"Where's my grandmother?" Doug growled.

Jermaine's smile turned into a scowl. "Your grandmother is where she is supposed to be. Now, once you do your thing, you'll see your grandmother. You feel me?"

Sean now had a look of desperation. "Jermaine, can we see her now?"

"Sean, you need to go sit down and enjoy the fight. You heard what I said. After the fights, *then* you'll see your grandmother. I'm not going to tell you again."

Doug balled up his fists and was about to hit Jermaine, but Benita placed her hand on his wrist, holding him back. "Come on, Jermaine, can't you do something? The brothers just want to see their grandmother."

Without missing a beat, Jermaine took a step closer to her. "You know what, Benita? How can I say no to someone as fine as you? Damn, girl. Look, I kept my end of the bargain. Grandma is here. Even got her a nice outfit to wear. Nothing will happen to her if your boy keeps up his end of the bargain."

"Okay. Thank you," Benita seductively answered him.

Doug pressed his lips together and remained quiet.

"Good. Now that we got that settled, I think it's time to get ready to rumble. You set? 'Cause I'm sure as hell ready to see you in that cage up there kicking some ass."

Benita turned to Doug and squeezed his hand. "You can do this." She kissed him on the cheek.

"Ah, that's so sweet. Damn, I would love to have those lips on me. Doug, you're a lucky man. Now, follow me, please."

Just as Benita was going to leave with them, Jermaine stopped her. "No, sweet cakes. Only Mr. Boxer and me. You all have to stay here."

"Wait, Jermaine, I'm not letting him go anywhere without me," Benita protested.

"Well, unfortunately, that's not going to happen. He's a big boy. He'll be all right."

Benita looked at Doug.

"It's all good, Benita."

"Damn, we ain't gonna kill him before he gets in the ring. Only afterward," Jermaine went from a serious face to a big smile again. "Just playin'. Your guy will be a'ight. Now, if you will please excuse us, we gotta prep for his first fight. JJ, escort them to their assigned seats. I'll be back when it's time for Doug's fight."

Jermaine, Doug, and one of the bouncers disappeared behind heavy black curtains, leaving Benita, Evan, Luciana, and Sean standing on the side of the cage. The bouncer moved people out of their way and showed the group to their seats. The smoke-filled room was extra packed with a mixed crowd of boxing enthusiasts and gangsters watching the brutality of the illegal fights. The group was rowdy and urged the fighters to grab, kick, and beat each other to a pulp without any repercussions.

Benita noticed Sean was looking around the room as if he were searching for someone. "You okay, over there?"

"I don't know. Something doesn't feel right. Where's A-Roc? What if he did something to my grandmother?"

"I'm sure she's fine," Benita replied.

Slouching in the chair, he folded his arms. "You don't know that."

"Well, Sean, we've come this far. And I'm sure that Jermaine is not trying to mess up a good thing. Just sit back and relax for a minute. And look out for A-Roc when he comes in."

Crossing her legs, Benita leaned forward, tapping her earpiece again. "Huey, do you hear me?"

"Yup. I thought that you forgot about me."

"How could I do that? I'm sure you saw us talking to Mr. Smooth earlier."

"That room is bananas. I can't really see anything that's going on. Can you stand up and look around for me?"

Benita adjusted her glasses and stood up to get a better view of the crowd. "Were you able to track down A-Roc yet? We haven't seen him, and he's supposed to be bringing Doug and Sean's grandmother to the fight."

"No, not yet. But I tapped into the surveillance system that covers all of the rooms and hallways throughout the building. Listen, your guys are not playing around. There are over thirty cameras in this place."

"What about outside the building?"

"Right. Looking into those now. This guy Jermaine ain't no joke. He's got things locked up tighter than Fort Knox."

"Well, if anyone can break in, it'll be you. Okay, keep us posted with whatever you find. I cannot wait to bust these guys. I'll hit you in a bit."

Benita leaned back in her chair next to Sean. "Hey, you good?"

"Nah. I'm not. I won't be good until after we get my grandmother back," he mumbled.

"Sean, when I first met you, I saw a complete asshole. But now I see that you care about your family. Have faith, will ya? We've come this far, and I'm not going to let these assholes win." Benita looked up to see Doug finally entering the cage. Suddenly, her body stiffened as she prepared to see the first punch. "Okay, here we go. It's showtime."

DeAndre nervously walked into the room where Mrs. Gibson had been held captive. He had spent a lot of time getting to know her, and now he was sad she was leaving. It was the first time he'd developed a real relationship with someone who cared about what he wanted in life. She was more than a stranger like when he first grabbed her at her car. He viewed her as one of his family members now. He was surprised how much he cared for her, and he wanted nothing more than for her to go home and pick up where her life left off. But he was scared that A-Roc would not keep his word and let her go. He overheard the conversation that his boss and his number two, Snake, had about getting her ready to go to the fight, but he didn't have a good feeling about what the outcome might bring.

"Yo, DeAndre. Here's a few dollars. Go pick up a nice outfit for Ms. Gibson. She gotta look tight for her grandson tonight."

"We're taking her to the fight?"

"Man, you are a smart one, ain't he, Snake? Yeah, we taking her to the fight. Now, go. No time to waste."

"Where am I supposed to get an outfit from?" DeAndre asked his boss.

"Nigga, don't you got female family members at your house? Damn, do I gotta think of everything? Just go to Target or something. They got lots of clothes. Damn."

Just as the young man was walking out of the room, he overheard Snake mentioning that maybe the old lady can wear the dress to her funeral. DeAndre stopped dead in his tracks, turned around, and looked directly at Snake. "What did you say?"

"Nigga, if you don't keep it moving . . ."

"Nah, nah. Why don't you say that again?" DeAndre stated as he became more defiant.

"Hey, DeAndre, Snake is just joking. Right, Snake?" A-Roc jerked his head at DeAndre.

"Yeah, A-Roc. Nigga can't even take a joke."

"Now, De . . . just go pick up that outfit, will ya? We gotta go soon."

DeAndre nodded back at A-Roc and headed out the door. He was so pissed that he ignored Simon, who was calling out to him.

"Hey, De, where you going?"

"I gotta make a run. I'll be back," DeAndre said without turning around.

He headed straight to the nearest Target, where he found a beautiful white and blue dress for Ms. Gibson. Before he purchased the dress, he asked a female shopper about the same build as his captive what size she wore. Once he was satisfied by his fashion choice, he picked up some makeup and other products that she would need to get herself together. He finally headed back to A-Roc's place, thinking about what Sean and Doug must be going through since their grandmother had gone missing. He had promised himself that nothing would happen to Ms. Gibson while he was watching her, and he planned on keeping that promise . . . even if that meant he would take A-Roc out to save her.

He unlocked the door where he found Elsie sitting in the chair with her eyes closed as she meditated to keep herself calm. She opened her eyes to see DeAndre standing with a Target bag in his hand.

"What do you have there, DeAndre?"

DeAndre walked into the room, where he slowly shut the door behind him. "Ms. Gibson, this is for you. You're going to see Doug tonight."

Elsie slowly stood up and faced DeAndre while biting her lip. She hadn't seen her grandson in over a week and was slowly losing hope she would ever see him again. She had been praying for this day, and it had finally come.

"Listen, I've got to be honest with you. I'm not sure what my boss will do after the fight, but I need you to trust me. No matter what happens, I'm going to have your back. I'll be back in about thirty minutes."

"Thank you," she said.

"Okay. Well, I'll be back. Ms. Gibson, I don't want you to worry. Doug's gonna come through for you. And so will I." DeAndre walked out of the room, leaving Elsie to examine what was in the bag. She continued to pray that everything was going to turn out the way it was supposed to.

Benita stood up and made her way through the crowded room to position herself close to the roped-off cage. Security guards were standing directly in front of the cage to keep people at a distance. She stood near the cage and began waving at Doug, trying to get his attention.

Doug was happy when he saw her and pulled out his mouth guard. He took a few sips of water and nodded when Benita mouthed, "You got this. *We* got this."

Doug placed his mouth guard back in and turned toward the other fighter. Unfortunately, this poor sap wasn't prepared for a fight with Doug. Not only was he a scrawny little guy who was wearing red boxer shorts that were two sizes too big, but also, there was no way that he was going to win against a more seasoned and well-trained boxer like Doug. Wearing his black boxing gloves, Doug tapped them together and started bouncing around the cage. With music playing in the background, this was a setup for a well-choreographed dance between an amateur and a champion. He gave Benita one more glance as he prepared to fight against an extremely unmatched opponent.

She watched as Doug pounced all over the skinny guy in the oversized shorts. Clearly, he took out his aggression on the poor guy in the cage. How this little guy ended up in the ring was beyond her, but then again, people would do anything when it came to money. She remembered when she broke up the fight between Doug and his brother. Doug was so filled with rage that he wouldn't stop hitting Sean until he was dead. He was like a pit bull who attached itself to someone's leg, not letting go. If she hadn't pulled Doug off of Sean, his brother would probably be dead right now. More importantly, Doug would be in jail. Her heart went out to Doug because it was clear that he loved his grandmother and hated his brother. It was sad because he only had one sibling, and if anything happened to his grandmother, he would truly be alone.

All she could think about was how Doug was in a cage fighting for the life of his grandmother. She knew that every blow had a bigger meaning. Every win would get him closer to seeing his grandmother again. She prayed that the tactical team would find the woman alive and well, and they could finally bring down this illegal boxing ring. But for now, the only thing one could do was take the emotion out of the situation and stay focused on the task at hand.

She watched as Doug performed crippling body blows to his unsuspecting victim. Finally, the poor guy fell to the canvas and didn't move. The referee called the fight for Doug Gibson by raising his arm in the air. Just like that . . . The first fight was over. The audience gave a lackluster response because it was indeed a mismatch. The second fight would begin soon, and Doug didn't have any time to rest. She looked down at her phone, but still nothing from Miguel. She then looked back at Sean, who was expressionless.

Evan slid over next to him. "Hey, you see A-Roc yet?"

"Nah, he ain't here. I'm beginning to wonder if he's even coming. I mean, this is Jermaine's shit. What if they don't keep their word?"

Evan looked at Sean with compassion. He finally started feeling the pain and anxiety that Sean was exhibiting. "We're gonna find her, Sean. Just hang tight."

Sean nodded in agreement with Evan, and they went back to watching Doug begin his second fight. As soon as the fight started, Doug threw one hard punch, and the second fighter fell backward and hit the mat with a loud thud. The crowd went wild as the referee announced Doug as the winner again.

"Holy shit. Your brother's on fire," Evan said to Sean.

"That's the one thing I never had to worry about concerning my brother. He has always been a fighter. I feel sorry for those guys. He's not going to quit until he gets to the end."

Benita was shocked by how fired up Doug was. He had turned his desperation into aggression, demonstrating his commitment to take down every one of his opponents. When she tried to move closer to the cage, the bouncers blocked her path and ordered her to stay back. "Look, I'm his manager. I need to talk to him."

"I don't give a shit who you are. You need to step back."

"Doug," Benita yelled. "Slow it down. You got two more fights. Don't wear yourself out."

Doug looked over at her and pulled out his mouth guard. "Hey, let her through. She's my manager. Please."

The bouncer reluctantly moved out of the way, letting Benita enter the area around the cage. She placed her fingers through the mesh. Doug bent down to get closer to her. "Is she here yet?"

"No. But the team is all over it. I promise we'll find her."

Frustrated by the news, Doug violently slammed his gloves together. "Damn it. The quicker I finish these four fights, the sooner they'll let her go."

"I know you wanna believe that, but there's no proof that'll happen," Benita replied.

"And no proof they won't."

"Doug, please. You need to slow down the next two fights. Give my team time to do their job."

The boxer gave Benita one more sharp look. "I can't promise you that, Benita. I gotta do what I gotta do to bring my Nana home." He placed his mouth guard back in and started dancing in the cage. Benita let out a sigh and looked at her phone again but still no messages from Miguel. She was about to make her way back to her seat when she saw Sean yelling at a large, burly A-Roc who was now standing next to Jermaine.

"Where's my grandmother, you piece of shit?"

What the hell is he doing? Benita maneuvered her way through the crowd to get to Sean. She hadn't anticipated this kind of confrontation, especially coming from him. She needed to do something—and do something fast. If she didn't, the entire operation could blow up in their faces.

Chapter 39

Sean watched as Benita talked to his brother at the cage. He knew that his brother wasn't speaking to him, but he couldn't help but feel jealous of this stranger who had Doug's ear. He was the one who should be handling things, not Benita. He bit down on his gnarly fingernails and started jiggling his left leg. Looking around the room, he finally spotted A-Roc walking through the door. It was then when Sean decided to confront A-Roc once and for all.

"Hey, where are you going, Sean?"

Sean turned around to face Evan, but he ignored him. He made his way out of the crowded row of seats to get a better look at the room. There was currently a DJ playing rap music from the second floor while many people in the crowd were dancing in their seats and dancing where they stood. This place was more like a party scene than a fight club, and it was time for Sean to shake things up. If anyone was going to find his grandmother, it was going to be him.

He found A-Roc standing next to Jermaine, and he walked up to them. Evan followed after Sean, but he was blocked several times by the crowd.

"A-Roc, can I holla at you for a minute?"

Barely acknowledging Sean, A-Roc half spoke to him. "Whatchu want, nigga?"

"I wanna know where my grandmother is, nigga. *That's* what I want. I kept my end of the bargain, and now, it's your turn."

A-Roc smirked and folded his arms. "You think I'm done with your ass? I don't answer to you. And you damn well don't tell me what the fuck I'm supposed to do. You betta fall back before you get your ass got."

"I'm not going anywhere until you tell me where my grandmother is. Like right now," Sean demanded.

A-Roc turned to Jermaine, who was shocked by the altercation. "Is this fool really stepping to me? Jermaine, you see this shit? This little nigga trying to do something. He wasn't saying that when he decided to get that paper from me and couldn't pay me back. It was all begging and shit to give him more time to pay it back. But you know what? I can respect a man who tries to step to me."

"I'm not playing around, A-Roc. Where the hell is my grandmother?"

Jermaine motioned for his bodyguards to grab Sean. "A-Roc, is this fool crazy or something? I'm sick of this nonsense. Trev, you and Ray take this asshole outside and keep him there until after the fight. I don't need him messing up A-Roc's and my business," Jermaine told the guards.

"*I'm* messing up your business? I'm gonna do more than that if you don't let my grandma go—like right now."

Benita finally made her way over to where the men were standing. Seeing Evan making his way to Sean from the opposite direction, she injected herself into the conversation. "Sean, hey, what the hell's going on?"

Trevor pushed Benita back and grunted. "Yo, you need to step back and mind your own business."

"Listen, man, this *is* my business when it comes to my fighter and his brother. Believe that. Now, I think *you* betta step back."

Evan pushed Trevor and stood next to Benita. "Hey, hey. You don't touch her," he screamed. "Ever."

"Listen, fellas. You ain't gotta take him outside," Benita pleaded.

A-Roc laughed. "Little girl, his brother is killing the competition, and big bro Sean here is making an ass of himself. He lost that right to stay in this here establishment when he came at me the way he did."

"I don't need for you or anybody to speak on my behalf. I'm my own man, and I brought my brother into my shit. A-Roc, we had a deal, and I want you to honor it right now."

"Sean, shut the fuck up. This is not the place for you to demand anything from my partners or me. You will get what you want once your brother finishes the fight. And then, maybe *just* maybe, you will see your precious Nana."

The crowd started screaming when Doug lifted the third fighter and body-slammed him to the ground. For a brief moment, Benita and the rest of them looked on as Doug easily won the third fight. The crowd went wild, and the DJ started pumping up the music as the announcer screamed Doug was the winner again. However, this time, Doug left the cage and went into the crowd.

"What the hell?" Benita's mouth fell open at the speed the fighter showed even with the battles he'd already won. Doug came out of nowhere and punched both bodyguards in the face with several quick jabs, causing them to fall to the floor.

"Now . . ." Doug turned to A-Roc, "where's my Nana?"

"You owe me one more fight," A-Roc replied.

Jermaine pulled out a gun and pointed it directly at Doug, Sean, Benita, Luciana, and Evan, forcing the four to raise their hands. After the two bodyguards stood up, Trevor pulled out his weapon, and Jermaine put his away. Jermaine was no longer the friendly, sophisticated, and charismatic man that Benita first met. His demeanor had changed, and he had turned mean. "Now, do you want my boys to bust a cap in your ass, boxer man? You need to go back in that cage and finish the fourth fight, or your grandmother won't be the only one who ends up dead."

"Jermaine, what the fuck are you doing? Doug, you need to calm down." Benita tried defusing the situation, but Doug ignored her.

"You threatening me? Where's my Nana? Is she here? Benita, we need to find her. I'm not fighting until she's released. *Then* I'll finish up that damn fight," Doug screamed at Jermaine and A-Roc.

"Damn. You know what, Jermaine? I'm tired of this shit. Let's just take them outside and have my guys cap their asses. I'm fucking tired of hearing their mouths."

"Nah, nah, A-Roc. I got too much riding on this little punk ass. What we're going to do is take these idiots to the back room until I get my last fight. Listen, if you just do what you're told, you will see your damn grandmother. Just one more fight, all right? And then I'll make sure that we keep all of these fine folks safe when you're done."

Benita watched as Doug begrudgingly returned to the cage to finish his fourth bout. As he walked away, he looked back to see her, along with the rest of the group, being forced to leave the fight area. Benita thought about her next moves, but she didn't want to get anyone hurt or killed in the crossfire. She looked back at Luciana and Evan, who were preparing for a fight once they left the large crowd. Hopefully, they would eventually find Elsie Gibson. She tapped on her earpiece and watched Doug getting ready for his last fight. "Listen, fellas, you don't have to do this. We just want to make sure that we resolve all of this." Benita felt the butt of a gun in her rib and quickly turned around, facing one of the bodyguards. "Hey, you need to watch where you're pointing that thing."

"I suggest you keep walking before this gun puts a hole in your back," Trevor replied.

Meanwhile, Huey saw the entire event play out as he heard the conversation between Benita and one of the bodyguards. He watched as Benita and the team were escorted out of the arena toward the back of the building. He quickly called Agent Cole and Miguel, who were waiting outside the building, ready to storm the place. "Agent Cole, Benita and the team are in trouble. They're being escorted out of the area by several large men."

Huey began speaking into Benita's ear as she watched Doug enter the cage. And to her surprise, Doug's last opponent was almost twice his size. "Hey, I see things are going a little crazy right now.

I've alerted Agents Cole and Perkins. They are aware that you need assistance."

"Great. I know how we're going to end this tonight," Benita replied as she tried not to alert Trevor that she was talking to Huey.

All of a sudden, Sean became irate when he also saw the monster fighter. "Jermaine? What the hell is going on here? That's Iron Man Mike. You got my brother fighting that crazy fucker?"

Jermaine laughed. "Hey, what can I say? I love a little drama and mystery. Let's see how your brother makes out after getting his ass beat by that muthafucka."

"Man, you've outdone yourself tonight. I was wondering when you were going to unleash the beast," A-Roc chimed in.

Evan whispered in Luciana's ear. "What the fuck is wrong with these dudes? They're straight-up psychopaths."

"Yeah, we got to put an end to this as soon as we get out of this place. We can take them." Luciana cracked her knuckles as she looked over at Benita, who was waiting for the signal to fight.

They walked into a small, luxurious lounge seating area with 55-inch screen HD televisions strategically hung throughout the room, a custom chandelier, ceruse oak paneling with silver leaf detailing, and stately wood floors. The sectional couches encircled a large, customized, rectangular

oak table, and between the televisions on the walls
were a valuable collection of one-of-a-kind sports
memorabilia. Jermaine was the first to sit down
and invited his guests to join him. "Now, why don't
we all get comfortable and enjoy the fight?"

Trevor and two other bodyguards pushed Benita
and her team toward the couches. "Hey, I'm warning you to keep your hands off of me."

Rolling his eyes at the feisty woman, Trevor
snarled back at her, "Well, I suggest you sit your
ass down like the man said."

As the group watched the fight, Benita was
concerned for Doug even though he was pumped
up naturally on adrenalin. This Mike Tyson look-
alike towered over him and could probably put a
hole right through his heart. Suddenly, Benita was
scared for Doug. She turned to Jermaine. "Are
you serious right now? That dude looks like he's
stuffed with steroids. This is not going to be a fair
fight."

"This is the kind of fight that the crowd lives for.
I'm all about giving the fans what they want, and
that's a fight to remember. Nobody gives a fuck
what these dudes are stuffed with. But your baby
boy, Doug, better fight to the death because that
may be the only way he gets out of that ring alive.
You know what, A-Roc? I think you're right. We
just need to get rid of these folks right now because
they're messing with my vibe."

Benita looked over at Evan as she gently tapped her earpiece, making sure that Huey picked up on the cues. "You know what, Jermaine, I don't take well to threats. Where's Elsie Gibson?"

Jermaine, who was now exasperated by listening to Benita, finally relented. He looked over at A-Roc and shook his head. "Fine. It's a damn shame that you just couldn't sit back and look pretty. A-Roc, call your dude who's babysitting the Gibson lady. Bring her up here. I'm tired of hearing this woman's voice right now."

A-Roc frowned when he couldn't get Snake on the phone. The call went straight to voicemail. "Damn, Snake ain't picking up."

"Well, try again. Jeez."

A-Roc redialed Snake's number, but the phone went back to voicemail.

"A-Roc, go check on him."

"Hey, I wanna go with you—" Sean started to stand up, but Jermaine pointed a gun at him.

"Ah, you need to sit your ass down and watch your brother fight. You ain't going anywhere. Don't worry. A-Roc is gonna take care of your grandmother."

Frustrated, A-Roc walked toward the door. "Yeah, I'm out. Something ain't right. Hang tight." He exited the VIP room with one of the other gang members. Angry that he couldn't reach Snake, A-Roc stormed down the hallway and headed outside to the van. Even after texting Snake to meet him at the back of the building, he received no response. He signaled several of his gang members to escort him outside to see what was going on. He knew that something was wrong because Snake never ignored his calls.

DeAndre was sitting in the back of the van with a scared Elsie Gibson while Snake drove around the neighborhood after dropping off A-Roc at the club. He had clear instructions to keep driving until he got the signal from his boss to "take care of the cargo." It was clear that they had no intention of bringing Ms. Gibson inside the building or ever letting her go. Even though she was knocked out with chloroform, she began to stir and heard A-Roc and Snake's conversation. DeAndre placed his hand over her mouth, whispering to her to remain quiet and stay still. "I'll get you out of here. Trust me." DeAndre began to make his way to the front of the van but looked back one more time, placing his finger to his mouth, which signaled Elsie not to move.

"Hey, Snake, why are we driving around? I thought we were supposed to bring her into the building."

Snake sneered at DeAndre without looking back at him. "You need to mind your own business. And that is to make sure the lady stays asleep."

"I know, but this is not what I was told—"

"You were told to make sure she doesn't wake the fuck up. *That's* what you were told. Now, get the hell back and follow directions."

When Snake got to the stoplight, he picked up the phone to see that he had a few missed calls. "Damn it. A-Roc is gonna kill me." He saw the text message letting him know that he should bring the Gibson woman into the building. "Cool. DeAndre, wake up the lady. She's about to make a grand entrance into the club."

Just as Snake was about to pull up to the building, he saw A-Roc being thrown to the ground. "What the—"

Suddenly, DeAndre made his move and began to struggle with Snake. Elsie screamed for help and tried to get out of the van, but there was no door handle. Snake elbowed DeAndre, but DeAndre was committed to getting the better of him. This was one time that he was not going to let up on the oversized gangster. He finally got his arms locked around Snake's neck, causing Snake to press his foot on the gas pedal, making the van ram into another vehicle. Snake finally passed out. DeAndre jumped into the passenger seat and opened the door. Then he opened the rear to the van and reached for Elsie's hand, but she was reluctant to go with him. "Come with me if you want to stay alive," he screamed. "Please, Ms. Gibson. We gotta go."

***

"Snake, where the fuck are you? I've been trying to call you. Check your damn messages."

Just as he pushed the door open, A-Roc and two of his gang members were thrown to the ground by several DTCU agents who held AR-15s to their heads. Other agents placed handcuffs on their wrists. Miguel walked over, bending down, looking directly in A-Roc's face. "Well, if it isn't Abril Roco. Fancy seeing you here. Now, you wanna tell me where Elsie Gibson is?"

"Fuck you. I ain't telling you shit," he snarled.

"Damn, why do people always want to make things harder than they need to be?"

Miguel stepped on A-Roc's back, causing him to scream out in pain. "Now, do you want to try this again?"

"I don't know, man. I've been trying to call my guy, but he's not picking up."

"I don't believe you." Miguel kicked A-Roc in the side. "Where is Ms. Gibson?"

"I'm telling you the truth. I don't know. Snake is supposed to be bringing her inside the building, but he's a no-show."

"You better not be lying to me. Take his ass to the van."

Just as A-Roc was taken away, a van crashed into another car, which startled Miguel and the other agents. Miguel and several members of the tactical team ran toward the vehicle to find Snake passed out in the driver's seat. One of the agents pulled him out of the van as a young man holding on to an elderly woman dragged her across the street. Miguel quickly recognized Elsie Gibson and started running after them. He and another agent pulled out their 9 mm guns and pointed at the assailant.

"Hey! Stop! Federal agents! Stop!"

DeAndre and Elsie hid behind a car in a dead-end street while Elsie was trying to catch her breath. Miguel slowly walked toward them. "Ms. Gibson, I'm Agent Miguel Perkins. We've been looking for you. Your grandsons, Doug and Sean, have been worried about you. Please come out. Show yourself."

Elsie looked over at DeAndre, who was scared to move. She patted him on his face. "It's okay, son. You saved us. They're not going to hurt us. They're here to help. Come on. It's okay."

"We're coming out. Please, don't shoot. This young man saved my life. I don't want anything to happen to him."

Elsie and DeAndre walked out of the dark alley with their hands up in the air. Miguel, who had his gun pointed in their direction, slowly lowered it. "Ms. Gibson, are you all right?"

"Yes. I'm fine. Where are my grandsons?"

***

Benita tapped Sean on his thigh. "Look, everything is going to be okay. Don't worry. We got things covered."

Jermaine laughed long and hard at her words. "Do you really *got things covered?* Woo. What a relief. I was hoping that things could have ended up differently, but you don't know how to play by the rules."

"And just what kind of rules, Jermaine? I mean, you've got what you wanted, but still, you want more."

"That's right, sweetheart. I want it all. But, unfortunately, I got a lot of money riding on your boy losing. No way is he going to last with Iron Mike. Sorry, honey, but business is business."

"Why, you son of a bitch. I'm going to kill you," Sean screamed. Just when he was lunging at Jermaine, he was clipped on the side of his shoulder with a bullet. "Aaaah, my arm."

"What the fuck, man? Are you crazy?" Luciana yelled at Jermaine.

Benita examined Sean's wound to see how serious it was. "Let me see. Let me see. Hold still. Okay. You're going to be okay. It looks like the bullet just grazed you. Jermaine, was that necessary?"

"Ah, it's just a little nick. It's not like he got shot for real. He's all right . . . At least until after the fight."

Benita side-eyed Luciana as she looked down at her purse. "Well, can we at least get something to stop the bleeding?"

Leaning back on his couch, Jermaine said, "What bleeding? Jeez, such a baby. Hey, Trevor, can you please get one of those towels from the bathroom? And also bring a Band-Aid from under the sink as well since that's all he needs."

"You got it, boss." Trevor walked to the bathroom, where he bent down under the sink, looking for the medicine kit.

Benita slowly took off her glasses and opened up her small purse to pull out the eyeglass case. "You know, Jermaine, I am highly disappointed in you right now. I honestly thought you were a man of your word."

"Lady, I'm a businessman who will do whatever it takes to get that paper. But sometimes, as a businessman, you have to eliminate the bullshit to accomplish your goals. And right now, you all have become more trouble than you're worth."

Sean chuckled between the waves of pain. "You ain't shit, Jermaine."

"Tsk tsk tsk. Muthafucka. I'm not the one who sold out his brother," Jermaine taunted him.

Benita fixed her wig to cover her ear. "So, what's taking so long to bring in Mrs. Gibson?"

Trevor came out of the bathroom and threw the towel and a few Band-Aids at Benita and Sean.

"Here. Why don't you shut the fuck up and clean up your ass. We're trying to watch the fight."

"Hmmmm. It is taking awhile, isn't it? Trevor, can you check on them, please? A-Roc's been gone too damn long. Thanks."

Trevor left the room, leaving only Jermaine and the other bouncer to watch over the agents. Benita motioned for Evan and Luciana to get in position to take down the men once she got the signal from Huey. But just when they were going to make their move, Trevor came back inside the room.

"I sent Wally to check on him."

"Good. I guess you didn't want to miss the rest of the fight, huh? Cool. Cool," Jermaine replied.

Benita tapped her earpiece and started speaking to Huey. "Come on. I need something."

"The tactical team gained entrance to the lower level of the building. They're making their way up to the second floor. Need a few minutes. Agent Cole said to hold tight until he gives you the signal," Huey replied.

Benita wiped off the speck of blood from Sean's T-shirt and placed the large Band-Aid on his shoulder. She continued to make eye contact with Evan and Luciana, letting them know that they needed to fall back. "You know it's going to take a bit more time, but I know that Doug can do this. And then everything will be okay, 'cause help is definitely on the way."

Evan had been extremely quiet while watching the bodyguards standing close to him and the ladies. He was preparing himself for the takedown but knew that their next moves depended on timing. Once Benita gave him the greenlight, he would focus on the guard closest to him.

As they watched the fight, Doug was getting banged up in the cage. Things were not going well for him because Iron Man was a beast and extremely dangerous. No matter how many times Doug came for him, his punches bounced off the oversized fighter. After Iron Man gave Doug a devious smile, the monster man lifted Doug, then slammed him to the mat.

"Oh my God, Doug," Benita swore.

Doug slowly tried getting up but slipped in his own blood. He finally stood up, ready to rumble again. However, this time, the man of steel came right at him and rammed his body into the cage.

"Come on, Doug. Come on, Doug," Luciana yelled. "Beat that grizzly bear's ass."

Jermaine looked over at her and flashed one of his pearly smiles. "Whew. Come on with it, girl. Why don't you come over here next to me?"

"No, I think I'm good right here." Luciana never took her eyes from the fight.

"That wasn't a request," he stated as he tapped the space next to him.

Luciana reluctantly stood up and sat next to Jermaine where she was now seated directly across from Benita. She pulled back her long, black hair and twisted it up in a bun. She was also getting ready to take down this guy when she got the go-ahead.

"Damn, you are fine. You know that?" Jermaine whispered in Luciana's ear.

"Yeah, that's what I've been told, papi," Luciana smirked back at him.

"Well, as soon as this fight is over, how about we head over to Baby Ruth's and grab something to eat?"

"I'd like that. I'm always down for a good meal."

Benita tried not to laugh because she knew that Luciana wasn't lying. That girl loved to eat, and no matter what she packed away, she remained the perfect size six. She was happy her female colleague was there because she definitely could hold her own. Benita continued to watch in horror as Doug was taking a major pounding. She prayed that he didn't die in that ring because he was not giving up no matter how many times he was hit.

"Doug, you can do it. Please think about what this means if you lose," Benita yelled.

Doug hit the floor with a thud. And this time, he wasn't moving.

"Oh my God, Doug," Benita screamed. She stood up, intending to head to the door, but Trevor pushed her down again.

"Nope. You stay here," he warned her.

Benita turned around and was about to slap him, but she thought twice.

"Hey, I'm not going to warn you again. You need to let go of her," Evan said.

"Nigga, you need to calm the fuck down," Trevor countered.

"You know what? I'm fucking tired of this shit. I'm about to bounce," Jermaine stated.

Suddenly, Sean jumped over the table and started wildly punching at Jermaine while trying to hit him in the face. Shocked, Jermaine grabbed him by his collar and threw him over the sectional.

"Who the fuck do you think you're messing with? Huh? I'm gonna whup your ass." Then Jermaine began pounding on Sean, causing Benita and the team to spring into action.

"Huey, you better tell me something because we can't wait any longer."

"They are in the arena," he replied.

"Good, because I'm about to kick somebody's ass."

Doug and Iron Man saw Agent Cole and other agents dressed in DTCU gear come into the arena from the corner of his eye. This allowed Doug to throw a few successive punches, finally knocking Iron Man out because he became distracted. Then

Doug quickly ran out of the cage and headed toward Agent Cole.

"Doug, nice. Do you know where Benita and her team were taken?"

He pointed to a set of black curtains. "Jermaine and his goons took them back there. There's a hallway leading to a different part of the building. That's where I was sent to change when I first got here. Have you found my grandmother?"

"Yes. She's here. Agent Perkins is leading the team to get her right now. I want you to stay here with our agents, and I'll let you know when we have her."

"I'm going with you," Doug shouted as it was hard to hear over the unruly crowd.

"Okay, let's go. Doug, stay behind Agents Paul, Cruz, and me. I don't want you to get hurt in case anything goes down."

As the group took off behind the curtain, Agent Cole tapped on his earpiece. "Huey, we're headed to the back of the building. Can you help us out here? We're going in blind."

"Yes, sir. There should be a stairwell at the end of the hallway leading up to the second floor. That's where the private lounges are located. Wait, I see two bodyguards standing at the top of the stairs, protecting the entryway."

"Duly noted. Thanks, Huey. Okay, Doug, I need you to stand back and remain quiet, okay?"

Doug nodded. When Agent Cole and the other two agents made their way to the second floor, Cole shot a gun out of one guard's hand, knocking it to the ground. Just as the other thug was about to point his weapon, Agent Cole yelled out to him, "I wouldn't do that if I were you. That is . . . if you want to live. Now, take me to your bosses—like now."

Benita elbowed Trevor in the throat, followed by a roundhouse kick to the groin. Just as one of the other bodyguards came bursting into the room, Evan grabbed the thug and threw him to the ground, punching him in the face and throat. Luciana had pulled out her gun from her purse and tasered Jermaine on his back, causing him to yell out in pain. Then she pulled Sean to safety as he was about to be trampled by the many kicks and punches Benita and Evan were delivering to the thugs.

"You okay?" she asked Sean, who was shaking off the punches that Jermaine had given him.

"Yeah, I'm fine," he smiled.

"Good, because I think my colleagues need my help."

Luciana sprang into action when another bodyguard came through the door. She quickly removed one of the framed memorabilia on the wall and hit him over the head. Five thugs suddenly appeared in the room in front of Benita, Evan, and Luciana, who were fighting. The agents were in full-fledged combat mode as they threw a succession of punches and kicks, taking out each of the oversized goons. Sean was catching his breath when he saw Jermaine trying to escape the chaos. He tried grabbing Jermaine's leg, but Jermaine kicked him in the face and hurried out of the room.

As Benita observed Jermaine leaving, she saw one of the gang members coming after her. She blocked his punch, then tripped and kicked him in the side for good measure. Just as Benita turned her head toward the door, she saw Sean running out of the room in hot pursuit of Jermaine. "No, Sean. Wait!" She looked over at Evan and Luciana, who had finally taken down the final thugs.

Agent Cole and Doug finally made their way into the VIP lounge just as Benita knocked out the gangster on the floor.

"Agent Jenkins, you guys good?" Cole asked.

"Yes, sir, always up for a good fight. Sean jetted out after Jermaine."

"He did *what?* He's going to get himself hurt. We gotta get him. Where's Nana?" Doug asked.

Agent Cole got a text message from Miguel. "She's fine. Agent Perkins has got her. She's safe. Agent Jenkins, let's go get Sean."

"Yes, sir. Doug, stay here with Agents Green and Rodriguez," Benita said.

"Nope. Like I told Agent Cole, I'm going where you're going. And you can't stop me," he replied.

"Okay, let's go," she said.

Agent Cole pulled out a 9 mm from his back and handed it to Benita. "Thought you might need this."

"This might be the nicest thing you've ever said to me." She turned to Luciana and Evan, who were tying up the criminals. "You guys all right?"

"Yeah, go," Evan said.

Benita, Agent Cole, and Doug hurried down the hallway to find Sean and Jermaine, praying that nobody gets hurt.

Chapter 40

"Huey, tell me something. We need your eyes. Where are Jermaine and Sean headed?" Benita spoke into her microphone.

"Give me a second. There are a million cameras throughout this place. Wait. I see them. Jermaine and two of his bodyguards are headed down two flights of stairs leading to a dead-end street. Sean is right behind them."

Benita turned to Agent Cole and Doug. "Damn it, Sean. Agent Cole, can you contact Agent Perkins? He's gotta stop them before they get away."

As they took off toward the stairwell, they heard several gunshots coming from the first floor, causing Doug to yell out to his brother, "Sean, Sean, you okay?"

With guns drawn, Benita and Agent Cole quickly started shooting when two of Jermaine's bodyguards tried to put holes in them. Benita was first to hit one of them in the stomach, and the other bodyguard was shot in the shoulder by Agent Cole. When he tried to aim and fire again, Cole finished him with a bullet to the heart.

When they finally made it to the bottom of the stairwell, they stepped over the men, tried to open the door, and found it locked. They peeked out the window, where they saw Jermaine holding a gun on Sean. However, Jermaine didn't see the agents because he was facing away from them. Plus, he and Sean were standing about 500 feet from the door.

"Hey, Jermaine's got my brother. How we gonna get to him? The door's locked. I don't want him to die."

"Listen, they're surrounded. He's not going to hurt Sean," Benita promised a scared Doug. She noticed that the door needed a fob key to open it. She looked back at the two gang members and checked their pockets. "Doug, look through that guy's pockets. We need to see if they have a fob key."

Unfortunately, neither man had a key, and Benita quickly tapped on her ear, but her earpiece fell out during the rush to the stairwell. She then pivoted, tapped on her watch, and began yelling into it. "Huey, can you hear me? Need your help right now. Can you do what you do and open this damn door?"

"Benita, it's not like I'm Houdini. I can't just clap my hands and make things happen."

"I know, but you're a genius. I've seen you do some of the most incredible things. Unlocking a door should be a piece of cake."

"Listen, tell Huey to figure out something and do it now before Sean gets himself killed," Agent Cole yelled at Benita.

"Huey, do something, *please*."

"Okay, I'm on to something. I need to see if I can link up the radio frequency identification to open the door."

"Well, hurry up."

While they were trying to get out of the building, they heard Miguel yell at Jermaine to put down his weapon.

Jermaine laughed. "I think you need to think again if I'm going to let this dude go. He's my meal ticket out of here. Maybe you just need to get out of the way. Let us leave. I promise I won't hurt him."

"You know we can't do that, Jermaine." Miguel pointed a gun at him.

Jermaine held Sean close in front of him with the gun to his head. "You know how much money you have caused me to lose, Sean? I mean, you lucky that I need you alive because none of you Gibson people would survive otherwise."

"You're a piece of shit. You know that, right?"

Meanwhile, as Huey was working on unlocking the door, Benita gave Doug a stern look. "Listen, Doug, I need you to stay inside because I can't worry about you getting caught up in the crossfire. Understand?"

"Yeah. Yeah, I got it."

The door clicked, and Benita quietly opened it. She and Agent Cole tiptoed out while Jermaine was still being defiant toward Miguel and the other agents who had guns drawn on him. The two agents hid behind a huge dumpster and got into position to take out Jermaine.

"Jermaine, why don't you make this easy for yourself? Put down your weapon before you get hurt," Benita yelled.

Agent Cole kept his gun steady on him as Benita continued to try to get Jermaine to surrender. "Jermaine, did you hear me? You got nowhere to go. You're surrounded. It's over now. Put down your weapon," she yelled.

"Shoot him," Sean yelled out.

"You know what? Maybe I'll just shoot your ass first. How would you like that, asshole?"

All of a sudden, Doug jetted out of the door and yelled, "You need to let my brother go, you dumb fuck."

Jermaine turned toward Doug, and just when he was about to point the gun at him, Sean struggled to get it but got shot, collapsing onto the ground. Benita leaped into action and quickly kicked Jermaine in the stomach, causing the gun to fall from his hand. When he turned on his side to reach for it, she kicked him in the face and then kicked the gun out of the way.

Agent Cole ran over to Jermaine with his gun drawn. "Don't even think about it, you dumb fuck."

Benita turned and ran over to Doug, who was holding Sean's head in his lap. Tears started streaming down his face. "Sean, I'm sorry, man. You're gonna be all right. Don't you die on me. Please, don't die."

"It's all right, little brother. Tell Nana I'm sorry for everything. I deserve what I got," Sean gasped and started spitting up blood.

"No, Sean. No one deserves any of this. Why? Why did you do it?"

"I suddenly remembered what it means to be a big brother." Sean smiled as blood bubbled from the corner of his mouth.

Miguel called for an ambulance while another agent took off his shirt, handing it to Benita, who quickly pressed it against Sean's stomach. "Doug, help me put the pressure on this wound." Doug nodded as the tears streamed down his face.

Suddenly, Elsie Gibson ran through the crowd of agents who had been holding her back. She was yelling at them to let her pass. "Let go of me. Those are my grandsons over there. Let go of me."

Miguel looked at the agents and told them to let her through.

Doug was shocked to see his grandmother, who immediately fell to the ground to hold on to both of her grandsons. "It's going to be okay, Sean. Nana's here."

"Nana? You're okay?"

She touched her grandson's face and smiled back at him. "Yes, baby, I'm okay."

Both Doug and Elsie wiped away tears as Doug continued to press on Sean's wound. Benita looked up to see the two paramedics rushing over with a stretcher. Once they strapped him on and carried him away, Doug and Elsie quickly followed behind them. Benita headed over to Agent Cole and Miguel as other agents took away a captured Jermaine, who was wobbly from the last kick that Benita had given him. She kept thinking about the bittersweet reunion between the grandmother and grandsons. This made her think about how much she couldn't wait to see her own family.

"Well, Agent Jenkins, you did a helluva job closing this case," Agent Cole said to her.

"Doug almost got himself killed. I told him to stay put, but he didn't listen."

"Just like someone else I know," Miguel commented.

"I know, I deserved that, Agent Perkins." She gave him a smirk.

After a few silent moments, Agent Cole spoke. "Listen, why don't you go home and get some rest, Benita? I'm going to head over to the hospital and check on Sean and his grandmother. Let's talk in the morning."

"Yes, sir," Benita answered as he walked away, leaving Miguel and Benita to talk.

"Benita, I'm sorry for how things went down between us."

Just when she was going to respond, Luciana and Evan made their way over to them as the rest of the tactical team surrounded the building, arresting members of A-Roc's crew and Jermaine's bodyguards. Benita smiled when she saw her colleagues and was glad that they made it out safely. "You guys good?" she asked.

"Yeah, all is well," Evan answered.

"We saw the EMTs taking Sean away. Is he going to be okay?" Luciana questioned.

"I think that he's one lucky man. One thing is for sure . . . The Black Hole is no more."

Benita continued talking to her team as Miguel slipped away without saying goodbye. He wanted her to relish in closing down a major illegal boxing ring in the New Jersey area. And it was more important that she shared this moment with her team instead of him. As much as he wanted to be with her, he knew how to separate being an agent and being her lover. He would leave her a message, letting her how proud he was.

Out of the corner of her eye, Benita watched Miguel walk away, but she couldn't say that she was sorry that he left. All she could think about was how Doug almost got hurt, and that didn't sit too well with her. Amid this tragedy, though, there was still joy. Doug's grandmother was safe. Doug was safe. And hopefully, Sean would come out of this having a second chance at life. She was grateful that the Gibson family was reunited.

And that made what she did all worth it.

Chapter 41

Benita was up early, getting prepared for her busy day. Even after only a few hours of sleep, she felt more energized than she had felt since starting this case. The first thing on her agenda was to stop by the hospital to visit Sean and his family. Even though Sean had been seriously shot, she had spoken to Doug, who let her know that Sean was out of surgery and was going to be okay. Hopefully, when he got out of the hospital, he would rebuild his relationship with his family. This was his second chance to make everything right.

When she arrived at the hospital reception area, she was directed to the waiting room, where she found Doug and Elsie sitting beside each other, holding hands. He looked up when he saw Benita dressed in a beautiful yellow, flowing blouse, jeggings, and platform shoes standing there holding a beautiful bouquet of roses. She was a ray of sunshine, and he couldn't help noticing just how gorgeous she really was. She had been his protector despite how difficult he had been early on, and he would be forever in her debt.

"Hello," Benita smiled.

Standing up, he gave her a big hug. "Benita, what are you doing here?"

"I just wanted to check on you and the family. And to see how Sean was doing."

"Nana, this is Agent Benita Renee Jenkins. She's the one I was telling you about. She was responsible for getting you to safety. If it weren't for her, none of us would be here right now."

Elsie looked at the lovely young lady and smiled back at her. "Oh my goodness. You're an agent? But aren't you the young lady from the gym?"

"Yes, ma'am. That's me. You remembered me?"

"Of course. I never forget a pretty face. I may have even asked Doug who you were."

"Nana, you're embarrassing me," he blushed.

Benita looked at Doug and winked at him. "You did, huh? He never mentioned that to me. Well, I'm so happy that you're okay. Doug was very worried about you."

Elise looked at the bruises across Doug's face and hands. "Oh, my grandson has always worried about me. He's such a good boy. I'm just sorry that he ended up all bruised and busted on that handsome face. Look at you. My beautiful boy fought in those matches for me."

"Nana, I'm fine. You don't have to fuss."

She thought about how blessed she was to be alive. Even though she had been through a traumatic experience, her focus was on her grandsons. She was happy to see Doug comforting her while they waited for Sean to get out of recovery. Thankfully, he would be okay, and they could all start rebuilding the trust that had been destroyed. Her heart was heavy for him, but she was optimistic about the future.

"Any word on Sean?"

"He should be going into recovery any minute now. We got word from the main surgeon that they removed the slug from his stomach," Doug explained.

"Thank goodness for that news."

"Agent Jenkins, may I ask you a question?"

"Yes, ma'am. Anything."

"What's going to happen to the young man named DeAndre? He took care of me, and I don't know if I would have survived another day had it not been for him."

"Unfortunately, DeAndre will be brought up on charges due to his involvement in your kidnapping. But since he helped you escape, I'm sure the district attorney will take that into consideration."

Elsie was shocked when she heard this news. "I am so sorry to hear it." She started crying as Benita continued to explain. With tears streaming down her face, she stood up and headed to the bathroom. "Excuse me. I need to go to the restroom. Thank you again, Agent Jenkins, for everything."

"You're so welcome," Benita said.

Just after Elsie stepped away, Benita turned to Doug. She was having a hard time holding things together because she felt the grief Mrs. Gibson was feeling. Suddenly, she became so overwhelmed with grief that she knew it was time for her to leave. "Doug, I have to go. Please say goodbye to your grandmother for me."

Not wanting her to leave, he pulled her close to him and gave her a big hug. "Thank you. There's so much I want to say to you right now, but I just can't find the words."

Benita gently laid her head on his shoulder and held on to him for what seemed like an eternity. Once they separated, she kissed him on the cheek. "Goodbye, Doug. Take care of yourself and your family."

She barely made it out of the hospital to her car before she broke down into tears. After crying for what seemed like hours, she pulled out the computer and thumb drive her father had left at her apartment building. She put in the thumb drive and read an encrypted email containing all of the information needed when she arrived in Connecticut. She then texted him a message from her burner phone, letting him know that she was on her way. Anxious to see her family, she made sure she followed her father's instructions to a T, hoping that everything would go as planned.

***

Doug stood outside his brother's door listening to his grandmother saying a special prayer over Sean as he continued sleeping. He wasn't sure what he would say to him after seeing him take a bullet. They had gone through a rough ordeal, and both needed time to rest and reset. Suddenly, Elsie yelled for Doug to enter the hospital room.

"Doug, Doug, Sean is waking up."

He walked into the room where he saw Sean slowly opening his eyes and his grandmother holding his brother's hand. She was fighting back tears, happy to see her once-estranged grandson alive. She patted his hand. "Sean, you scared me half to death."

"I'm sorry, Nana. I seriously didn't mean to do that." He chuckled between the pain in his stomach. Then he looked up to see his brother standing by the door. "Hey, Dougie boy. Man, you look like shit."

Doug gave him a half smile as he shoved his hands into his pockets. "You should see the other guys." He tried laughing, but he flinched a little from the pain in his side.

"Well, I'm just so happy to see both of my grandsons are here with me. Dougie, come closer."

Doug slowly walked to the other side of the bed, still a little gun-shy from last night's events. "You know what, big brother? Why would you jump in front of me like that? You seriously wanted to die, didn't you?"

"If that's what it took to save my baby brother, I would take a thousand bullets." Sean closed his eyes when a sharp pain ran up his arm.

It broke Elsie's heart when she saw how uncomfortable Sean was. She wanted to wrap her arms around him and make all the pain go away. As Sean attempted to sit up in the bed, she helped reposition his pillow. "Let me help you, baby. You okay? You want us to call the nurse to give you some pain meds?"

"No, I'm good. But could you get me some water? My throat is so dry."

"Of course, baby." Elsie poured him some water from a small pink pitcher.

Doug sat on the corner of his brother's bed, relieved that Sean didn't sustain a life-threatening injury. Then, tapping Sean on the leg, he tried to lighten up the conversation. "Sean, I'm sorry, man. You didn't deserve this. I mean, you *did* deserve this, but I'm glad that you're okay." Sean laughed at his words and then groaned loudly.

"Doug, please don't make your brother laugh. You two still play too much."

"It's okay, Nana. I deserved that. I just want to thank you for coming through for me. You didn't have to do that. I appreciate you. And, Nana, I didn't mean for you to get in the middle of all of this mess."

"Sean, what's done is done. Now, I need for you to rest up and get better. We gotta lot of work to do to get us all back on track. I love you, sweetheart."

"I love you too, Nana."

"Now, Doug and I are going to let you get some rest. We'll see you in the morning." Elsie kissed him on his forehead while Sean slowly drifted off to sleep. She whispered to Doug, "Let's go, baby."

Doug watched his brother sleep for a minute, and then he followed his grandmother out of the room. "Do you think he'll be okay? Should we stay and watch him?"

Elsie gently tapped Doug on his cheek. "Baby, he's gonna be all right. God has seen fit for him to see another day. And I believe in my heart that your brother will be fine. Now, it's time for us to go home and rest ourselves."

"Nana, I'm sorry that I was so stubborn. I should have listened to you and made amends with him a long time ago. If I just helped him, none of this would have happened."

"Well, it's a good thing it did happen because now we have a second chance. A second chance. This is not all on you. Your brother made choices that had serious consequences. You are a loving, kind, and caring soul. You put your life on the line for your brother and me. Life is too short to think about the past. It's time that you start to let all of that anger and resentment go. You also have a second chance at life, baby. I want you to start living it."

As they walked out of the hospital hand in hand, Elsie began humming to him to help ease her grandson's mind. She remembered when his mother left him and his brother at her house and never returned. Doug had always been the sensitive one, and she made sure that she paid extra attention to him. No matter how old he got, he would always be her little Dougie.

"Now, why don't you tell me about that little agent who was responsible for finding me."

Doug smiled but, at the same time, was embarrassed. "Nana, it's a long story."

"Well, we got plenty of time. Why don't you start at the beginning?"

Doug chuckled and began the story of how he met a beautiful yet annoying woman at the gym who wanted to spar with him, but he wanted nothing to do with her. Elsie enjoyed having her grandson near her, and she listened intently to every word that came out of his mouth. She thanked the Lord for bringing them back together. And now, she enjoyed every minute that she had with him.

Benita drank her double espresso to help her stay awake as she drove north on Interstate 95. She had a long time to think about the past twenty-four hours, and she couldn't believe that she had done the unthinkable. Not only had she gotten Doug's grandmother back safe and sound, but she had also closed the Black Hole case. On her way home, she gave her father the great news. More importantly, she would now be able to meet him in Connecticut. Not only was Leroy thrilled by this news, but he was also very proud of his daughter and how she achieved her mission.

When he asked how she left things with her bosses, she told him that Agent Cole was happy at the outcome, but she and Miguel had not dealt with the trust issues. Leroy warned her that she needed to tread lightly when it came to Miguel because it was essential for her not to tip her hand. "Benita, whatever you need to do to smooth things over, you need to do it now because you can't have him not trusting you."

Benita agreed with him and made the call to Miguel. They talked for about twenty minutes, and she apologized for the way she had been treating him. She explained that it had been an emotional couple of weeks and that she just asked if he would give her some space, to which he agreed. She let him know that she just needed some time to decompress. That seemed to be enough for Miguel to back off for a bit, and she would take advantage of that time away from him.

She then had a video chat with Evan and Luciana, thanking them for standing by her throughout this case. It was more than she had ever bargained for, but if it weren't for them, they would have never shut down the Black Hole. She again apologized for bringing them along when she first decided to find Elsie Gibson without the agency's approval. They both agreed that if they had to do it all over again, they would change nothing. Benita was very grateful for their friendship, and they decided to have dinner to celebrate.

"Maybe we can even invite Huey."

Benita chuckled as Evan argued that he didn't like that idea. Benita and Luciana loved to tease Evan because he had a hard time dealing with Huey due to his eccentric behavior. But then Evan finally acquiesced and told them that he was okay with him coming to dinner. She eventually ended the call by telling them that she had decided to head to a day spa in Connecticut to decompress. She would be out of pocket, but if they needed her, just call.

Now that she had reached out to the DTCU folks, she prepared herself for her exciting day. She pulled out her phone and looked up her things-to-do list. She had called Miguel. Check. She had called Evan and Luciana. Check. She created a cover story, letting them know that she was headed to a day spa. She did her morning run just in case anyone was watching her. Check. Check. She lay down for a few hours as she prepared herself to see her family.

Once she finally arrived at the boutique hotel, she took out her overnight bag that held two different outfits, a wig, baseball hat, sunglasses, and her new black Christian Louboutin Tiketa Slip-On Red Sole Runner Sneakers and headed inside. She checked in, and the hotel receptionist handed her a package that was left for her. Benita made her way to room #615, where she was pleasantly surprised that Leroy had booked her a beautiful suite with a view of a tennis court and a hiking trail. Dropping her bag on the neighboring chair, she checked the time on the phone. Then she sat down on the couch and opened the package containing two maps—one of the hotel with all of the exits marked and one for the stadium where she would meet the family. She also pulled out a set of keys to a white Mustang and a photo of a young woman— who looked almost identical to her—same weight, hair, and features—that she would be meeting in the women's locker room at the spa.

Benita pulled out a bottle of water from her bag and began drinking it. She didn't realize how thirsty she was, and after finishing, she placed the empty bottle back into her crossbody bag. She picked up her bag and walked to the bedroom, where she pulled out a black, long-sleeved T-shirt, black jeggings, and black sneakers. She quickly changed out of her clothes, folding her outfit on the bed, and grabbed a white fluffy robe and slippers from the closet. Putting her robe over her clothes, she slid on her slippers and threw her sneakers, wig, and glasses into her bag.

She checked into the spa and was escorted into the women's locker room located between the sauna and pool. She took off the robe, pulled out her wig, makeup, and sneakers, and got ready to head out to the stadium. Out of the corner of her eye, she saw her doppelgänger walk out of the sauna room dressed in a similar robe. Benita gasped when she saw how much this woman looked like her. She'd seen a photo, but it was uncanny because this young woman could be her identical twin.

"Hi. You must be Benita. I'm Sophia," the young woman said.

"Ah yeah. That would be me. Nice to meet you, Sophia."

"Leroy didn't mention how beautiful you are. The man definitely has great taste."

"Okay. Well, thank you. Same to you. I'm assuming Leroy sent you instructions for today's events?"

"Of course. Listen, this isn't my first rodeo, Benita. And you don't have to worry. I follow directions well. Plus, how hard can it be to play the role of Benita Johnson? It'll be fun playing you.

Don't worry; you're all good. I love a good spa day."

"Thanks. So, when is your last appointment? I mean, when is *our* last appointment?" Benita looked in the mirror, putting the finishing touches on her makeup.

"My last appointment is at four o'clock. But I would suggest you get back before 5:00 p.m. and head to the sauna. I'll meet you there." Sophia pointed down a hallway. "It's located through there. Hope you have a great day. I know I will."

"Thanks."

Sophia smiled and walked away, heading to the sauna before her first massage appointment. Benita placed her crossbody bag over her shoulders, folded up the gym bag, and stuffed it into one of the open lockers. She punched a password into the keypad, took one more look in the mirror, and walked out of a connecting door opposite the reception area. She headed to the stairwell exit, walked down two flights, and departed the building, where she found a parked white Mustang in the hotel parking lot.

"Damn, Daddy. You sure do know how to set things in motion," Benita said.

She was extremely impressed with how her father had handled things. She had only known him to be the strong, silent type, but now, she saw how skilled he was as a former agent, helping her set things in motion without getting caught. Pulling out the set of keys from her bag, Benita pressed the button and opened the door on the driver's side. Once inside the vehicle, she found a secret compartment underneath the driver's seat, where she pulled out a small burner phone. Quickly turning it on, she found there was a message blinking, and she played it.

"Hey, my dear Benita. If you found this phone, I'm guessing that everything is going as planned so far. You will be driving for about thirty minutes until you arrive at the stadium. Once you're there, go through the security line and let them know that you are with the Leroy Jones group. They're expecting your arrival. Once you get inside, park the car on the north side of the stadium, and you'll see an entrance that reads Participants Entrance. You'll find a black jacket, baseball cap, and a special badge located in the trunk of the car, which you will wear to show that you are one of the security volunteers working the stadium. Once you get to the main door, show your badge. Okay, let's hop to it. See you soon, my darling daughter. Your grandmother and brother are here waiting for you. Love you, my dear."

Benita played the phone once more, listening to every detail that her father had left for her. Then she finally headed over to the jujitsu competition located at the Webster Bank Arena. Once she arrived, she saw thousands of people attending the National

Brazilian Jujitsu Championship Tournament sponsored by the Gammet Corporation. As the visitors and contestants walked toward the arena, Benita followed signs leading to the security line, where she made it through to the north side of the building.

Getting out of the car, she opened up the trunk and put on the security jacket and cap on top of the spare tire. Once she found the badge in her pocket, she headed inside the building, where she hurried down the corridor toward a room where Leroy, Grace, and Wes were waiting for her.

"Grams?" Benita yelled.

"Benita? Oh my Benita." Grace held out her arms for her long lost granddaughter.

Benita ran into her embrace, and tears of joy spilled over Benita, Grace, and Wes.

"Oh my goodness, let me look at you. I cannot believe how skinny you are. You're not eating enough. Don't they feed you where you are? Oh my dear baby. My dear baby."

Benita couldn't stop crying as Grace cradled her first grandbaby. Benita looked at Leroy and mouthed, "Thank you." He nodded and walked over to Wes, who was staring at his sister while wiping away his own tears. He placed his arm around the young man and nodded for him to go and spend time with his sister. Leroy knew that he had done the right thing bringing the family back together. He would do anything to make sure that Benita was happy. His heart nearly broke when he saw how sad she was after the last case, and he promised himself that he would do what he could to bring a smile to her face.

As for Grace and Wes, they had endured a lot of time without seeing Benita. Even though Leroy knew that Grace hated him for abandoning both Benita's mother and his daughter, she agreed to the plan to bring them all together. Grace told him that she would do whatever it took to see her granddaughter. No questions asked.

Between the tears and the laughter, he had done a great thing. He walked out of the room, giving the family time to catch up during this special reunion. Time felt like it stood still while the Jenkins family caught up on everything that had happened in the past year. Grace asked Benita a million and one questions, and she tried to answer every one of them. Wes asked a few questions as well, but he made sure that he didn't reveal that he had already been in communication with his sister, wanting to hide the pain that it would cause Grams if she ever discovered that he had kept secrets from her.

After about two hours, Leroy came back into the room, letting Wes know that it was time for him to compete. Although he was nervous, the young student was excited to participate in his first competition. He turned to Benita and smiled. "Are you going to stick around to watch me?"

Benita flashed her pearly whites. "Of course, I wouldn't miss my baby brother competing in his very first match."

"Well then, let's go. Can't keep the opponent waiting," Leroy said.

As Grace and Wes walked out the door, Benita pulled Leroy back from her family. "Sensei Leroy, can I speak to you for a minute?"

"Sure, Benita. What's going on?"

Benita couldn't form the words and simply gave her father a huge hug and a kiss on the cheek. "Thank you for making this possible. I don't know what I would have done if I didn't see my grandmother and brother again."

They stood there for a few minutes longer before Wes peeked his head back into the room. "Ah, I hate to break up this love fest, but I *do* have a match to attend."

Benita looked at her brother and shook her head. "You know what, little brother? You're so right. Let's go see what you got going on." She placed her arm around her brother's shoulders and began whispering in his ear as they walked toward the arena competition area, with Grace and Leroy following.

Grace looked over at Leroy and gave him a half smile. "Well, Mr. Jones, I must say that I'm impressed with you. So I guess you're not all bad."

"Why, thank you, Grace. That means a lot coming from you."

"Don't get too cocky, sir. I said, not *all* bad. You and me are still *not* friends. Remember that."

Leroy let out a hearty laugh and simply shook his head at the courageous older lady. She was definitely a lion protecting her cubs, and she was always looking out for them, no matter what. He appreciated that she finally came forward last year telling him that Benita was his daughter, and for that, he would be forever grateful.

After spending more than an hour and a half watching as Wes competed, Benita witnessed her brother winning his first match. She was beyond ecstatic by his accomplishment. She found herself joining the crowd and jumping up and down after seeing him win his latest match. Grace was clapping hard and looking back and forth between her grandson on the floor and her granddaughter sitting next to her. She was so happy to see Benita, but a sense of sadness soon followed when she realized that her grandbaby had to leave soon.

Benita looked over at her grandmother and saw the somber look on her face. "Don't be sad, Grams. I promise that we'll see each other again."

Grace rubbed her granddaughter's leg as a way to help comfort herself. "I know we will, honey. But it's just so hard for me to see you go. I miss you already." She gave Benita one last hug and told her that they should go back to the room to say their goodbyes. Benita agreed. They walked back to the room where Leroy and Wes were already waiting for them.

"Did you see me, Grams? I won," Wes gleefully commented as he held out his first-place medal.

"Yes, baby. I saw every move. I am so very proud of you." Grace hugged him and then turned to Benita. "And how lovely was it for your sister to see you win."

Benita grabbed her brother and playfully slapped him on the back of the head. "I am so happy right now. You did a phenomenal job, little brother. But, ah, don't get too cocky, you hear me?"

"Now, was that necessary? But thank you, sis. If it weren't for you, I wouldn't be here. I mean it. Thank you."

After they hugged, she sadly said her goodbyes, followed by a few more hugs from Grace, Wes, and Leroy. Then Benita headed back to her car, opened the trunk, and placed the jacket and cap back inside. Just as she was about to open the car door, she saw someone who looked like T-Bone attending a tailgate party. She wasn't entirely sure, but she decided to get a closer look. However, just as she was ready to make a move, her phone beeped. She checked it. It was her father telling her to make sure she drives safely back to the hotel.

When she looked up, the T-Bone look-alike was nowhere to be found. She decided to table that situation for another day because she would see him pay for getting Joe shot and helping to send her to jail one day. She would exact her revenge. Then she looked at her watch and jumped into the car. She used the fob key to gain entrance into the building and headed back to the spa, entering from the same door adjacent to the reception entrance.

She went to the women's locker room, pulling out her bag, removing her wig and other clothes that she wore to the match. Quickly, she grabbed a robe and slippers from the locker and put them back on. Just when she was about to walk to the sauna, Sophia came toward her fully dressed.

"Hope you had a great day 'cause I know I did," Sophia commented.

"I did. Thank you very much. Oh, Leroy wanted me to give you this envelope." Benita handed Sophia an envelope full of cash, and Sophia gladly received it.

"Why, thank you, Ms. Johnson. Look, I'm going to leave through the employee exit before anyone spots me. You enjoy the remainder of your evening."

"You too." Benita said her goodbyes and walked to the spa reception area, where Genie, the only one at the desk, greeted her.

"Checking out, Ms. Johnson? Hope that you had the perfect spa day with us," Genie commented.

"Oh, I did. It was amazing. So, how much do I owe?" Benita smiled back at the young woman.

"Oh, you're taken care of. Your spa day was prepaid, even with the tip."

"Well, great. Just great. Thank you so much for everything."

"You're so welcome. Enjoy your stay," Genie smiled.

Benita walked back to the suite, peeled off her clothes, ran a hot bath, and ordered room service. This was truly one of the best days of her entire life, and she owed it all to her father, Leroy. He planned the perfect meeting for her and her family, and she was genuinely grateful. He was heaven-sent, and she was lucky to have him in her life. When she thought about all she had lost, he was there for her. Not only did he comfort her during her lowest point, but he had also made it clear that she was not alone in her journey.

She finally lay on the beautiful king-sized bed and was about to close her eyes when she heard a buzzing sound coming from her phone. It was a text message from Miguel simply saying, I'm sorry. Benita replied, I know. It's all good. Have a good night. She placed her phone on silent and thought about today's events. Things couldn't have gone any better, and at that moment, she was the happiest she had ever been.

She felt normal, if only for a few hours, and she would take that any day than not to have her family in her life. There were no people more important than her grandmother, her brother, and now, her father. She would make sure that she stayed in touch with them no matter what. She closed her eyes to the sweet smell of lavender coming from her pillows and sheets. She smiled as she got comfortable in the bed. She was thankful for many things in her life, and she would never take them for granted. Not for a single day. She knew that she had to deal with Miguel, but not tonight. She just wanted to dream sweet dreams. Tomorrow would soon come. But tonight, it was simply about her.

Chapter 42

Benita walked into the DTCU offices, where she had a meeting with Agent Cole and Miguel. She was happy that they had given her a day to unwind before being debriefed. She loved her "me" time and used it to disconnect from thinking about cases, assignments, and the Agency. Before her planned meeting, Benita had breakfast with Evan and Luciana, who discussed their debriefings with their bosses. They both reassured her that the meeting was simply a formality and had gone smoothly. It was nothing more than a check-in to make sure that they were mentally coping. In fact, Agent Cole praised the team for having the fortitude to close one of his cases. Luciana mentioned that it was the first time she saw Agent Cole beam with joy, which was because of Benita. She had taken her role seriously and had led them to victory. Benita was hopeful that her meeting went as well as her fellow agents' because she had been reminded of her ability to go rogue.

Once she arrived at Miguel's office, she noticed that Agent Cole was also there waiting for her.

"Knock, knock."

"Hey there, Benita. Come in. Shut the door."

Benita slowly closed the door and sat down beside Agent Cole, who was holding a notebook and a pen.

"Did you have a good night's sleep, Benita?"

"I did. Thank you, Agent Perkins, for pushing back my briefing for another day. I didn't realize how much I needed to decompress."

"Well, that's why we have rules in place, Agent Jenkins. Once you finish up an assignment, it's important to take a breather before getting back out there. Look, Agent Perkins and I wanted to discuss your actions as they related to this case," Agent Cole commented.

Benita braced herself for any reprimands that they may have for her part in taking on a case that the DTCU did not sanction. She was ready to accept whatever punishment that was coming from her bosses. It was time that she started playing the role of a compliant subordinate if she wanted to reach her goals. Leroy had prepped her for the meeting, and she was ready to put on a show that would appease her bosses and plead her case, if need be.

"Yes, sir," Benita answered.

"When Agent Perkins first told me about you, he mentioned that you were some sort of loose cannon. You know, I have to tell you I was concerned when I first met you. It burned me up because I assumed you were hard of listening to the truth when it came to how important it was to follow orders. I know it's difficult because we've all been there at one point in our careers. But you, Agent Jenkins, need to understand that being an agent takes not only skill but also collaboration. There needs to be a level of respect for your higher-ups and your colleagues. But, more importantly, you need to understand that your actions can end up getting someone killed. So, the biggest thing for you is to learn how to check your emotions."

As Benita listened to Agent Cole, she knew she wasn't going to stop doing what she was doing because it was the right thing. However, she would think about a different approach to get what she needed from her bosses. Although she was watching his lips, she had tuned him out as soon as he went on his tangent about being a good agent. Sitting there with a straight face, Benita showed very little emotion. If that was what he wanted, then that was what she would give him. In fact, she would act like a robot and, as he said, check the emotions at the door.

"Are you listening to me, Agent Jenkins?" Agent Cole asked.

"Yes, sir. I will bring my enthusiasm down a notch and only work on cases assigned to me. I have learned my lesson, and that is to make sure that I follow the proper channels and not recruit my fellow agents so as not to put them in danger. And more importantly, it's showing my respect to my superiors. Did I miss anything?"

Agent Cole was about to speak, but Miguel interjected because he knew his friend would hold them captive for at least another hour. He had watched as Benita quietly sat there listening to Willard without saying a word. He felt bad for her because she was not fully engaged, although he noticed that she was holding it together. Maybe Sean Gibson getting shot took a bigger toll on her than he thought because she acted differently right now. Never had he seen her so subdued before. She was a firecracker whose flame was burning low. Had she finally realized that this job was not a game and that she could end up seriously hurt . . . or even dead?

Today, she looked tired. He didn't want Willard to deflate her completely. He watched as the flame in her eyes was quickly fading. "Benita, I just want to say that, in the end, you did an excellent job in shutting down this illegal fighting ring case. We wanted to acknowledge that."

"Thank you, Agent Perkins. I appreciate that coming from you. I have had time to reflect on my actions, and I agree with both of you. I was stubborn and hotheaded and only seeing things my way. But if I'm here to work as a team, I need to collaborate with my colleagues. I knew in my heart that something was going on with Doug and his family, and I just had to do something about it. However, after thinking it over, I should have just come to you, Agent Perkins, and explained my concerns. I'm truly sorry if I caused you any problems. It won't happen again."

Agent Cole looked at Miguel with pride. He felt confident that Benita had learned her lesson and took full credit for her turnaround. "You know what, Agent Jenkins? Let me be the first to say that after seeing you in action in the field, I fully recognize that you handled yourself as a true professional. I think that you're well on your way to becoming a helluva agent. Right, Agent Perkins?"

"I agree with you wholeheartedly, Agent Cole. Agent Benita Renee Jenkins is one helluva agent. I'm confident that she now knows what it takes to navigate the pitfalls of being an agent. And I also think that she understands we are a team and must work together if we're going to solve these cases. We have to make sure that we're all in lockstep."

"Absolutely, Agent Cole. I will never go out on my own again without going through the proper channels. We're a team here, and I can promise you that going forward, I'll go by the book."

"Well, that's what I want to hear, Agent Jenkins. Miguel, you have a real one here. I would also like to mention you did an excellent job out there. You kept your cool while trying to talk down the suspect. But, unfortunately, sometimes, there are casualties that we can't control."

"Agent Cole, may I ask you a question?"

"Of course. Ask away," he commanded.

"So, what do you think would be the one thing that I can do to get to the next level? I mean, I know that I only have two cases under my belt, but I see myself taking on a bigger role in some of these cases. I'm grateful you believed in me to be the lead. I would love to work with you in the future, if you would allow me, sir."

Suddenly, Agent Cole's face lit up, and he poked out his chest in pride. "You know what, Benita? You have to be a visionary and be able to think three steps ahead in any case. I saw you cared about that young man and were hell-bent on helping him find his grandmother. That is quite admirable. Quite admirable. So, the best thing you can do is to continue to listen to Agent Perkins to make sure you observe and think things through before you step out there on your own. But more importantly, I would love to have you on some of my other cases."

"Thank you, sir. Agent Perkins?"

Miguel stared at Benita with a stone face. Although he was very pleased with her behavior today, he didn't want Benita to work on other cases with his buddy, Willard. That would mean that he would have less control over her career.

"Although things started a little rocky, in the end, you did a great job pulling the team together and creating a strategy that worked for everyone. That is all to say that like Agent Cole here, I'm pleased with your work."

"Thank you, Agent Perkins. That means a lot . . . from both of you," Benita answered.

She had now been in the office with both men for over an hour and was getting anxious to spend time with Samantha, her mentor. Samantha was the only one besides her father that Benita felt she could be honest with about her feelings since coming to the DTCU. She had always told her the truth, and she had a great deal of respect for her. Benita also appreciated the fact that Miguel couldn't control her relationship. She finally decided to end the meeting.

"This has been extremely helpful. Do you need anything more from me? I have completed my paperwork, and it has been sent to Huey. I now have an appointment with Agent DeVreau, and I don't want to be late."

Agent Cole perked up when he heard Samantha's name. "Agent DeVreau? She's definitely one helluva an agent."

"Yes, sir, she is. If it weren't for her, I don't know if I would have survived the first year here at the Agency."

"Please tell her that Agent Cole said hello."

"Of course. Well, if there isn't anything else . . ."

"No, I think we're done for now," Miguel replied.

"Thank you both," were Benita's last parting words before heading over to Samantha's office.

She knocked on Samantha's door, and without looking up, the agent motioned for her to enter her office. Samantha had trained Benita to become a superagent. She had taught her to use her femininity to gain an advantage over her subjects. But more importantly, Samantha had created a more refined Benita, and that always pleased her. "Agent DeVreau? What's happening?"

Samantha looked up from her reading and pushed her glasses up the bridge of her nose. "Benita. How's my favorite pupil?"

Benita looked around the office and was amazed at how pristine it was. Samantha was a minimalist who cared more about quality and less about quantity.

Leaning back in her oversized black swivel chair, Samantha crossed her arms as she smiled at Benita. Benita's behavior always amused her. She'd taught Benita a lot about being a buttoned-up agent while Benita taught her how to loosen up and enjoy life. "So, how are you feeling after finishing up your last case? Was it everything you thought it would be? But I guess the real question is, how does it feel to stick it to your bosses?"

"Actually, this time, it didn't feel so good. I mean, I know that I tend not to follow the rules, but this time, things felt different. I guess I'm just tired of being reprimanded by the higher-ups. Of course, I want to stay true to myself, but at the same time, I'm learning that I don't have to jump the gun on everything I do. You know what I'm saying?"

Samantha placed her glasses down on her desk. "Well, I'm happy that you came to that conclusion. And you are right. You don't have to do everything alone. Or make decisions on your own. You're part of a team. And it's always important to protect your team at all costs."

"I appreciate your advice, Agent DeVreau. I will definitely keep that in mind."

"You do just that." Suddenly, Samantha's phone rang. "Excuse me for a minute, Benita. Hello. Samantha DeVreau. Bertie, how are you?" After a long pause, a look of confusion crossed her face, then a look of fear. "Wait. Slow down. Say that again."

Benita read Samantha's face as she continued talking to someone named Bertie. Samantha's entire demeanor had changed, and that suddenly made Benita's heart rate accelerate. She wasn't sure what was going on, but she knew that something wasn't right.

"Slow down, Bertie. You're talking too fast. What are you saying? Oh my God. Okay. I'll be there as soon as I can. I promise."

Hanging up the phone, Samantha turned white as a ghost, as if all of the blood drained from her face.

"Agent DeVreau, are you okay?"

"Actually, I'm not, Benita. How would you like to go with me to New Orleans?"